D1003869

THE
SILVER
ECLIPSE

AKKRON
- BOOK 1 -

KRISTY DIXON

Akkron

For Xander, Brevan, Isabelle, Grant, Malia,
Ellena, Sonnet, Azalea, and Ford

CHAPTER 1

W ren closed the door to Professor Dovin's office, being careful to make as little noise as possible. She left it unlatched and slightly ajar to ensure no one could enter the connecting classroom without her knowledge. If she got caught, it would not be pleasant. As a precaution, her friend Ming Li was keeping watch outside the classroom and was ready to alert her if anyone came close. The office was a mess. Papers blanketed the desk, and the floor was littered with garbage that hadn't quite reached the bin. Wren inched to the desk as quietly as she could and pulled open a drawer. It was full of smudged old papers. She reached for one, but froze when she heard the creak of the classroom door.

"We can talk in here," came Professor Dovin's smooth voice from the connecting room. Wren shuddered at the familiar oily tone. He was many students' favorite professor, but something about him always reminded her of a pre-owned alicorn salesman.

"Are you sure?" An unfamiliar woman's voice asked. "A school doesn't seem like a private place."

"No one comes into my room at lunch. I don't allow it." Arrogance dripped from his lips, as if he was the only teacher to carry out such a basic feat.

Wren squeezed her eyes shut and tried to stay focused. She could get suspended for coming into his office without permission. She looked around desperately for an escape. There was a window to the outside, but they were on the fourth floor. Levitating wasn't one of her strong points, so if she tried to lower herself down, she would probably break her head. Fortunately for her, the windows between the office and the classroom were clouded. Since she couldn't see out, she hoped that meant they couldn't see in.

"I'm getting tired of not being told things," the woman complained. "I've done everything you asked, and I've gotten nothing in return! Do I get to meet the leader of the organization? When do I get to meet the other Dark Cl–"

"Shhh," Professor Dovin interrupted. "You have to be patient, Melly." Wren could imagine him smiling in the annoying, superior way he always did. "We will tell you more when we come to trust you. Trust takes time."

Wren sucked in sharply. *The Dark Cloud*. That must have been what the woman was about to say. Sweat trickled down her back. Professor Dovin and Melly continued to talk quietly, but Wren wasn't listening anymore. She was too busy panicking. The Dark Cloud was dangerous. If she was discovered now, it would be worse than being expelled.

She could open a portal, but that was forbidden, not to mention dangerous. Unpredictable and uncontrollable, there was no way to know where the portal would open, and one could find oneself in another world entirely. Returning home from a different world was easy. You could always return to the place where you made your first portal. Nothing else about them could be controlled.

Where was Ming Li? She should have been keeping watch. Wren shouldn't have gone along with her friend's scheme to sneak into the office. They had suspected that Professor Dovin was up to something, but had never imagined this.

"The paper is in my office," Professor Dovin said, breaking Wren out of her anxious stupor. Quick, heavy footsteps moved across the floor in the direction of the office. Wren decided. It would be better to fall into the ocean than to be caught by The Dark Cloud. Putting her pointer fingers and thumbs together, she quickly pulled them apart, opening a shimmering silver portal. The door to the office squeaked, and she jumped through without looking back.

Wren fell out of the portal and landed hard. Her hands and knees scraped as they barely stopped her from smacking her face against the cement surface. She inhaled deeply through her nose, ignoring the pain in her hands and the way her arms were shaking. Going through a portal was draining, and she wasn't sure she could stand yet. The wind blew long strands of red hair into her face, obscuring her vision. Thunder rumbled above, but thankfully, there was no rain. Wren had hoped to make a new portal to return home as soon as she landed, but her magic felt exhausted.

A rhythmic, pounding sound, like something smacking against the earth at an even pace, rang in her ears. Once she realized the pounding wasn't only in her head, Wren pushed herself into a kneeling position and took a moment to get her bearings. She was in a park. The houses across the road were crammed together, and in various stages of falling apart. Weathered fences with red words painted across them were surrounded by yards that were green, but overtaken by weeds.

After a few false starts, she managed to get to her feet. Now that she was standing, she could locate the source of the pounding. A boy, a little older than her at fifteen or sixteen, was bouncing a ball up and down and throwing it through a suspended net. Behind him was what appeared to be a children's play area, also covered in red writing, and behind that a grove of trees.

The houses didn't look inviting, so Wren walked carefully across the untended grass towards the boy. In a practiced motion, she pulled a handful of dust from her pocket and sprinkled it over her head. It only took a small amount to make her invisible. She silently thanked her father for always insisting she carry it in case of an emergency. The boy wouldn't be able to see her, but if she made too much noise, he would hear her. She stopped when she reached the cement rectangle he was playing on and observed him.

He was wearing a strange blue shirt. It was silky and hung loose on his tall frame. The shirt was sleeveless, and on the back it had the number 12 with the word "*Dryson*" printed across it. Wren had never seen clothing with writing on it. She had also never seen a shirt with no sleeves or britches that only went to the knee. She wondered if he was trying to show off his muscles.

Wren watched as the boy threw the ball in the net over and over. He never missed. Sweat beaded on his warm brown skin, but he didn't seem to mind. Wren shivered. She hated sweating worse than anything. Being smelly and sticky were things she avoided. The boy was extremely good looking, and if it wasn't for the fact he couldn't see her, she would be embarrassed by her staring. Another wave of exhaustion hit her. It would be awhile before she could go back home. It couldn't hurt to stay here observing the handsome boy. There were definite advantages to being invisible.

Graham sighed. The girl was still hovering nearby, watching him. The air was getting heavier, and the wind had picked up. Any second it might rain, and he wanted to go home. Going home would mean passing her. He threw his basketball into the hoop and snuck a glance over his shoulder. What was she wearing? She looked like someone out of a movie. Her long green dress and black cape blew dramatically in the wind, and her tangled red hair flew wildly around her face. If he didn't get home soon, Aunt Temperance would be fuming, if she wasn't already.

Graham retrieved his ball and sighed again. Tucking the ball under his arm, he walked in the girl's direction. When she saw him coming nearer, she fidgeted with a long, thin gold necklace. She looked like she was younger than him, but not by much. She was pretty, but definitely not Graham's type. People in capes were probably a little odd, in his opinion.

"Hey," Graham said, stopping approximately five feet in front of her. He held out the ball, not sure what to do. "Do you wanna play?"

She looked around, eyes wide, as if he wasn't staring right at her. "Ummm ... me?"

Graham wondered why he didn't just walk around her and go home. "Yes?"

"You can see me?" she whispered, taking a step back.

"I can see you," he said, raising an eyebrow. There were always crazy people in this park. "You should probably go home. It's going to rain soon."

She looked at the dark sky and shivered. "I can't go home right now." She gave her necklace another little tug. "I'm kind of lost."

Graham followed her gaze up to the sky and wondered how this peculiar girl had suddenly become his responsibility. "You're bleeding." He pointed to one of her scraped hands. She dropped the gold chain and looked down, assessing the damage. She quickly folded her arms, hiding her hands in her cape.

"I fell. They're fine."

"Do you live around here? What's your address? I can help you." He pulled his phone out and brought up maps. She shrugged and looked at the ground.

"You might want to wash your hands. There's a restroom over there." Graham pointed to the small brick park bathroom covered in graffiti. "It's probably not very sanitary, though." The girl didn't look up.

"Graham!" a familiar voice yelled. "You are in T-R-O-B-L-E!" Graham's ten-year-old cousin Kaylee was hurtling towards them at full speed, black braids flying.

"You missed the U," Graham said, wishing the little busy body would leave him alone for once. The mysterious girl took a few small steps back.

"I never know what the heck you're talking about," Kaylee growled, putting her hands on her hips in the universal gesture of annoying ten-year-olds everywhere. She looked like her mom, right down to the thin-lipped sneer. "Mom said you were supposed to get home an hour ago to wash Walter."

"She never told me," Graham protested, as he continued to watch the caped girl out of the corner of his eye. She had taken another step back, and she was nervously chewing on her bottom lip.

"Well, how could she?" Kaylee said with a smirk. "Mom didn't know he was gonna go roll around in the mud. And you didn't do the dishes. You're so lazy. Mom's gonna take away all your dumb books if you don't straighten up. You ain't ever gonna go to doctor school, anyway. You are too

D-U-M. Mom said you better come home right now. I hope you don't though, cause then I get your lunch."

Graham wondered if Kaylee would ever pass out from talking so fast. He bent over, resting his hands on his knees so he would be at her level. "Tell Aunt Temperance I'll be home after I help this girl."

"What girl?" Kaylee asked, looking around suspiciously. Each turn of her head sent her braids whipping through the air, nearly catching Graham in the face.

Graham held up his hands protectively and rolled his eyes. "The only girl here besides you." Despite getting along with her most days, when Kaylee channeled her mom, she could be one of the most annoying people on the planet.

"I'm Graham Dryson," he said, turning his attention back to the girl. "What's your name?" A raindrop hit Graham's nose and ran onto his cheek.

"I'm Wren," she muttered, looking at Kaylee and stepping back again. She was making distance and was now a good nine feet away from them. Wren inclined her chin at Kaylee. "I don't think she can see me."

"She's just being annoying. It's her favorite thing to do."

"Stop trying to trick me," Kaylee said, crossing her arms. "How did you make that girly voice? You better come home. Mom's already thinking of your punishment for not cleaning Walter."

Graham was sure she was. Aunt Temper, as he liked to call her, liked nothing better than punishing him. They had the cleanest house in the city because of how often she had him clean it.

"I should go," Wren said, her eyes focused on Kaylee.

Graham pointed at her hand. "You need to put something on that to stop the bleeding." A small line of blood was dripping down the side of her dress. She clasped her bloody hands together and nodded. She walked forward at an angle to move around Graham without passing too close to him and moved towards the trees. "Do you have a phone? Should I call someone for you?" he called after her, holding up his cell phone.

"Why are you such a freak?" Kaylee said, baring her teeth. "I'm telling mom you were trying to scare me." She grabbed a stick and chucked it at him. It whizzed past his head and barely missed Wren. She looked back with wide eyes and started running.

"Nice," he said, side-eyeing Kaylee. "You scared her. She's lost; we should help her."

"There is nobody there and I AM TELLING!" Kaylee yelled, as she ran across the park. Graham ran after Wren.

"Wren, wait!" he called. "Let me help you!" Wren looked over her shoulder and ran faster, cape billowing behind her.

Graham should let her go, but there was something wrong about her. Maybe she was on drugs, or maybe she hurt her head when she fell. Graham couldn't help it. After being raised by Aunt Temper, it was hard to see someone in trouble and not help. That was one reason he wanted to be a doctor. Doctors could help people in a way a normal person couldn't.

Wren ran into the trees. Thanks to years of running laps for basketball, Graham had almost caught up to her when she shouted something he couldn't understand and flung her arms out wide. A bright, silvery light flashed, and she disappeared into it. Graham tried to stop, but he was going too fast and plowed through after her. He felt himself falling, and before he had time to wonder what had happened, he slammed into the ground.

CHAPTER 2

The ground smashed into Wren's back this time, knocking the air out of her. She rolled to her side and wheezed, struggling to catch her breath. Getting up would not be an option for a while, but the portal had opened! Spending the night in the woods wouldn't be too bad. At least it wasn't raining here. This was the first place she had ever opened a portal, and so it was the place her returning portal would always open. It was only a five-minute walk home, but Wren wasn't sure she would make it. She felt like something had ripped apart her insides.

"Are you okay?" Graham asked, gently shaking her shoulder. Wren jolted up, grabbing her head as it began pounding. She had brought Graham back. This was possibly the worst thing she'd ever done. Not even Ming Li had ever managed this level of trouble.

"Did you see that lightning?" he asked with a confused glance at the now clear sky. "It was right in front of us! I've never felt anything like that. Did you hurt your head?"

Wren looked at him through squinted eyes. "I only need to rest." What was she going to do?

Graham was kneeling over her, looking concerned. "I think you need a doctor. Is there someone I can call?" He held up a rectangular device, the same one he'd waved at her when he'd asked that question earlier. "Oh man, I cracked the screen when I fell. It doesn't look like it's going to turn on."

"I can't go anywhere until I rest. I think I might need to stay here until morning."

"No, I'll go get help," he said, standing. He looked around and frowned. "I'm a little disoriented."

Wren's head hurt worse as she thought about telling Graham he was probably stuck here forever.

"I'll go home and get help." He scanned the trees.

"You can't," Wren said, wondering how he was missing the fact that the trees had changed from oaks to aspens. It wasn't raining here, and it was much warmer than his world had been.

"Why not?"

"Because we ran through a portal."

"A portal?" Graham's face screwed up in confusion. "Like a black hole that takes you to a different dimension?"

"No, like a silver hole that takes you to a different world."

Graham pursed his lips. "We need to get you help. I can't figure out why I feel so confused. Which way is North?"

Through her pounding headache, Wren channeled her most authoritative voice. She didn't want him to panic, but he needed to understand his situation. "Look around Graham Dryson. We are not in your world." She scooted herself up against a tree for support.

"I must be turned around," he said, as if she hadn't spoken. He walked around in a big circle. Worry lines creased his forehead, and he was fidgeting with the odd gadget in his hand.

"I opened a portal, and you followed me."

"There's no such thing." He squinted into the trees, drumming his fingers against his leg. "You landed pretty hard. You're probably just feeling a little confused."

"*I'm* a little confused?" If she had the energy, she would laugh. With his head tilted and his dark brown eyes so full of questions, he looked like a lost puppy. Wren glanced at the sky, and her brows puckered. The sun was sinking below the treeline and the splatters of orange and pink were already deepening into purple and black. Being stuck in the dark woods with a confused Graham was not appealing.

"In the morning, we can go to my house. My dad might know what to do," she said, doubting her own words. Despite being a great guy, her dad wasn't one for solving problems, which was surprising, considering he was a counselor to the governor.

"Why is it getting dark?" he asked, squinting at the sky. "It's the middle of the day."

Wren sighed, unsure how to deal with Graham's denial. "Day and night can be different in different worlds, and going through a portal can completely mess you up. You can lose entire days. It's best to not even try to think about it."

"I'll carry you," Graham said, with a decisive nod. "You must have a head injury. Once we get out of the trees, I'll know where we are."

She crossed her arms. "I don't have a head injury and you can't carry me. It's five minutes to my house."

"Five minutes?" he scoffed. "That's nothing. I can carry you that far."

"But ..." Wren protested as he scooped her up. She was sure her face was bright red. Hopefully, it was dark enough he wouldn't notice.

"Which way?" he asked. She pointed, and he walked. She tried to relax in his arms, but it wasn't easy. It was turning out to be the worst day ever.

This day was strange. That was the only way Graham could describe it. If his friends could see him now, they would tease him for eternity.

The wind had stopped, and it was almost completely dark now. If it wasn't for the brightness of the moon, he wouldn't be able to see anything in the heavily wooded area. Not for the first time, he wondered if he was okay. There weren't this many trees at the park. They should be out by now. There was nothing to do but keep walking. Wren had her arms around his neck and was looking anywhere except at him. In the dim light, he could just make out the red in her cheeks. She looked like she was going to die of embarrassment. He might have smiled if he wasn't so worried. His left leg was aching. He must have hurt it when the lightning hit.

"We should be out of the trees," he muttered. "This doesn't make sense."

"The forest keeps going until we get to my house," Wren said, eyes still averted. Graham shook his head. He must have hurt himself more than he thought when he fell. Maybe he had gotten knocked out and was having a crazy dream. It was possible, but it felt way too real. He wanted to ask questions, but he didn't know what to ask first.

"We're almost there," Wren said. Graham was happy to hear it. He wasn't sure what was happening, but his arms were burning and even with the moon, it was getting hard to see.

Graham stepped into a grassy clearing. In front of them was a large stone mansion, three stories high. It was white and had so much outdoor lighting it almost seemed to glow. The only time he had ever seen a house like this was when his English teacher made them watch a boring Jane Austen movie. Definitely not something that should be in the park.

Wren's eyebrows drew in with concern as she took in his stunned expression. "Are you alright?"

"Yeah," he said, blinking a few times, "I don't know how I've never seen this house before. Me and my friends know the city inside out."

"Wren!" a man's voice called. Graham saw a tall, wiry figure running towards them from the mansion. He put Wren on her feet, supporting her as she found her footing.

As the man came closer, there was no mistaking his resemblance to Wren, with his red hair and wide eyes. Graham would almost bet this was Wren's dad. The man was also wearing a black cape.

"What happened?" the man asked, scooping Wren into his arms. He looked her over and turned to Graham. At this distance, Graham could see that the man's eyes were bloodshot, and his brow was furrowed.

Graham wondered if he should offer to carry her, because this guy didn't look steady.

"It's a long story," Wren said, glancing at Graham and away.

"Let's get in the house, and you can tell me what happened. I've been so worried," he said as he ushered them to the door. Graham didn't know what else to do, so he followed.

"The school sent a message that you missed some of your classes. When Ming Li didn't know where you were, I was frantic. I have people looking all over Akkron for you."

They arrived at the house and the door opened to reveal a large, muscular man, whose face looked like it owned a permanent frown. His shaggy brown hair made Graham think of his dog, Walter, but that was where the cute resemblance ended. A long, jagged scar ran across his face, starting at his eyebrow and running diagonally over his eye and nose and ending in the middle of his cheek. By the look of it, it was a miracle he still had his eye. Graham tried not to stare. This man was also wearing a cape. What was with these people and capes?

"Thank you Karlof," Wren's dad said. "Can you please go inform everyone that Wren has been found safe?"

"Of course," the man said, with a deep, raspy voice that put Graham in mind of a heavy smoker. Wren's dad walked through the door, and when Graham hesitated, Karlof motioned for him to follow. Graham shuddered. Karlof was not a man he would want to meet in a dark alley ... or a light one, for that matter.

"Come this way," Wren's dad said, entering a large sitting room. He placed Wren on a white sofa and pointed to a matching chair across from it. "Please sit."

Graham sat and wondered how many months Aunt Temper was going to ground him for. Two at least. One for not coming home and one for breaking his phone. The room was enormous, and so bright he had to squint. He wondered what their electric bill came to every month. A crystal chandelier hung in the middle of the ceiling, and several matching crystal lamps were hooked to the walls. Graham's entire house could fit inside this room. The overall whiteness of the room made him think Wren was an only child. Nobody in their right mind would have white furniture with little kids running around. Kaylee spilled almost every single time she ate, and she wasn't even that young. Even the carpet was a light beige color. If it wasn't for the colorful abstract art that adorned the walls, the room would be too hard to look at.

"What happened?" the red-haired man asked, as he took a seat next to his daughter. Wren looked at her hands in her lap. They were covered in dried blood. "You're bleeding," he said, his mouth pulling down at the corners.

"Not anymore," she muttered. They sat in silence for a moment before the man held out his hand and blew into his palm. A wet rag appeared as if by magic. He handed it to Wren, and she began wiping the caked blood away. Graham's eyes widened. Now he was seeing things. Where did that rag come from?

"I don't think we've met," the man said, realizing his daughter wasn't eager to talk. "I'm Drew, Wren's dad."

Graham was happy to let an adult help with this problem. "My name's Graham Dryson. I found Wren hurt in the park."

Drew shot his daughter an exasperated look. "Well, Graham Dryson, my daughter doesn't seem to be in a talkative mood. Can you tell me what happened?"

Graham looked at Wren. She ignored him and kept wiping her hands.

"I was playing basketball, and I saw Wren. She was lost and hurt, so I tried to help her. My cousin scared her and she ran away. I followed to make sure she was okay and lightning must have hit super close to us. We both got knocked over. It must have shaken her up, because she couldn't stand. That's why I carried her here."

Drew frowned. "Lightning? There hasn't been any lightning today." He leaned forward and studied Graham with his kind green eyes." May I ask where you are from Graham Dryson? I can't place your accent."

"I've always lived in Missouri," Graham said, shifting in his seat.

"And where is Missouri?" Drew asked, looking pale.

"We're in Missouri?" Panic gnawed at his stomach.

Drew sighed and turned to his daughter. "Wren?" he asked. "What's going on?"

"Shouldn't we talk about this tomorrow?" she asked, a pleading look in her eyes. "I'm kind of worn down."

"Wren. Now." He sounded annoyed, but not like when Aunt Temperance was angry. Graham could tell he was at least trying to stay calm.

"Okay." She sighed. "So … I was in one of my teacher's offices without permission when I heard something I shouldn't have. I didn't know what to do." She looked helplessly up at Drew.

"I knew I couldn't be caught, so I opened a portal and went through, and accidentally brought Graham Dryson back with me."

Drew pinched the bridge of his nose and leaned back on the sofa. "I was afraid of something like that."

"I think she hurt her head or something," Graham explained. "She keeps saying crazy stuff like that."

"Why didn't you make a portal from the school to the woods? A five-minute walk beats a detour to another world."

Wren's eyes widened. "I didn't actually think about it. I was scared. I wasn't thinking clearly!"

Great. Now Drew was talking about portals.

"Is there magic in Missouri Graham Dryson?" Drew asked.

"No … and you guys can call me Graham." His head was starting to hurt.

"Oh. I thought you said it was Graham Dryson," he said.

"It is, but Dryson is my last name."

"Last name? How many names have you had?" Drew frowned, running a hand over his head. "Never mind. We will deal with all of this tomorrow. You both look done in. You can stay with us tonight and we'll get this whole situation figured out in the morning."

"I can't stay," Graham said standing, "My aunt is going to be mad enough that I'm so late."

"I'm sorry, Graham," Drew said, shaking his head. "You won't be able to go home today. It's too far away."

"Can I use your phone?"

"I don't know what a phone is," Drew said softly. "I'm sorry to say this, Graham, but you have traveled to a new world. There isn't anything we can do tonight. I would suggest you sleep and tomorrow we'll deal with this."

"There's no such thing as magic." He wished he would wake up right now in his own bed. "If there was, couldn't you just open a portal and take me back?"

"It's not as easy as that," Drew said with a sad smile. "In fact, it's quite complicated."

Graham stared into the darkness. He couldn't believe he was sleeping in a strange bed, in a strange house, with so little explanation. The bed was the most comfortable thing he had ever laid on, and the room was at least five times bigger than his own. It felt odd trying to go to sleep with so much space.

It was equally hard to believe he was wearing a night-gown, or the closest thing he had ever worn to one. He'd thought Drew was joking when he handed him the long, drapey thing, but Drew hadn't been smiling. With the silly thing dangling around his legs, he felt like Ebenezer Scrooge.

Drew had promised to help him tomorrow. Tomorrow felt a million miles away. None of this made any sense. Magic wasn't real ... but he had seen the flash of light and felt himself fall. And there was the rag that Drew made appear ...

Aunt Temper was going to lose it. He wondered if she would call the police. She probably would. If she lost him, she lost her maid, cook and dog washer. She would probably make him quit basketball. She already hated how practice and games took him away. He was only allowed to do it because it gave her something to threaten him with.

"Oh no, basketball!" he said out loud as a realization hit him. He put his hands over his face. If he wasn't back for practice tomorrow, the coach might throw him off the team. It wasn't likely, because Graham was good, but you never knew what Coach Williams would do to make a point. If Graham didn't get a scholarship, there was no way he could go to medical school.

His eyelids felt heavy, but he wasn't sure if he'd be able to sleep. He wasn't sure if he *should* sleep. Drew didn't look dangerous, but Karlof sure did. How are you supposed to sleep when something this crazy happens? No matter

21

how hard he tried, he couldn't come up with anything that made sense. The more he thought about it, the more his stomach hurt. Hopefully, he'd wake up tomorrow and find out this had all been a wacky dream.

It couldn't be morning, could it? Graham felt so tired. He could feel Walter breathing on his face, and Walter knew better than to bug him until morning. Something wet dripped onto his cheek.

"Gross Walter!" he groaned, wiping at it. He opened his eyes, and instead of seeing a sloppy, bright eyed golden-doodle he saw ... a dragon? "AHHHHHH!"

Graham bounded off the bed, knocking the blankets to the floor. He backed away as the creature's pitch black eyes followed him. It was definitely a dragon. It wasn't any bigger than a small dog, but it had sharp teeth, green scales, and wings.

"Graham? Are you okay?" Wren called from the other side of the door.

"There's a dragon!" he yelled, not taking his eyes away from the creature. It tilted its head and watched him. The door opened and Wren peeked in. "Ahhh!" he yelled again, grabbing a blanket that had fallen from the bed. He wrapped it around himself. He didn't want to be killed by a dragon, but he really didn't want Wren to see him in a nightgown, either.

Wren laughed as she stepped into the room. "Don't worry," she said, scooping the dragon off the bed like it was a house cat. "Ben is a bantam. He can't breathe fire, and he's full grown." The creature curled up in Wren's arms and seemed to purr. Graham relaxed as much as he could, but it was a dragon!

Wren momentarily distracted him. She didn't just look pretty today; she was beautiful. The light hit her now neat, red hair and her green eyes sparkled like emeralds. Her long purple shirt and black leggings didn't look much different from what people back home wore. No cape today. She kissed the top of the dragon's head and moved closer to Graham. "Do you want to pet him?"

"Maybe later," Graham said, not wanting to lose his blanket. If dragons were real, then magic must be real, and he had gone through a portal. Why was his biggest worry about what he was wearing?

"Ahh, you are both awake," Drew said, entering the room with a bag and a pair of boots in his hands. He placed them on the bed. Where Wren was looking refreshed, Drew looked worse than yesterday. His reddish hair was poking out, and his clothes were rumpled. Dark circles ringed his eyes. He looked like he hadn't slept all night. "I bought you some clothes that will be better suited for today. After you get dressed, come to breakfast and we will talk." He nodded and left the room.

"Do you remember where the kitchen is?" Wren asked. Graham nodded. He was pretty sure he could remember where he had devoured a sandwich the night before. "The dining room is to the right of the kitchen." She smiled and left with Ben, shutting the door behind her.

He walked to the bag and pulled out a curious-looking shirt he wanted to call a tunic. It was long and blue, with a v-neck and a criss-cross drawstring. Or a lace. Maybe a cord? Was he supposed to tie it at the top or leave the laces hanging down? He shook his head and sighed. The pants weren't bad. They almost looked like cargo pants, but they didn't have pockets. There was also a belt and a black cape.

"Well, if anyone can pull off a cape ..." He joked to himself. "And who names a dragon, Ben?"

It was hard not to stare at Graham as he entered the dining area. He looked so much more handsome now that he was wearing normal clothes. The short britches he had been wearing yesterday had been borderline ridiculous. He wasn't wearing his cloak, but had it draped over his arm.

"Sit," Drew said, standing and motioning to the empty chair across from Wren. Graham sat and looked relieved to see they were eating fruit, hot chocolate, and toast. Wren wondered what he was thinking. He grabbed his toast and took a bite.

"I was glad to see you were still here this morning, Graham." Drew winked. "I worried you might slip out at night, thinking we are all crazy people."

"The thought might have crossed my mind," Graham said, with a half grin. "After meeting Ben, I'm finally convinced."

"There aren't dragons in your world?"

"No. Only in stories."

"That sounds like a sad world," Wren said. She loved dragons. She couldn't imagine a place where Ben didn't exist.

"It's strange, the things you have that I've seen so far, and the things you don't."

"What do you have we don't?" Wren asked, leaning forward.

"You don't have phones," he said, holding up the rectangle object he had showed her yesterday.

"What does it do?"

"Everyone has a different number. If you put a person's number into your phone, it will alert that person and you can talk to each other by holding it to your ear. You can talk to them from anywhere in the world."

"Wow, that's amazing!" It sounded like magic to her. "What are some things that are the same?"

"Electricity and running water," Graham said, smiling. "I was relieved to see the flushing toilet. Your house doesn't look much different from the houses where I'm from."

Wren raised her eyebrow. "The houses looked different to me."

"Yeah, well, that's because you saw the ghetto. I don't live in the nicest area of town. I've never seen a house as fancy as yours. It wouldn't make me think I was in a different world, just a different zip code."

"Zip code?"

"A different neighborhood."

Her dad yawned. "I have to leave soon, so I'm going to talk while you two eat." Wren drank her hot chocolate faster than was probably good, but she figured she couldn't eat and listen at the same time. Too many things could go wrong today.

"Wren, you aren't allowed to open portals," he said, tapping his foot on the shiny wood floor.

"But–"

"I understand that you think you had to," he said, holding up a hand. "I don't want to know why you did it. The less I know, the better. The less I'm told how you proceed the better." He looked at Graham. "I have an important position with the governor. I'm one of seven fleet members. We counsel the governor. I'm not sure which of the members I can trust, so sometimes being ignorant is a blessing. Wren could get into a lot of trouble for this. A lot of trouble."

Wren slumped in her chair and stared at her plate. She didn't know who had it worse. She could go to prison, and Graham was stuck in a world that wasn't his own. The worst part of the whole situation was that it was all her fault.

"I've decided the best thing to do is to send you both to talk to my friend Brake. I want you to tell him everything that happened."

"But he's creepy," Wren protested. She couldn't see any way this could be a good plan.

"He's not creepy," Drew said with a pointed look. "Reclusive, yes, but he has his reasons for that. He wasn't always that way. You suspect things are wrong in Akkron. Things I've told you not to worry about. Brake shares some of your suspicions. I think he's the best one to help us. He can do things without drawing suspicion."

"So we can trust him?" Wren asked, fiddling with her napkin.

Drew nodded, popping a grape into his mouth. "Completely. Tell him everything. Even whatever it was you heard your teacher say."

"But it was about The Dark–"

"No!" Drew said, slapping his hand on the table. Graham raised his eyebrows and Wren clenched her teeth. She hated the way her father always ignored her concerns about The Dark Cloud. Everyone in Akkron pretended the group didn't exist. If she didn't think the governor was involved, she would take her suspicions straight to him.

"I cannot know anything, Wren!" He ran a hand through his already mussed hair. "I've decided, and this is the best plan. You need to go as soon as you eat. The faster you figure this out, the better you can prepare."

Arguing would be pointless, so Wren tried to eat a piece of toast. Breakfast wasn't her thing. Her Dad told her hot chocolate wasn't a complete breakfast, but it was what she usually had. Hot chocolate was a new thing that her best friend's mom shared with them. She wasn't excited to talk to Brake. The few times she had were always awkward.

"Don't talk to anyone on the way if you can help it." Drew wiped his mouth with a napkin and left the room.

"So, that was weird," Graham said, raising one eyebrow.

"Yeah," Wren agreed, tapping her fingernails on the table. "He doesn't want to know anything. It makes me more sure about things."

"What things?"

"Just some suspicions me and my friend have involving the governor. I don't think my dad trusts him, but he doesn't want to tell me."

"I guess there's corrupt government officials in every world," Graham said.

"Everyone senses something's wrong, but everyone's ignoring it. The governor is only allowed one term of two to six years, depending on how many votes he gets. Once he is in office, he can make any law he wants. They voted Governor Briggs in for six years. He had more votes than anyone has ever had. The first law he made was that the governor can stay in office as long as he wants."

"For real?" Graham chuckled. "That's the dumbest thing I've ever heard. That didn't pass, did it?"

"He's been in office for seven years now." She shrugged. "Some people grumble about it, but for the most part, no one has done anything. His popularity has gone down, but no one goes against him. I probably shouldn't be telling you any of this, but I suspect he is part of ..." she hesitated. She didn't know Graham. Why was she telling him things only she and Ming Li had discussed? She felt pretty sure he was a good person. He did try to help her when she was acting crazy.

"Part of what?" he asked, leaning forward.

"There's a rumor about a group that's trying to take over. Not just take over Akkron, but the entire world."

"Akkron, is this city?"

"Yes."

"What's your world called?"

She raised her eyebrow. "Um ... the world?"

"Oh. That's kind of boring."

"Well, what's your world called?"

"Earth."

She raised her eyebrow. "Earth? Like dirt? Okay ... Anyway, this group is called The Dark Cloud."

"Why are they called that?" he asked.

"A few unexplainable things have happened that we think they are behind. Each time something bad happened, the sky would cloud and turn black. Not even at night, in the middle of the day. It was like they used dark clouds to hide what they were doing, or to distract us. A few people disappeared. A couple of crazy fires broke out. Most people think it was only a storm and a coincidence. Nobody wants to believe it could be something malicious. Me and my friend Ming Li thought that our teacher Professor Dovin was up to something."

"That he was part of The Dark Cloud?"

"No, we didn't think anything like that. We've seen him sneaking around the school, looking suspicious. We actually thought he might be stealing money from the school. Ming Li is always trying to get me to do stupid things. She dared me to sneak into his office and see if I could find anything.

"She was supposed to be watching outside the classroom. I wonder what happened? She wouldn't leave me on purpose ... unless she saw a cute boy ... Anyway, I snuck in. I ended up hearing things I shouldn't and now I'm pretty sure there is a Dark Cloud and that Professor Dovin is part of it. I was scared and jumped through a portal," Wren said, wringing her hands.

"So I guess we go tell all of this to some guy named Brake?"

"I guess so." Wren wished he would blink. Graham was turning out to be the king of eye contact.

"Do I need to wear that cape?" he asked, wrinkling his nose and looking at the cloak on his chair.

"It's a cloak, not a cape," she said, picking it up. "See how it has a hood?" She held it out.

"Okay, but do I need to wear it? I feel funny enough in these clothes," he said, holding out his tunic.

"It's better if you do. When we go out, we wear a cape or a cloak. If you aren't wearing one, people will wonder why."

She grabbed her own cloak off a hook on the wall and fastened it. He reluctantly put his on. Wren thought it was funny that he thought these clothes were strange. No clothes were weirder than what he had been wearing yesterday. She smiled to herself as she remembered the look on his face this morning when he tried to hide behind his blanket. She couldn't believe her dad had given him a nightshirt. Most people didn't wear them, but her dad had no sense of fashion.

CHAPTER 3

Graham felt like he was taking things pretty well. He should probably be freaking out. Yesterday, magic didn't exist and today it did. Sure, he freaked out about the nightgown and the dragon, but who wouldn't? As soon as he got home, he would be in tons of trouble, but he'd deal with that later. Now here he was, walking through more trees, with a mysterious girl, wearing a cloak.

"Does everyone live in houses surrounded by trees?" he asked, breaking the silence.

"No," Wren said, stepping over a log. "My grandparents built our house out here because they liked their privacy. They liked the convenience of the city, so we aren't far out. It's only a twenty-minute walk to town. We're headed in the opposite direction though. Brake lives out here because he's weird. He doesn't go out much. At least to town. He goes off to other places, doing who knows what. My dad visits him a lot when he's home."

"Why doesn't he go to town?"

"No idea. My dad said I wouldn't judge him if I knew his story, but he won't tell me what it is."

"Why do you think he's weird?"

"It feels awkward to be around him. He stares at me like he can see what I'm thinking or something."

"Is that possible?" Graham asked, wincing. He was feeling his sore leg again. He hoped this was a short walk. "Can people here read minds?"

"No, thank goodness," Wren said, shuddering. "There are stories that say that hundreds of years ago, people could communicate telepathically, but nobody knows if that's true or not. Sometimes I wonder if my dad can do it. He knows when the governor wants him to do something, even when he hasn't seen him."

"What kind of magic can you do?"

"Uhhh, nothing too impressive," Wren said, following the dirt path around a large tree. "I can open portals, obviously. That's my strongest power. Most people can't do it, and there isn't a lot of reason to try since it's forbidden. I can levitate things, but nothing too big. I haven't practiced that like I should. It would have been helpful yesterday. I've never learned to summon anything either. I tried for a while, but I gave up."

"So you can learn magic?" That would be cool.

"If you have the gift, you can."

"So, not everyone here is magic?"

"No. Most people are. Now and then, someone isn't. We rarely talk about it because it makes everyone feel weird."

"Why aren't you allowed to open portals?"

"Portals aren't very stable. It would be easy to close one on yourself. You can't actually decide where the portal opens, either. You could end up jumping into a volcano or something."

Graham shuddered. It sounded like he was lucky he got through the portal before it closed. "So can you, like, pull a rabbit out of a hat?"

"No ... and I'm not sure why anyone would want to," she said, looking sideways at him. "Rabbits reproduce fast enough without bringing more. I guess you could pretend to pull it out, if you could summon one into the hat. I don't see the purpose though. Actually, that wouldn't work. You can't summon living things. At least I've never seen anyone do it."

"Do you use magic wands?" he asked, wondering why he kept asking such dumb questions. Talking seemed to keep things lighter. He wondered if Wren would think he was a big dork.

"No ... Well, some people do. It's kind of nerdy. You feel the magic inside of you and kind of push it out. Everything I do feels like it comes from inside of me and goes down my arms and out my fingers. You can use an object like a wand, but people who do that are made fun of. The wand doesn't help, it's just for show."

They walked in silence for a time. There was so much to think about.

"Hey," Graham said, having a thought, "Why can we understand each other? If we come from different worlds, shouldn't we speak different languages?"

"I have no idea," Wren said, shrugging.

"It seems odd that we both speak English."

"I don't know what English is. When we enter a portal to another world, we usually go to worlds that are like ours. Maybe that's why?"

"Could be. It seems strange though," Graham said, thinking. There were a lot of languages on Earth. It was hard to believe Wren would happen to go to the place that spoke the same language as her.

"I can always understand people when I go through portals ... Not that I go through many. A lot of worlds must have the same language."

"Are you missing school today?"

"No, it's an off day. We go for four days and have three days off."

"That's awesome. In my world we go to school for five days and get two days off."

Wren made a face, "That sounds terrible."

"It's not that bad. Better than hanging out with my aunt." Sometimes he wondered if he liked school, or if he enjoyed getting away.

"There it is," Wren said, pointing at a house and interrupting his thoughts.

Graham whistled. "That house is enormous! I imagined a little shack with a scary little hermit inside. This looks more like a castle."

Wren scanned the house. "It isn't that big ... Well, I guess it seems big compared to the houses I saw in your world."

"It even has towers and turrets! You could fit my house in that thing, like, fifty times," Graham said, shaking his head. "Your house is pretty big, too."

"Most of the houses in Akkron are."

"What type of jobs do people have here?"

"Teachers, politicians, shopkeepers, healers. I don't know, lots."

"What does this Brake guy do?"

"I'm not sure. He used to be a tutor. There are people that will pay good money to help their kids with magic."

"He has a house this big from being a tutor?"

"He probably inherited it. A lot of people in Akkron have money, but it's not because of their jobs. Their families have had money for generations. If you think this is impressive, you should see the governor's house. It looks like a castle."

Graham wondered what it would be like to have money just because someone handed it down to you. "Whoa, look at that." He pointed to the sky above the enormous house. It looked like a bird, but different. It was big. "Is it a dragon?"

"No," Wren said, squinting at the creature. "We don't get dragons that size around here. My guess is a pegasus or an alicorn. It's too far away to be sure."

"Wow, I can't believe I'm seeing all this awesome stuff and I won't be able to tell anyone."

"Why not?"

"Nobody would believe me."

"So you don't have alicorns, pegasi, or dragons? Do you have animals in your world?"

"Yeah, but nothing like those. I have a dog."

They walked up to the large castle-house. After pausing, she knocked on the door. It was quiet for an uncomfortable moment, and then the door slowly opened. A tall, dark man, with deep black eyes and thick curly hair, stood before them. His red shirt had the same ties as Graham's.

Wren didn't say anything, and Graham wasn't surprised. This man's eyes were sharp, and he didn't blink as he looked from Wren to Graham and his mouth stayed in a straight line. This man didn't look like any hermit Graham had ever seen ... not that he had seen many hermits. He thought he would be old, but he couldn't be over thirty-five and he was what most people would call attractive. He looked a lot like a young Morgan Freeman.

"Wren," the man finally said in an even tone. Graham thought his voice would be deep and scary, more like Karlof, but it was a smooth baritone that carried a friendly warmth to it. "And Wren's friend," he nodded at Graham. "Is something wrong with your father?" he asked, looking back at Wren.

"No," she said, a little more high pitched than normal. "My father sent us, though. We have a problem and he told us we need to come tell you about it."

"Come in." Brake stepped back to allow them entry. Graham didn't miss the way Brake eyed the woods suspiciously before bolting the door behind them. Graham tried not to squirm.

Brake led them through a large stone entryway and into a sitting room that was big enough to hold at least twenty people. The large crystal chandelier hanging in the center made Drew's chandelier look like a lamp in comparison. The furniture looked old-fashioned, but new. Exactly like something Graham would imagine being in a castle. Wren and Graham sat on a sofa and looked around awkwardly. "So, what is your problem, and why would it involve me?"

"I'm not sure why my father wants us to tell you," Wren admitted. "He didn't want to know the details."

"He seemed scared to hear it," Graham added.

"Tell me," the man said, sitting across from them. Wren summarized the past day, starting in her teacher's office. Brake didn't move or change expressions throughout the entire story. Graham could tell it was unnerving for Wren, the way he stared at her. When she finished, he didn't speak for a full minute. He looked at Graham and back to Wren and rubbed his chin.

"Opening a portal is an arrestable offense," he finally said. Wren looked at her lap. "I understand why you did it. If you had been discovered, you would most likely be dead now," he murmured quietly. Wren gasped. Given what she had told him earlier, Graham didn't think it was something she didn't know, but hearing someone else say it must have been scary. "I'm surprised to hear about Professor Dovin. He taught me in school, and I wouldn't have expected it ... Why didn't you open the portal by your house?"

"I wasn't thinking clearly. Do you have any ideas on how we can get Graham home?" she asked.

"I think you know as much about portals as anyone," he said, drumming his fingers on his knee. "I remember when you opened your first portal. You couldn't have been more than three. Your father was terrified of the trouble you might cause. I remember he taught you everything he could to make sure you knew the seriousness of it."

Wren nodded and looked away.

"I get that it's forbidden," Graham said, "But couldn't she open one really fast and let me jump through? Nobody would have to know I was even here."

Brake shook his head. "It doesn't work like that."

"I can't choose where a portal opens," Wren told him. "Once you open a portal into one place, it's highly unlikely that you'll ever open the same one again."

"Anywhere on Earth would be okay ..." That was what he said, but his thoughts didn't agree. There were plenty of places on Earth he wouldn't want to end up. Wren had already explained the whole 'might end up in a volcano' thing. There was nothing comforting about that. The chances of falling in the ocean were also pretty high.

"Wren doesn't get to decide what world to open a portal into. There are infinite amounts of worlds and dimensions," Brake explained.

"Couldn't we open a bunch and look through until it looked familiar?"

"No, you can't see through a portal," Wren said, looking at her boots. Graham didn't want her to feel guilty. It wasn't her fault he chased her.

"That's one of the biggest reasons portals are forbidden," Brake added. "They are incredibly dangerous."

"So you're saying I'm stuck here?" Graham asked, unsure how to feel.

"I'm afraid so," Brake said softly. "People have wasted lifetimes trying to find a certain world. It never ends well."

"Why did my father even send us here?" Wren asked. "I thought you must have some insight I didn't."

"Your father is in a very important position right now with the governor. Anyone with half a brain is aware the governor is up to no good. Your father needs to stay close to see if he can figure out what that is. He doesn't know who to trust. The less he knows regarding certain things, the better. If you don't know something, you can't tell others. Your father is a good man, but his poker face is abominable."

"Okay, so I'm stuck here." Graham took a deep breath. "What should I do?" He tried to look natural, so they wouldn't see the panic that was bubbling in his stomach. He was pretty sure he should win an award for looking calm when he wanted to scream or cry.

"You will stay with me for now," Brake said calmly. "We need to create the least amount of gossip possible. We will tell everyone that you are my nephew from Boztoll. Everyone knows I have a sister there. Her husband has no magic, and Boztoll is much kinder to those people than Akkron. That will explain why you have no magic yourself." Brake studied Graham with a sympathetic stare. "I am sorry for you, Graham. It will be hard to live among a magic people and not have it yourself. Some will ridicule you."

"I can take it," Graham said. He was sure it couldn't be much worse than Temperance and Kaylee. How would he give up basketball, though? And what about becoming a doctor? Did they even have doctors here? How were some of his teammates going to pass math if he didn't help them study? He took a deep breath and tried again to push the panic down.

"I'm also sorry that you'll never see your family again," Brake said, rubbing the back of his neck.

"I live with my aunt and cousin, and they never liked me, anyway." He paused. "I'll miss my friends ... and school. Will I be able to go to school here? Do they teach anything besides magic?"

Wren giggled, and Brake even smiled.

"They don't teach magic at school," Wren explained. "That's something we have to learn at home."

"So what do you learn at school?" he asked.

"Math, reading, science ..." Wren said, shrugging.

"Oh," Graham said, embarrassed. "Any sports? Basketball?"

"There are sports, but not that one. Is that what you were playing when I saw you?"

"Yes," Graham said, feeling more regret. He swallowed the lump that was trying to choke him. "I was hoping to get a scholarship playing basketball so I could go to a good university." He could get an academic scholarship as well, and with multiple scholarships, he had hoped he would have a free ride through college.

"We have octaball," Wren said, tapping her lip. "That's the most popular sport. People pay a lot to go see the professional teams play. The governor's fleet members get free tickets. I'm sure my dad would take you sometime, if you want to go." She cringed. "He makes me go at least once a year."

"He makes you go? Isn't it fun?"

"Meh," Wren shrugged. "If it wasn't for the snacks, it would be a complete waste of an afternoon. It's better to watch it than to play it though. Coach Zalliah makes us play octaball in gym class at least every other week. I think she enjoys humiliating those of us with no coordination."

"Why's it called octaball?" Graham had a funny picture pop into his head. "Is the ball shaped like an octopus?"

"No. There are eight people on a team. I think that's why it has octa in it."

"I used to love it when I was young," Brake said. "You have to be fast to compete well."

"I'm pretty fast. I was one of the best players on my basketball team. They're going to be short-handed without me. Our alternate players aren't very good, but there's always someone to step in."

"I'll try to tell you about our world before you go to school, so you'll be prepared." He put a comforting hand on Graham's shoulder. The accompanying warmth made him feel a little better.

"Can't Graham stay at my house?" Wren asked. "I'm sure my dad wouldn't mind. We could say he's my cousin. That way, I can teach him all the things that happen at school."

Brake and Graham looked at Wren for a few seconds and Graham let a small laugh escape. "No one is going to believe we're cousins," he said with a crooked smile.

"Why not?" Wren asked, causing Graham to smile even wider. He grabbed Wren's pale arm and put his own next to hers and pointed at them.

"Even if you tan for days, we aren't going to look like cousins."

Wren blushed, "Right," she mumbled. "But you and Brake aren't exactly the same color either."

Brake laughed out loud. "Perhaps not, but that can be explained because my sister's husband is white. No one will question Graham, being a little lighter than me. Your family is well known and it couldn't be easily explained."

"Can't Graham pretend to have magic?" Wren said, trying to change the subject before her mistake had her cheeks turning any more red than they already were. "Some people do it."

"It always comes out," Brake said with a shake of his head.

"But we aren't allowed to do magic at school, so would anyone need to know?" Wren asked, looking at Brake. "And there's a trick that me and my ... someone do. I cup my hands," she said, her eyes bright with excitement, "And I bring up light." Her hands filled with a ball of light.

"Wow!" Graham said, leaning forward.

"Cup your hands, Graham," she instructed. He cupped his hands. "Okay, I'm going to transfer the light to your hands and it will look like we're passing it, even though I'm doing it all."

An orb of light leaped into his hands.

"That was so cool!" Graham said, looking at the orb. It felt warm.

"That was impressive," Brake said, looking at the light.

Graham looked at Wren and smiled. She was looking at him with wide eyes. "What's wrong?" he asked.

She held up her orb. "I didn't pass you the light."

Chapter 4

Wren leaned back in her chair and made pictures out of the swirly patterns on the ceiling. If yesterday was the weirdest day ever, today was the most boring. Brake had been trying to get Graham to recreate the light orb for the last four hours. Brake made him try it while standing, sitting, comfortable, uncomfortable ... Wren wondered if it would be rude to go home.

"I don't understand," Brake frowned, sitting on a chair facing Graham. "You did it so easily the first time."

"Maybe I didn't do it," Graham mumbled, rubbing his eyes.

"Are you sure you didn't do it, Wren?" Brake asked, for at least the fifth time.

"I didn't do it," she said, not bothering to look at them. She found a shape on the ceiling that looked like a lopsided unicorn.

"Well, I didn't do it. That only leaves you, Graham."

Wren's stomach growled. The only break they'd taken was at lunchtime. She shuddered at the thought of calling what they ate lunch. It was a type of sandwich. What kind? She had no idea. How anyone could make a sandwich taste that bad was beyond her. It was mushy and hard at the same time and she couldn't identify anything about it except the bread. Brake was no chef. Even the drinks he served tasted like a sugarless mix of lemons and water trying to pass itself off as legitimate lemonade.

One thing Wren had learned today was that she had misjudged Brake completely. After watching him for a while, he seemed as normal as anyone. He was still intimidating, but not nearly as scary or unapproachable as she'd spent the last several years imagining him to be. He seemed to care about what happened to Graham.

"Do you want another sandwich?" Brake asked her.

"Oh, no thanks," she said quickly.

"Do people from other worlds usually have magic?" Graham asked.

"Sometimes," Brake said, "But not usually. If your world doesn't have magic, it's highly unlikely you would."

Something was stirring in the back of Wren's mind, but she wasn't sure what.

"That's it!" she said, popping up from her recumbent position. "You are different from people in your world! When I was little and I started opening portals, it totally freaked my parents out. My dad gave me some dust that would turn me invisible, but it only works on people who aren't magic. I put some on right before you saw me. You shouldn't have been able to see me!"

"That's right," Graham said slowly. "My cousin Kaylee couldn't see you."

"But you could," Brake muttered, rubbing his temples.

Graham leaned forward with his elbows resting on his knees. "So that's why you were staring at me all creepy. You thought I couldn't see you."

Wren scowled. "What do you mean, all creepy?" She didn't know why she asked. She had been staring at him like a creep.

He laughed. "I was ready to go home when you walked up. You have to understand, your clothes are ridiculously different from what I'm used to, and you were standing there with your cape and hair blowing all over the place ... You looked kinda freaky."

Wren's lips curled up in a smile as she leaned back into her chair. It was funny to think of Graham being scared of her. He was at least seven inches taller, and way stronger, but she had probably looked peculiar. "I guess I did look crazy."

"Why were you staring at me like that, anyway? I swear you didn't even blink."

Wren's smile disappeared, and she racked her brain for an answer that made sense and wouldn't be embarrassing. She didn't want to tell him the real reason she had watched him. Brake had a small, knowing look on his face, and his brown eyes twinkled as he looked at Wren. She could feel heat creeping up her neck and ears. He could at least have the decency to look away.

She fiddled with her sleeve and didn't look at Graham. "I hadn't ever seen anyone play a game like that before ...

with the ball ... and stuff." It wasn't a lie. Just an omission. She didn't have any interest in sports, in this world or any other.

"You seem to be taking all of this well," Brake said, putting a comforting hand on Graham's shoulder.

"Yeah, well, it still doesn't seem real. I hear you saying I can't ever go home, but something in me refuses to believe it."

"It's true there might be a way, someday," Brake said, as he removed his hand, "But right now there's nothing I can think of." He gave Graham a speculative look, "You said you were raised by your aunt? May I ask what happened to your parents?"

Graham leaned back and looked at the ceiling. "I don't even remember them. They went on a boat for their anniversary. I think it was a cruise or something. A huge storm arose, and the boat capsized. My aunt was my only relative, so she was stuck with me."

"I'm sorry," Brake said sincerely. Graham nodded. "Where are your parents from?"

"My guess is Missouri. My aunt won't talk about them at all. She used to get really mad if I mentioned them. I was planning on trying to find out some things about them someday, but I never got the chance. If my parents were magic, wouldn't my aunt be too?"

Brake tapped his heel against the floor. "I'm not sure. I've never heard of anything like this before. Missouri. I feel like I may have heard of it. It isn't close to California, is it?"

"No."

Before Wren could ask Brake how he knew anything of Graham's world, a loud knock on the door made them all jump. "Wren!" a girl's voice called from the other side of the door.

Wren hopped up. "That sounds like Ming Li!" She hurried into the entryway and unbarred the front door.

Ming Li grabbed her in a tight hug. The petite girl came to Wren's chin. "What happened to you?" she asked, stepping back and tossing her long black hair over her green cape. "I looked away for two seconds and you disappeared!"

"You were supposed to be keeping watch!"

"I was."

"Why didn't you stop Professor Dovin from coming in?"

"Oh, no!" Ming Li exclaimed, putting her hands to her cheeks. "I swear, I only looked away for a few seconds. He must have slipped in behind. I saw him and a woman come out and I figured you must have gone in, seen him, and left. I couldn't figure out how you got past me. Did he see you?"

"Almost, but I got out."

"How?" she asked, putting her hands on her hips. "You didn't open a portal, did you?"

"I didn't really have a choice."

"We promised to never go through a portal again, remember? And if you are going to break the rules, you should only do it when I'm with you. I don't want you getting arrested alone."

Wren crossed her arms. "Yeah, well, if The Dark Cloud found me eavesdropping on them, I could be a lot worse than arrested."

"What does The Dark Cloud have to do with anything?"

"Professor Dovin is part of The Dark Cloud," Wren said. Ming Li's eyes widened at the revelation. "That's why I had to open a portal."

"I'm so sorry, Wren," Ming Li said, giving her another quick hug. "I can't believe I looked away."

"Who were you looking at?" Wren asked, raising her eyebrow.

"What do you mean? You just assume I was looking at a boy?"

"I know you were looking at a boy."

"Oh, fine, it was Tal."

Wren groaned and rolled her eyes. "Come on! Anyone but Tal. He's evil."

"He's not evil. His dad is evil. He's only a conceited jerk. That doesn't mean that he isn't incredibly good looking."

Brake cleared his throat, and Wren jumped. She had forgotten about Brake and Graham, and now they were standing behind her.

"Hey, Uncle Brake," Ming Li beamed, stepping through the door into Brake's arms.

"Ming Li," Brake said, patting her on the back. "It's been awhile."

"Uncle?" Wren blinked. "I thought I knew everything about you."

"It's more of an honorary title," Ming Li said, with a curious sideways glance at Graham. "Brake is good friends with my mom."

Brake was good friends with Drew, but Wren barely knew the man. She had spent more time with him today than the rest of her life put together. It seemed odd that Ming Li had never mentioned it before. They spent most of their free time together.

"Wren, you shouldn't be telling anyone that you opened a portal." Brake said, fixing her with his gaze. He motioned them all back into the sitting room. "If it leaks out, you will be in a lot of trouble."

"I only told Ming Li. She was supposed to be my look-out yesterday."

"And we tell each other everything," Ming Li said.

"Except about honorary uncles, apparently." Wren glared playfully at her friend.

"I really am sorry," Ming Li said. "I only looked away for a second. Even you have to admit Tal is good looking ... and speaking of good looking, who is your friend?" She smiled as she gazed at Graham from under her lashes. Graham twitched, and Brake rolled his eyes.

Ming Li never knew when to keep something to herself, and she never had the decency to get embarrassed. Wren was always getting embarrassed and sometimes suffered second hand embarrassment for her friend.

"I'm going to be in the next room if you need me," Brake said, shaking his head, and opening a door off to the side.

"This is Graham," Wren said, trying to ignore the blatant way Ming Li was smiling at him. "Graham, this is Ming Li. She's my best friend."

Graham shifted from one foot to the other. "Hey. Ming Li? Is that Chinese?"

"Chinese?" Ming Li asked, scrunching her forehead.

"Nevermind. Sorry." He looked awkwardly around the room.

"No, Ming Li is sorry," Wren said, sitting. "She's at least partially to blame for your being here."

"What do you mean?" Ming Li asked, still staring at Graham.

"Sit down and I'll tell you." Wren pointed at the seat next to her. Graham sat on a sofa across from her, and Ming Li sat on the chair. She quickly told Ming Li everything that had happened in Professor Dovin's office and everything that had happened after she went through the portal ... Well, almost everything. It didn't seem necessary to tell her about staring at Graham, especially with him there. She ended with Graham following her through the portal.

Ming Li wasn't smiling anymore. "I'm so sorry, Graham. I should have guarded the classroom better. There isn't any way I can ever make this up to you."

"Everyone keeps telling me they're sorry," Graham said. "Don't worry about it. Things happen. My life wasn't that great before I came here. This could be a good change for me."

Wren hoped he wasn't just saying that to make them feel better.

"You owe me, though. This means you both have to be my friends, right?" When he smiled, Wren could feel her insides melting into a gooey mess. He had a really nice smile.

"We aren't the cool kids or anything," Ming Li admitted. "I mean, we aren't losers or anything, but we won't make you popular."

"That's okay. I've been popular, and it isn't that great."

"I'll take your word for it."

"You can help us try to capture The Dark Cloud," Wren said.

Ming Li laughed. "Capture The Dark Cloud? How exactly do we do that? I thought we were just going to turn Professor Dovin in."

"Turn him in? To who?" Wren asked.

"Ummmm ... good point. Nobody would believe us or care, most likely. Did you hear what happened last night?"

"No. What?"

"You know Jayan from our math class? He was out of town with his family, and when they came back, everything in their house was packed. They had a note telling them they had one hour to leave. They decided to wait until morning and that night their house burned down. Everyone got out, thankfully. There's no question in my mind about who did it. They are getting more brazen. The note had a picture of a cloud on it."

Wren shook her head. "That doesn't make sense. Jayan can do magic. I've seen him."

"Yeah, but his grandma can't, and she lives with them. The governor said it was all an accident, and he isn't going to look into it because no one was hurt. My mom is so mad ... and scared. That was really close to our house."

"So, what do we do?" Graham asked.

"I'm not sure," Wren admitted. "There isn't much a bunch of kids can do. A lot of people pretend The Dark Cloud doesn't exist. I think everyone is scared. No one wants to risk anything."

Ming Li raised her hand. "I'm always ready to take a risk. My permanent seat in detention will tell you that."

"I've always wanted to make a difference," Graham said. "Back home, there were people who thought they could do anything, and people pretended it was okay. It made me mad, but I didn't do anything. I don't know much about The Dark Cloud, but it sounds like destroying their group would make a difference. I'm in."

"We would be on our own, though," Wren said, shifting her weight. "Everyone is pretending everything is okay."

"Well, someone has to take a stand. If we do, others might follow. I mean, it's not like we can arrest someone or anything, but we can make people more aware. It doesn't matter if a million people say that something is okay. Right is still right and wrong is still wrong. I think this could be my chance to make a difference in the world ... even if it's not my world."

"What do we know for sure?" Ming Li asked, her brown eyes shining. She always liked to have a plan, even if it wasn't a well thought out plan.

"That Professor Dovin is in The Dark Cloud," Wren said. "That's at least something."

Ming Li nodded. "And since he's at school, we can watch him."

The door opened a crack. "No portals," Brake called from the other side. He shut the door, and they all chuckled.

"We also know that someone named Melly is working with Professor Dovin," Graham added.

"Right," Wren said, wondering how she had forgotten about the woman. "Ming Li, did you see what she looked like?"

"Ummm," Ming Li said, tapping her finger on her chin and looking at the ceiling. "I wasn't thinking about her, because I was wondering where you were. I remember thinking she wasn't pretty, so I was surprised Professor Dovin was with her. He usually hangs out with the hot teachers. She was really skinny, like too skinny."

"So we're looking for a super skinny, ugly person?" Wren asked, wrinkling her nose. "That's not a lot to go on."

"She wasn't ugly, just not pretty."

"And we have her name," Graham added. "Shouldn't that be useful?"

"Brake!" Ming Li called, "Do you know anyone named Melly?"

"No!" Brake called from behind the door.

"How did you find me today?" Wren asked Ming Li.

"Your dad told me you were here," she said, eyes twinkling.

"I'm surprised he told you where I was. He didn't want anyone to know what happened."

"He didn't want to tell me," Ming Li admitted. "I told him I would wait on the porch until you came home. I sat there and sang *The Goblin Who Fell into Fifty Puddles of Mud* as loud as I could. After fifteen minutes, he came out and told me where you were."

"I bet," Wren giggled. "That's the worst song."

"It probably helps that I can't sing worth anything," she said, shrugging. "I don't think your dad likes me very much."

"He just doesn't like you getting me into trouble."

Graham raised an eyebrow. "So you aren't the popular kids or the losers, you're the troublemakers?"

"We aren't that bad. It's mostly Ming Li. She only pulls me in occasionally."

The door opened again. "No more trouble, Ming Li," Brake said, peeking out. "If you are at all serious about tracking The Dark Cloud, you shouldn't bring attention to yourselves. I know you think you are alone in this, but you aren't. There is a group trying to bring them to justice. You should listen to whispers, but not act. You need to be careful."

"We're always careful," Ming Li said, pushing her hair over her shoulder. Brake frowned at her and pointed at Graham. "We're almost always careful," she amended with a sassy smile.

"I don't want you to do anything without talking to me first. If you learn anything about The Dark Cloud, I want you to tell me and I'll pass the information on to this group. They have resources and experience that you don't."

Wren cocked her head. "We need to act, though! Nobody has so far. I don't want to hide in the background and pretend everything will fix itself. Not if I can help."

"Me either," Graham and Ming Li said at the same time.

"I understand you are all enthused, but you need to think. What will you do if you find someone from The Dark Cloud? Knock them out, tie them up, and keep them in your closet?" They all looked at each other. He had a point. "Just talk to me first. Please," Brake pleaded, looking at each of them. They all nodded. "Graham, I think I need to tell you more about our world. You'll want to be prepared for school."

"I'll walk you part way home," Ming Li said to Wren, as they stood and walked to the door.

"I guess I'll see you both around," Graham said, looking nervous.

Wren and Ming Li left the house and strolled quietly down the path.

"What are you thinking?" Wren asked as they walked.

"I was wondering why you didn't jump to the portal by your house. That would have fixed everything."

"Ugh. Does everyone have to point that out?"

"It seems pretty obvious."

"I've never made a portal from our world to another place in our world, so I guess I wasn't thinking. I hope Graham doesn't hate it here and resent me."

"He seems nice. I doubt he would hate you. It's not anyone's fault completely. I should have kept a better watch. You shouldn't have gone there, and Graham shouldn't have run after you."

"Do you actually think Graham will want to hang out with us once we get to school?" Wren wondered.

"He has to," Ming Li said, smiling. "We already called him."

Graham smiled at his makeshift basketball hoop. It wasn't bad for an hour of work. Brake had a basement full of odds and ends, and he told Graham he could use whatever he wanted. As soon as breakfast was over, Graham had gotten to work, though his stomach was still trying to recover from the atrocity Brake had tried to pass off as food. It might have been pancakes. It didn't taste like pancakes, or really look like them, but he watched Brake pour some kind of batter onto a skillet and burn it.

After locating a large bucket, Graham cut the bottom out. It was just big enough for a ball to slide through. Brake was letting him use a big room in his house for a basketball court. A fancy room. It looked like a room from a fairytale where people would have a ball or a party. There were several chandeliers, but there wasn't any furniture.

Graham felt bad using it, but Brake said it was a room he didn't use anymore. It had a wooden floor, which was better than the ground outside. He even let him nail the hoop onto the wall. It was nice of Brake to let him do this. It helped him keep his mind off the fact that his life had completely changed in a few hours.

Picking up his ball, he dribbled it a few times. The ball had been the tricky thing. He had to think hard to remember whether he had still had it when he ran through the portal. He finally decided he must have, and so he had gone out into the forest to find it. After coming back empty-handed, Brake had offered to go with him. He knew the place Wren had opened her first portal, so with his help, they found it pretty fast. The ball was under a tree and still full of air.

"Graham Dryson dribbles down the court," Graham narrated. "It's all up to him, with only seconds on the clock. Will he make the shot, or will he ruin it for his team?" Graham launched the ball at the bucket. "He shoots! He scores! Right at the buzzer, ladies and gentlemen! And the crowd goes wild!" Graham raised his hands in triumph and quickly stopped and turned towards the sound of laughter.

Wren raised her eyebrow. "Are you supposed to talk to yourself during the game?"

"Of course," Graham said, ignoring the heat creeping up his neck. Wren was wearing a long green shirt, and she had her hair in a neat ponytail. He grabbed the ball and tossed it to her. She caught it and her eyes lit up. "Try throwing it through the hoop," he said, motioning to the bucket.

"Do I have to talk?" Wren asked. "I think that will make it harder."

"No, just throw it in."

Wren looked at the ball and hoop. She threw it and missed by a good four feet.

Graham laughed. "Air ball."

"That was my first try. It doesn't count!" Wren ran and scooped up the ball. She went closer to the basket and tossed the ball underhand. It hit the rim and bounced off.

"That was closer," Wren said, nodding as she chased after the ball.

He shook his head and tried to keep any humor from his eyes. "That was called a granny shot. Even if you make it that way, people are going to laugh at you." Wren glared at him as she retrieved the ball. She threw it awkwardly at him and he caught it.

"Fine," she said, crossing her arms, "Show me how to do it." Graham grinned, amused at how unthreatening she looked. He shook his head, remembering how scary she'd seemed at their first meeting.

"First, I'll teach you to play horse," Graham decided, dribbling the ball. "It's easier than learning to play basketball."

She tilted her head as she looked at him. "I haven't played horses since I was five. I haven't even played unicorns since I was eight. It might be funny to see you running around pretending to be a horse, though."

"It's a game with the ball," Graham said, rolling his eyes. He quickly explained the rules. "Are you in?"

"Sure." He handed her the ball.

"I'm in too," Ming Li said from the doorway. She had a bright yellow shirt with a brown belt around her waist, and she was pulling her hair into a quick ponytail. She took off her cape and tossed it onto the floor. "Brake told me to come down."

"Okay," Graham said, "Let me tell you the rules."

"I already heard. It sounds easy enough." With complete confidence, she ran up and stole the ball from Wren and threw it through the basket.

"She shoots! She scores!" Ming Li called out, pumping her arms in the air.

"Why, shoots? You threw the ball. I don't understand the point of saying what you do," Wren said, shaking her head. "And that didn't count because it's my turn."

Ming Li grinned and scooped the ball up, tossing it to Wren. She caught it and ran closer to the bucket. Graham tried not to smile at how awkward and cute she was. She threw the ball and missed. Ming Li grabbed the ball before it could get away and tossed it through the hoop. She grabbed it again and tossed it to Graham.

"Okay, let's see what you've got!"

Wren sat against the wall, watching Ming Li and Graham play. She had only made one basket. She wasn't sure why it was called a basket when it was a bucket. Graham quickly won their game, and when they started playing a more competitive one, Wren decided to watch. She couldn't dribble the ball like Graham showed her and walk or run at the same time. She was also sweating, and she didn't want to take another shower today.

"Can I sit?" Brake asked from beside her. She was startled at his sudden presence.

"Sure."

He lowered himself to the floor and watched Ming Li and Graham. "Peculiar game," he murmured. "Still, I can see it catching on."

"I'm not very good," Wren admitted. "It's kind of fun, but I can't keep up with them."

"Things like that take practice," Brake said, rubbing his smooth chin.

"Ming Li is a natural, but she's a natural at all sports. I'm pretty bad at most of them."

"Everyone has natural talent for some things," Brake said, still watching the game. "If we were all good at the same things, life would be pretty boring."

"I guess I could get better at sports," she said thoughtfully, "But I don't care that much. Graham seems incredibly good at it. When I watched him before we came through the portal, he never missed."

"Everyone misses sometimes. It's part of life."

Wren wondered if he was still talking about basketball. A sudden cracking noise sounded and part of Graham's bucket fell to the ground.

"You broke it!" Ming Li exclaimed, wiping sweat from her forehead.

"Yeah," Graham said, panting and walking in a circle with his hands at his hips. "I figured it would happen, eventually. I'll figure something else out later."

Ming Li's eyes sparkled. "Wren can work on her dribbling."

"No thanks," Wren said, standing. "I think I've had enough today. You two don't need me to make you look better. I should probably go."

"Will you come back tomorrow?" Graham asked.

"I have to help my dad tomorrow, but I'll see you at school the day after?"

"Yes," Brake said, "I had a talk with the governor early this morning and he said Graham can start immediately. I was worried it would take more time. The governor seemed eager to help, which is not like him."

"I'll walk home with you," Ming Li said, linking arms with Wren. "Then we can talk about how cute Graham is when he plays basketball." Wren didn't want to see the look on Graham's face, so she steered Ming Li towards the door.

"Bye Wren. Bye Ming Li," Brake laughed. Graham didn't say anything.

"If you keep those two as your friends, you certainly won't get bored," Brake chuckled, patting Graham on the back.

"Yeah, I never know how to react to Ming Li," Graham admitted as they walked down the hallway and into the kitchen.

"Ming Li never hides what she's thinking. She's been like that since the day I met her. Wren is the opposite from what I observe. They are good for each other. I think they might be good for you as well." He opened the refrigerator and scanned the items.

"They seem nice." Graham grabbed two cups and put them on the table. "They feel guilty about me being here."

"You seem to be doing well."

Brake put some type of green vegetable on the counter. Graham wasn't sure what it was, or if he wanted to taste it. It looked like thick green worms with wilted stems.

"To be honest, it's been a lot better here than at my house," Graham admitted. "I wish I had some of my things, though."

"What things?" Brake asked as he scooped the green vegetables on two plates and added a blob of something white and lumpy. He placed them on the table and sat in front of one. Graham took the other seat and looked suspiciously at the food. He imagined it coming alive and eating him.

"I wish I had my clothes," he said, poking the white stuff with his fork to see if it would move. "It would be nice to have my books. I brought my phone, but I broke it. It wouldn't work here, anyway." He took a small bite of the white blob. It wasn't bad. It wasn't good either.

"Sorry, I'm not much of a cook," Brake said, "But I'm sure you have already realized that."

"It's fine," Graham said, as he tried to swallow the green thing. It was pretty gross, and it seemed to get bigger the more he chewed and it was coating his teeth in slippery scum. If he thought about it too much, he was going to gag.

"The bizarre thing about being here is the way this world seems so different from my world, but has some things that are exactly the same. I mean, your fridge looks exactly like the ones back home. And your toilets. It seems like they would be different, even if they do the same thing."

"Not so long ago, it was easier to visit other worlds than it is now. Because of this, there are similar things in a lot of worlds. If a person visited a different world and found something they felt was better than what we had, they would learn everything about it and make it here. They could even bring supplies or laborers from one world to another."

"I guess that makes sense," Graham said, trying not to gag on another bite of green stuff. If any food could make a person cry ... this was it.

"Wait until dessert," Brake said, his eyes sparkling with anticipation. "Dessert is my weakness." He pointed his fork at a box on the counter. "That box has some muffins from Mali's Bakery. Mali is Ming Li's mother. She is the best baker Akkron has ever seen. Hurry and finish and I'll let you have one."

CHAPTER 5

The warm Akkron sun was shining into Graham's eyes as he walked to school. His brain was a little overloaded as he looked at a small map to the school that Brake had drawn for him. It didn't look too difficult to read. Graham sifted through all the information Brake told him about Akkron the day before. Akkron was the capital city. It only had around one hundred thousand people, but it was the most populated city in this world. The world needed a name. The world was made up of two continents. A governor and his seven fleet members ran all cities on this continent. They were called the fleet because they were supposed to be working towards the same goals, though Brake admitted that it rarely happened, and that it was getting worse all the time. They were supposed to work for the good of the people, but they didn't listen when anyone brought up suspicions related to The Dark Cloud.

A rumor circulated that The Dark Cloud was trying to get anyone who wasn't magic to leave Akkron. They didn't do it outright. Strange things would happen that caused them to move. Houses would burn, or they would lose their jobs. Some left without explanation. Brake assumed they were being threatened, but nobody wanted to say anything. Most moved to Boztoll, the city Brake's sister lived in.

Brake said that all types of magic were accessible to anyone who had magic. In theory, one person didn't have more magic than another. Some people were better at certain aspects of magic because they practiced more, while others were naturals, like Wren with the portals. Graham wished they taught magic in school.

Brake also told him about lost magic. There were some things that had been so difficult to learn that people gave up on them, and nobody knew how to do them anymore. Some people whispered that The Dark Cloud was trying to bring back some of this old magic. If they managed, that would put everyone else at a disadvantage.

Karlof, who turned out to be Wren's uncle, had come by the night before with a bunch of green tunics and capes for Graham. Green and black were the only colors they allowed at school. Graham wasn't sure how he was going to pay Wren's family back, and he worried about how long Brake would allow him to stay, although Brake assured him he could stay as long as was needed.

It wasn't long before Graham passed the forest and came to a dirt road. After following it for a few minutes, he came to a paved road with houses scattered here and there.

They were all big and fancy, but he didn't see any as big as Brake's.

He didn't know what he'd expected. It looked more like an old British T.V. show than a different world ... until he saw a unicorn trotting towards him. This wasn't a small unicorn either, and it was brown. Graham had thought all unicorns were white. Well, he'd thought they didn't exist, but if they did, he thought they were supposed to be white. A man was perched on top, wearing a blue cape. The closer the unicorn came to him, the more nervous he felt. He moved to the far side of the road to avoid it.

The nearer he came to the school, the closer together the houses were. There were more people and unicorns as well. There were several colors of unicorn, including black, brown, white, and tan. Some were even spotted. They were beautiful, but he didn't want to get too close. He made it a point to stay away from most animals, and these were huge! They were probably the size of a horse, but Graham had never been close to a horse either. It surprised Graham that there were paved roads when there weren't any vehicles. Maybe it was easier on the unicorns hooves.

Wren had been right. Everyone he saw was wearing a cape or cloak. He didn't feel as strange in his green clothes and black cape now. All the men he saw had different lengths of hair, but all the women had incredibly long and shiny hair. It was like being in a shampoo commercial.

As the road turned, he was greeted by a street lined with cozy shops. They were all connected and had big colorful signs above them. The shops didn't appear to be named, they simply described what they were. There was The

Clothing Shop, Wood Shop, Jewelry Shop, and Capes and Cloaks. Mali's Bakery was the only one that had a name.

The school was at the end of the road. The building was large and gray, with five levels. It seemed a little ... boring. It was rectangular, with no embellishments. After all the fancy houses, Graham was a little disappointed. There wasn't anything remarkable about it. Graham stopped and looked around. Kids his age were going into the building or lounging on the lawn, talking. If not for all the strange clothing, he could imagine he was anywhere on Earth.

Graham hoped to see Wren so he wouldn't feel so lost. He'd settle for Ming Li if he had to, but that girl's flattering talk made him feel uncomfortable. Obviously, she had good taste, but she was a bit too unfiltered for him. Not seeing either of the girls as he scanned the grounds, he decided to go in by himself. Taking a deep, resolved breath, he made his way to the school.

Inside smelled like an old musty hotel, but it looked decent enough. Trophy cases lined the white walls, and light gray tiles covered the floor. He walked to one case and looked inside. All the trophies were for the sport Wren and Brake had told him about called octaball.

"Hey," a boy around Graham's age said, coming to stand next to him. He pushed perfectly brown waves out of his eyes. He was almost as tall as Graham. Even though he wore the same color of clothing as everyone else, his looked more expensive. It fit like it was made for him. He stuck out his hand. "You must be the new guy. I'm Tal."

Graham shifted as he shook the boy's hand. "Graham. I didn't know anyone knew I was coming." This must be the boy Ming Li and Wren had been talking about.

"Well, I get more information than most people," Tal said with a cocky smile.

"Oh, and why is that?"

"Because the world revolves around him," Ming Li said, joining them. She crossed her arms and glared at Tal. "And his dad is the governor, so he thinks he's special."

"Hey Li," Tal said, still smiling. "It always warms my heart when you brag about me."

Ming Li rolled her eyes. "Whatever. And don't call me Li. I'm pretty sure we have had that conversation before."

"She actually likes me," Tal said to Graham. "She just likes to hide it."

"Just because your dad is the governor and you have incredibly nice shoulders, doesn't make you better than everyone else," Ming Li said, pushing her black hair behind her ear. Graham smiled. Hanging out with Ming Li might be more entertaining than he thought. Did she even realize all she had done was compliment Tal?

"Besides," she continued with a twinkle in her eye, "Now that Graham is here, there's someone as good-looking as you, so now you won't stand out so much." Graham's smile disappeared. Ming Li was only entertaining when she was focused on someone else.

Tal laughed. "That's true. Way to put me in my place Li."

"Ming Li. You can call me Ming Li."

"Do you know where Wren is?" Graham asked, trying to change the subject.

"I haven't seen her," Ming Li said, still glaring at Tal. "What's your first class?"

"I don't know if I have a schedule yet. Brake sent me with a map."

"Your schedule is the same as mine," Tal said, "My father made sure. He wanted you to have a friend in your classes."

Ming Li sneered. "Then why put him with you? I thought you were too good for friends."

"I have friends, I just have so many it's rare to see me with the same ones."

Graham wasn't sure what to think about Tal.

"If all of your classes are with jerk boy here, you have gym with me and Wren. We made sure we got the same schedule. I wish we could have the same schedule as you, but you're a grade ahead."

"Hi guys," Wren said, joining what was becoming a circle. "Did I miss something?" she asked, glancing at Tal.

"Tal thinks Graham has come to be his best friend," Ming Li said, rolling her eyes again.

Tal waved, unaffected by the attitude Ming Li was throwing his way. "Hey Wren. Maybe we can all be on the same team in gym today."

"We are not being on your team," Ming Li growled.

"Why not?"

"Because we want to win."

"Tal's team usually wins," Wren reminded her with a nudge.

"Yeah, well, we want to win honestly, and we don't cheat."

Tal raised his eyebrow, "Are you still upset about that time–"

"Yes, I'm still upset." Ming Li said, narrowing her eyes.

"For the record, I didn't cheat. It is possible for you to lose sometimes."

"I'm pretty good at gym," Graham said, hoping to defuse some of the tension.

Tal nodded. "Then the four of us will make a great team. Especially if we play octaball. Come on Li. You and me are the best. If Graham is good too, nobody will stop us."

"That might not be totally true," Ming Li said, glancing at Wren.

"Hey!" Wren frowned, crossing her arms. "I might not even want to be on your superstar team."

"You don't need to feel bad," Ming Li said, patting Wren on the shoulder. "I was only trying to help Tal understand that just because he's on a team doesn't mean he's going to win. I'm better than him at most sports, and I still lose when you're on my team."

Graham tried not to smile.

"That makes me feel better," Wren said, rolling her eyes.

"I will not ditch you to be on his team. I would rather lose with you than win with him. Besides, you need eight people on a team for octaball, so one person who isn't good won't make a huge difference. Also, Tal is not part of this group," she said, gesturing to herself, Wren, and Graham.

"Come on," Tal said, "You need me to be part of your group. I can be the funny one."

"What are you talking about?" Wren asked.

"You know," Tal said, with a lopsided smile, "When you have a group of friends you need to have the shy, smart one," he pointed to Wren, "The small, outspoken one, that's you Li," he winked, "The strong level headed one, I'm giving you that one Graham, since I don't know you, and that makes me the funny good-looking one."

"I'm not shy," Wren said, at the same time Ming Li said, "I'm not *that* small." Graham thought it was funny Ming Li didn't object to being called outspoken.

"And you aren't funny, or good-looking," Ming Li said, poking Tal in the chest with her pointer finger. Graham hid a smile. She must not remember that she had admitted she thought he was good looking a minute ago.

"We should probably get to class," Graham said, "I don't want to be late on my first day."

"Math is this way," Tal pointed. "See you two in gym class."

Graham waved at the girls and followed Tal down the hall. He sure hoped Tal was more pleasant than Wren and Ming Li seemed to think he was. If they had every class together, it would be hard to avoid him.

Catching up was going to be easier than Graham thought. There were a few words he didn't understand in math class, and the teacher used some different methods than he was used to, but math was math no matter what world you were in. There was something comforting in that.

"You don't have to show off on your first day," Tal whispered, when Graham raised his hand for the third time. He lowered it quickly. He didn't want to look like a know-it-all.

"You answered three already," Graham whispered back.

"I'm kidding, answer."

"Graham? Tal?" Professor Leana said, looking down at them. "Are you two visiting during my class, or are you discussing the question?" Leana wasn't a small woman, and it felt like she was towering over them.

"Discussing the question," Tal said.

"And the answer is?"

"Three hundred and thirty," they both said together.

"Let's do our own work from now on," she said, narrowing her wrinkly eyes. She handed out an assignment and dismissed the class.

"You're going to get me in trouble on my first day," Graham said, tossing his bag over his shoulder.

"Nah," Tal said, leading him out into the hallway. "Professor Leana never punishes anyone. She just likes to tower over people and intimidate them. I think she's too old to actually punish anyone. She's like two hundred years old, I bet. Did you see those wrinkles?"

"So, where to next?"

"Gym."

Graham felt odd walking through the plain halls, filled with kids in capes. The entrance to the school looked decent with all the trophies, but the halls were boring. It looked like royalty walking around the dungeon ... or a bunch of theater kids putting on a Shakespeare play.

They walked through the gym doors and saw Ming Li and Wren waiting for them.

"I hate having gym second," Wren complained. "It stinks having to take a shower at school. There should be rules against it."

"I don't bother with showering," Tal said, shrugging.

"What a surprise," Wren said sarcastically.

Tal clasped his heart. "Wow Wren, that hurt. Hey, I think that's the first time you've insulted me. Well, at least to my face." Wren turned red.

"Our dressing room is this way," he said, expecting Graham to follow him. Wren and Ming Li walked off in the other direction. They entered a locker room that looked like any other. So far, this magic world had a disappointing school.

Tal tapped on a locker. "This is you."

"I wonder if I should have checked into the office." Graham opened his bag and pulled out some clothes.

"No," Tal said, opening a locker close to Graham's. "When your uncle asked my father to let you start the school year late, and quickly, my father had everything arranged as fast as possible. I'm not sure why. I've seen kids start late before and it took my father a month at least to let them in." He unhooked his cape and placed it in his locker. "Five minutes talking to your uncle and my father was scurrying around like crazy, pulling strings for you."

"I wonder why." Graham looked at the clothes Brake had put in his bag and frowned.

74

"No idea."

"I don't think my uncle knows what gym clothes are." Graham held up a white tunic and black pants. The pants didn't look long enough to be pants, but were too long to be shorts.

"What's wrong with them? That's what everyone else will be wearing."

Graham quickly changed and sighed.

"I don't think I can go out like this. I feel ridiculous. How are these gym clothes? They seem almost like normal clothes."

"The shirt is shorter so you can move better, and the sleeves aren't as long," Tal said, motioning to his arm. Graham wasn't convinced. Tal's pants came to his ankles. Graham's were hitting him mid-calf. "What did you wear in Boztoll?"

"Something a lot different. I think my pants are too short."

Tal had a gleam in his eyes. "They are a little short. Most people won't notice."

They walked back out into the gym, where about twenty students were standing in groups talking. Graham headed over to Wren and Ming Li. Tal followed. Tal was right. Everyone was wearing the same thing. He'd have felt better if he wasn't the only one with short pants. It wasn't like he could do anything to fix them either, since he didn't have any money. First the nightgown and now this.

"Hey, Tal!" a feminine voice called. Graham looked over and saw three girls smiling at Tal and waving. "Come over and bring your friend!" the pretty blonde leader called.

"Not right now, Solia," Tal called back. "Leader's of my fan club," he explained, smiling, as Wren and Ming Li joined them. They shared a look. "What?" Tal winked. "You two are welcome to join."

"Not in this lifetime," Ming Li muttered, and Wren nodded in agreement.

"What's our school called?" Graham asked. "It didn't have a sign out front."

"What do you mean?" Wren asked, scrunching her forehead.

"It's the school," Tal shrugged.

"But doesn't it have a name?"

"The school?" Wren asked, smiling. "What kind of name would a school have?"

"How do you tell it apart from other schools when you are talking?"

"This is the school with the two gigantic trees," Tal explained, "Then there's the school without two gigantic trees, and the school with the odd shaped rock out front. Trust me, you are lucky to be at this one."

"It seems like it should have a name." They didn't name their schools, or their world. Graham wondered why no one seemed to find that confusing. Maybe they didn't like dealing with naming things if they could help it. That could be the reason they didn't have last names.

"Do you name your schools in Boztoll?" Ming Li asked, her eyes sparkling with mischief.

He didn't have to answer because a whistle blew and a tall woman in a green tunic and black leggings walked in. She must be Coach Zalliah. Her brown hair was pulled back into a tight ponytail. Graham would guess she was in her late thirties, but it was hard to tell with all the makeup she was wearing. He had never seen a gym teacher look so fixed up. Blowing the whistle again, she let it fall on the string around her neck.

She surveyed the room, and her eyes widened when she saw Graham. She glanced at Tal, Wren, and Ming Li, and back to Graham. For a second, she looked like she was going to be sick.

"New kid, to the front," she said in a tight voice. "Everyone else, laps." A collective groan rose as everyone began running or walking around the gym. Graham walked up to the coach.

"I'm Graham."

"Yes ..." she breathed. "Very interesting."

"What?" He didn't like the way she was studying him.

"You are Brake's nephew, I've been told?" He nodded. "And how do you like Akkron so far?" She rubbed her fingers over her whistle.

"I've only been here a few days, but I like it." He couldn't help wondering about the strange way she was looking at him. He couldn't tell what she was thinking. Different emotions seemed to play across her face.

"And you've made friends?" She glanced at the kids running around the gym.

"I think so."

She gazed at him. "You are from Boztoll? I haven't been to Boztoll in years. Things must be a little different from last time I was there, if that is where you are from."

"I am." Graham wished he had asked Brake for information on Boztoll. He didn't know enough to make up answers if people asked questions.

"This is interesting."

"What is?"

"I wouldn't expect someone like you to be from Boztoll."

"Why?" He hoped it wasn't a race thing. It couldn't be though, Brake's sister lived there, so everyone in Boztoll couldn't be white.

"When I was in Boztoll, most people weren't as healthy looking as you."

"Oh." Graham shifted uncomfortably. He wasn't sure where this conversation was going. Why wouldn't people in Boztoll look healthy? Maybe it was because there were so many people who didn't have magic. Was she against non-magic people? He hoped not.

"Well, it is what it is."

"What is?"

"Alright, you may join your class," she said, ignoring him and nodding towards Tal. Graham ran over to the side of the gym and started running. He caught up to Tal.

"How many laps am I behind?"

"No idea," Tal said, "All I know is that Ming Li has lapped me once," he laughed. "No shock there though. And I've lapped Wren twice. Also, no surprise."

"Yeah, she's not so fast," Graham agreed. "She had a good start on me the other day and I caught up to her pretty fast."

"Oh?" Tal raised an eyebrow. "And why were you chasing her?"

Graham mentally kicked himself. "I was trying to catch up is all," he said. "It seems like she'd be faster than Ming Li. Her legs are a lot longer."

"Nobody is faster than Li. She dominates gym class. For being small, she is incredibly strong and athletic. Gym is the only class she gets full marks in. I would never want to get into a fight with her, that's for sure, because she doesn't hold back."

"Wren said that your team always wins."

"Yeah, but if it isn't teams, Li wins. That girl is super competitive, but she's also super loyal. She wants to win, but she is always on Wren's team. Wren is pretty bad at every sport I've seen her do."

They ran in silence for a few minutes. Graham wasn't sure if it would be polite to pull ahead. He was curious to see whether he could pass Ming Li. They had already passed Wren, who had stopped running and was speed walking. Lots of kids were walking now.

"How long do we run?"

"Not usually this long," Tal panted. "I feel like I'm going to face plant." Graham still felt okay, but that was probably because he had started late. "Why does Coach Zalliah keep staring at you? She looks like she's spaced out."

"I don't know. People are walking pretty slow."

"Yeah, even Li has slowed down."

After a few more minutes, Tal slowed to a walk, and a few minutes after that, Ming Li even walked. Graham ran around a few more times and then started walking when he came to Wren and Ming Li.

"We're trying to decide what's wrong with Coach Zalliah," Wren told him. "She keeps looking at us all with that strange frown."

"I've noticed."

"Noticed what?" Tal asked, catching up.

"Coach Zalliah, staring at us." Ming Li said, "Should we stop? Almost everyone else has stopped." Coach Zalliah shook her head and seemed to come out of her trance. She blew her whistle.

"Everyone to the showers!" she called. "Graham, Wren, Ming Li, and Tal, I will see you in my office." She turned around and walked away.

"Class still has fifteen minutes," Wren said, raising an eyebrow. "Coach Zalliah never lets us stop early."

"I hope I'm not in trouble on my first day," Graham said, frowning.

Wren's stomach was knotting up. What could Coach Zalliah want? They hadn't done anything wrong. They hesitantly followed her to her office. She opened the door and motioned for them to enter. They all squished into the cramped office and stood in front of the spotless desk. Coach Zalliah slumped into her chair and stared at them. And stared. Wren fidgeted.

"No mistake," Coach Zalliah muttered. "But it's supposed to be five," she mumbled. "And you are all so young." She rubbed her temples, and Wren wondered if she had a headache. She was definitely acting strange. Wren was glad to see she wasn't the only one fidgeting. Even the mighty Tal looked uncomfortable, and he could make a joke out of any situation.

"Five what?" Wren asked.

"No matter," Coach Zalliah said. "If it's you, it's you." Her expression changed. She looked resolved. "Ming Li, you are fast and fairly strong. You need to work on keeping some of your thoughts to yourself and you would do even better."

"Did you bring us in here to give us a personal evaluation?" Ming Li asked, hands on hips.

"Wren. Oh Wren," Coach Zalliah said, shaking her head, and ignoring Ming Li. "I don't even know where to start with you. I've never had the heart to give you a low mark because you try so hard and you are persistent. That will have to pull you through."

"Pull me through what?" Wren asked, shifting her weight from one leg to the other.

"You need to run. Every day. A mile would be good," she said, nodding. "You should also do pull-ups. Lots of pull-ups. You need to work on your upper body strength. You never know when you are going to be hanging off a cliff and need to pull your body up."

"Ummm ... okay ..." Wren said, hesitantly. Why was Coach Zalliah acting so weird? "I'm not planning on hanging off a cliff."

"We don't plan for those things, do we?" She turned her attention to Tal.

"Tal, I'm not so sure about you. You are pretty strong, and probably fast enough. You should work on being a little more serious and less cocky. Too much confidence can lead to mistakes. I am the most shocked by you. Actually, I am completely shocked. Graham, I don't know you, but you look strong and you were running pretty steady."

Wren frowned. It looked like she was the weak link here, but the weak link for what?

"Okay ..." Tal said, with a slight smile that didn't reach his eyes, "Can we leave?"

"Yes, but I want all of you to come in early every morning. You all need to be stronger. Come in and I will have workouts for you."

"Why?" Wren and Tal said at the same time.

"We can't risk failure. Can't you see I'm trying to help you?" Coach Zalliah said, throwing her arms into the air. "You come an hour early. Your grades will depend on this."

"How is that fair?" Ming Li asked. "You aren't making the rest of the class do it."

"What does fair have to do with anything?" she said, squinting at them. "And do me a favor. Don't stand so close to each other. You might give a person a headache."

"Geography is not your subject," Tal said to Graham as they sat down at lunch. "You should stick to math."

Graham groaned. "Why was Professor Hedder picking on me? He sees a new kid and figures he better humiliate them on the first day?"

"He isn't usually that brutal," Tal said, pulling out a sandwich. "But seven continents? Even a five-year-old knows there are only two. And when you asked what they were called? Were you trying to make him mad?"

"I need a book on geography and I'll catch up." Graham grumbled as he pulled a soggy sandwich out of his bag. He grimaced.

"Wait, really? I thought you were messing with him. You don't know that stuff? I mean, I know Boztoll is kinda backward, but you should know basic geography."

"I guess it wasn't something I was interested in." Graham hated looking stupid. He should have asked Brake more questions. "So, if you're so smart, what are the two continents called? I didn't hear you answering when I asked."

Tal smiled a crooked smile. "What are they called? Do they have some bizarre thing in Boztoll where they have to name everything? There's this continent and the other continent. I've actually vacationed on the other continent."

"I guess you don't name the oceans either?"

"Since there's only one, why would we name it anything other than the ocean?"

Graham shook his head as he bit into his sandwich. He shuddered. It tasted bad. Like old corn mixed with tuna. He didn't even want to know what it was.

"I'm surprised the cities have names. Nothing else seems to."

"There are a lot of cities. It would be confusing to not name them."

"I thought Wren and Ming Li would be here."

"I don't know what Li did, but she has to spend one lunch a week cleaning Professor Ballina's classroom. Wren goes and helps her."

"Tal, why aren't you sitting by us?" The blonde girl from gym said, walking up to the table. She was crossing her arms and pouting.

"I'm helping my new friend Graham here," Tal said, not looking at her. "Have you met him?"

"No, I haven't." Her sparkling white teeth flashed as she smiled at Graham. "I'm Solia."

He nodded at her. "Graham." Tal kept eating his sandwich and seemed interested in something across the room.

"You are welcome to eat with us anytime," Solia said.

"Thanks," Graham said. Tal was still looking away. Wasn't this one of his friends? He didn't seem interested in talking to her. She stood there smiling for a moment before turning and walking back to her table.

"That was awkward," Graham said, taking a small bite of his sandwich.

"Was it?" Tal asked, looking bored. "I guess I didn't notice."

"Isn't she your friend?"

"Yeah, kind of. She's more like the girl who forces you to be her friend because your dad is the governor. I've been trying to get away from those girls forever. I'm hoping if I hang with you, Wren, and Li, Solia will leave me alone."

"She's that bad?" Graham gave up on the sandwich.

"Yeah, she's pretty bad. I put up with her for a while, but one day ... Nevermind. You don't want to hear that story. I

84

don't even want to hear that story. Now that you are here and everyone is curious, maybe she'll start bothering you instead," he said, his smile returning.

"I hope not."

"She won't. Solia hates Wren. I'm not sure why. If you keep hanging out with Wren, Solia will leave you alone."

Graham wasn't sure what to think of Tal. He didn't seem to be the person Wren and Ming Li made him out to be. He seemed a little stuck up sometimes, but Graham was thinking it was more of a joke.

"I hope you brought your pillow. We have magical equality next."

"So, it's boring?"

"I'm sure there are worse classes," Tal said, shaking his head, "But I haven't found one yet."

CHAPTER 6

G ym was so bizarre," Wren said, taking a bite of her apple. It had been hard to think of anything else all day. Coach Zalliah had been so strange. It was also unnerving going into Professor Dovin's class today. She was worried he would say something, but he acted the same as usual. He didn't even look at her funny. That relieved a lot of the stress she'd been feeling. He must not have seen her.

"You keep saying that," Graham said, sitting next to her in Brake's kitchen.

"It creeps me out," said Ming Li, sitting across from them. "I couldn't concentrate on school at all. It's possible I failed every assignment."

Tal smirked. "And that's different from usual?" He stood by the window, tossing his apple up and down.

Ming Li stuck her tongue out. "Who invited you anyway?" she asked.

"You don't have to feel like you have to hang out with us, Tal," Graham said.

"We might as well be friends," Tal shrugged. "We're going to be spending a lot of extra gym time together."

"If you are going to hang out with us," Ming Li said, "Then at least try to be less annoying."

"Deal," Tal said, as the door opened and Brake came in.

Looking around the room, he froze when his eyes rested on Tal, but he quickly recovered. "Good to see you again, Wren. Ming Li. And welcome Mr. Tal. How was your first day, Graham?"

"Good," he said, looking at Tal. "Not much different from my last school."

"Except it turns out they don't teach geography in Boztoll," Tal said, grinning.

"Yeah, but give me a month and I'll know it better than you."

"I suspect Boztoll is concerned with more practical matters," Brake said. He nodded at them and left the room.

"That guy makes me nervous," Tal said, shaking his head. "No offense, Graham. I know he's your uncle." Graham shrugged. Wren wondered if he was trying to figure out how to make them all leave. He looked tired, and they'd been awkwardly hanging out for the last hour. There were so many moments of silence, she wasn't sure how much more she could take.

"You didn't talk at all in history," Tal said. "Is that another thing they don't teach in Boztoll?"

"Just because I don't talk doesn't mean I don't know something," Graham said. Wren hoped Tal wouldn't pry too much.

"Well, you talked a lot in math and science."

"I'm more interested in those. Do you get to choose any classes here? Like electives?"

"Yes," Tal said. "They probably didn't let you pick anything since you came when the year was already in full swing. Well, that and my dad wanted us to have the same schedule."

"I took three years of a language," Ming Li said. "I was super excited because I'm good with languages, but I've never gotten to use it because only trolls speak it, and you don't see a lot of trolls running around Akkron."

"That's for sure," Tal said. "My dad is pretty anti-troll."

Wren wondered if Tal would keep hanging out with them. The more he was around, the more likely he would find out something wasn't right with Graham's story. The last thing they needed was the governor learning about it. She would try not to dwell on that.

"As fun as this is, I better go," Ming Li said, standing. "If we have to get to school an hour early, I'm gonna need to go to bed early. You can't skimp on beauty sleep."

"I'll walk you part of the way, Li," Tal said, tossing his apple to Graham. Graham caught it and sat it on the table.

"Ming Li," she said, glaring at Tal as she fastened her black cape. "Ming Li. Not Li. I thought you were going to be less annoying."

"Hey," Tal said, grinning, "You can't expect me to change in a day."

"I better go too," Wren said. "We all should get good sleep. Who knows what will happen tomorrow?"

There was no way Graham was going to sleep. He had worked too hard to do well in school and he would not blow it just because he was in a new world. All his friends on the basketball team used to tease him because of his good grades.

Aunt Temperance had always insisted he use good grammar. She never bothered Kaylee about it, but she insisted on it with Graham. It bugged him when he was younger, but now he realized it was one positive thing Aunt Temper had done for him. It was probably done to punish him, but it had helped instead. He knew his grammar wasn't perfect, but he was one of the few people on the team who didn't stress when he had to write a paper.

Graham pulled out his history book and started reading. He didn't want to feel like the only person who didn't know what was going on again. Geography and history had left him totally lost. He didn't want Professor Hedder to think he wasn't smart, and unfortunately, Professor Hedder taught geography and history. The strangest thing about the history book was that Coach Zalliah wrote it. Why would a gym teacher write history books?

At midnight, he turned out the lights. From what he could understand, there were four dominant groups in this world. There were humans, giants, trolls, and goblins.

They usually all got along. The goblins seemed to cause the most trouble, but usually kept to their homes on the far side of the continent up in the mountains. The trolls and giants had their own small cities and had been relatively peaceful throughout history.

Graham couldn't imagine meeting a goblin, troll, or giant. He wondered if he would ever see any. He hoped he never ran into a goblin if they looked like the art in his book. It was still hard to comprehend that these creatures he thought were myths were real. Lying in his bed, he tried to sleep. It was hard with so many things running through his head.

This continent used to have a large fleet of ships to protect them from the other continent. The history book even called them this continent and the other continent. Graham shook his head. The other continent didn't have governors and fleet members. It had two kings that ruled the entire continent. They had their own issues and there hadn't been problems between the continents in hundreds of years and the fleet eventually broke apart. The ships weren't even seaworthy anymore.

Graham closed his eyes. With luck, Professor Hedder would talk about the things he read tonight. It would only take a few more nights of late night reading to finish the book and then he might show Tal he could do history.

"I can't believe my dad thinks extra gym is a good idea," Wren complained, as they walked into the school the next day. She was tired and early mornings were not her thing. It didn't help that it had taken forever to fall asleep last night. Begging her dad to write a note to get out of it had been a bust.

"Brake does too," Graham said. "He thinks that it's curious Coach Zalliah singled us out, but he believes kids these days are too soft."

"No point in telling my parents," Tal said. "They don't know what time I go to school."

"How can they not know?" Wren asked.

"My mom is usually out of town and my dad is always busy."

"Sleeping in isn't my thing, so it doesn't bother me," Ming Li said. "I always wish gym could be longer. It's good to be in shape."

"That's a really strange opinion," Wren said, yawning. "And you guys are all in good shape. I'm the only one who isn't."

"You're in fine shape," Ming Li said. "You just aren't super coordinated."

Tal snorted, and Graham smiled. Wren sighed. She knew she wasn't coordinated, and it was going to stand out more with a smaller group.

They entered the gym and stopped when they saw the crazy sight in front of them. Coach Zalliah had transformed the gym into a huge obstacle course. There were ropes, cones, and high platforms scattered around.

"Wow," Tal said, looking around. "Someone didn't sleep last night."

"Not a wink!" Coach Zalliah said, stepping out from behind a makeshift tower. Her brown ponytail was messy, and she had makeup smeared under her eyes, but she was smiling.

"Should we change?" Wren asked.

"No, I want everything to feel natural."

"So naked?" Tal asked, raising his eyebrow.

"No Tal," she muttered, "I mean, if you are to fall into trouble, you won't have time to change into your gym clothes. You don't want to be distracted because you need your gym clothes."

"That makes sense," Ming Li said, nodding. "If you're crazy," she whispered.

"I can hear Ming Li," Coach Zalliah said, rolling her eyes. "Trust me, you will thank me someday."

"Coach Zalliah?" Wren asked. "Is there a reason you chose us to do this?"

"Okay, let's begin," Coach Zalliah said, clapping her hands, ignoring her. "Where are my alligators? Jaaz? Cal? Places!" Two boys stepped out from behind the tower. They were wearing masks that kind of resemble alligators, and they had green mittens. Wren wondered what they'd done to earn this punishment. Graham and Tal snickered quietly, and Ming Li laughed out loud. The boys walked over and positioned themselves between two platforms.

"This is a race," Coach Zalliah said. She pointed at a blue line on the floor. "Start at this line and follow the arrows. Run to the tower and climb it. Once you get up, climb down the other side. Run around the cones, and climb the platform. Grab the rope and swing across to the other platform. Don't let the alligators get you." One boy with the alligator mask waved and the other one growled.

"I think they're enjoying themselves," Ming Li said with pity in her voice.

Tal laughed. "Wand carriers, for sure."

"Climb down the platform, jump on the rocks," Coach Zalliah continued, "And climb that tree."

"How did you get a tree in here?" Graham asked, looking at the thick twenty-five foot tree at the edge of the gym.

"It looks like it's growing out of the floor," Wren said, impressed. It must be some type of magic.

"What does the winner get?" Ming Li asked.

"Satisfaction," Coach Zalliah said.

"Figures."

"As I was saying," Coach Zalliah explained, "Climb the tree. There are flags at the top. Grab one and come down. First one to finish wins, but everyone must finish." She glanced at Wren. "On my ready, get set, go!" She blew her whistle and Tal, Graham, and Ming Li took off. Wren sighed and ran behind them. Ming Li reached the tower first and used the handholds to climb to the top. Graham and Tal were right behind her.

"You can do it Wren!" Ming Li called.

Wren climbed as fast as she could. Thankfully, no one was behind her to see how much she was shaking. She had little upper body strength. From the thuds she heard a few moments ago, she assumed the others had jumped. She climbed down and ran around the cones until she reached the platform. A rope hung against the platform wall. With no footholds, she wasn't sure she would make it.

"Grab the rope, Wren," Coach Zalliah called.

"It's not that easy," Wren said to herself as she grabbed the rope and put one foot on the wall. When she raised her other foot, her whole body spun around and her back smacked against the wall.

"It's alright, try again."

Wren rolled her eyes. She tried again with the same result. The platform wasn't that high. She should be able to get up.

"Grab my hand," Graham said from the top of the platform. He reached his hand down. Wren reached up, and he grabbed her wrist. She grabbed his wrist, still unsure it would work. Tal appeared next to him and reached for her other hand, and they easily pulled her up. Ming Li was already climbing the tree. Graham and Tal must have come back for her. Tal grabbed his rope and swung across the alligators. Jaaz and Cal were enjoying their part, snapping and growling. Graham was right behind him. Wren grabbed the last rope. It was only six or seven feet across.

"Roar! Growl! Chomp!" yelled one alligator.

Wren tied a knot high on the rope so she could hold on above it. Sighing, she closed her eyes. She sprung forward and swung over the alligator's heads.

"Let go!" someone called out. Wren couldn't make herself let go. She swung backwards and fell right onto an alligator.

"That was one of the most awesome things I've ever seen," Tal laughed, as he and Graham sat in their math class. "I'm seriously going to be laughing all day."

Graham smiled as he pictured Wren falling on one of the alligator's heads. As soon as he'd recovered, both alligators growled and pretended to bite Wren. Wren screamed and flailed until Coach Zalliah called the boys off. One of them had a bloody nose, but didn't seem to care.

"What happened to you?" someone asked. Graham looked up and saw Jaaz enter the room with an icepack on his face. Tal laughed. Graham tried not to, but couldn't help joining in.

"I saved a beautiful maiden from a terrible fall," Jaaz grinned. His blond hair was going in all directions. Tal laughed louder, but Jaaz didn't seem to mind. He sat smiling in his seat with his ice pack.

The first part of the day flew by quickly, and it wasn't long before Graham was in history class. Getting by in geography meant keeping his hand and questions to himself. It was annoying having two classes with the same teacher. At least he had lunch and magical equality to break it up.

Professor Hedder wasn't bad, but it was boring listening to his monotone voice drone on for so long. It had been annoying the way he kept calling on him the first day. Graham wasn't sure what to make of him. His long, greasy, brown ponytail hung halfway down his back and it looked like he was trying to grow a beard and failing horribly.

He was one of the youngest teachers Graham had seen. Graham would bet he had gotten picked on when he was in school.

"Is something amusing you, Mr. Graham?" Professor Hedder asked, walking over to Graham's desk. Graham hadn't realized he was smiling.

"Nope," he said.

"I hope you aren't contriving ways to disrupt the class today."

"No."

"No?" he asked, frowning. "Don't you want to tell us about the seven continents again?"

"I was tired yesterday," Graham said, ignoring Tal, who was smiling next to him.

"You don't want to name the continents today?" Professor Hedder asked.

Graham swallowed. He hadn't made a friend in Professor Hedder.

"That would have been in geography," Tal said, cutting in. "It's history now."

Professor Hedder looked confused for a moment and turned and walked back to the chalkboard.

"I think you are on his bad side," Tal whispered.

"You think?" Graham muttered, opening his history book.

"Don't take it personally," Tal said. "He wouldn't like you even if you hadn't been so clueless yesterday. He doesn't like anyone that's bigger or better than him at anything. You must be at least five inches taller than he is."

"Mr. Tal," Professor Hedder said, through clenched teeth, "Would you like to share with the class?"

"Not even a little," Tal said, grinning.

"I hope you aren't telling Mr. Graham the answer."

"Nope," Tal said, shrugging. "I didn't even hear the question."

"I was asking who caused the war between the goblins and the trolls under the rule of the troll, King Azurk. Why don't you tell us? Actually, let's have your new friend tell us," he said, leaning against the wall with his arms crossed, smiling a mean smile. Graham changed his mind. He didn't like this guy at all.

"Um," Graham said, stalling for a second. He did the reading last night, but with all the extra he read, it took him a second to remember. "It was the goblins. They were upset because they felt like the trolls underpaid them when they helped them get rid of an infestation that was killing their crops. When they demanded more from the trolls, they refused to pay, because they had already agreed on a price."

Professor Hedder looked disappointed. "Yes. If Mr. Tal helps you again, I will have to assign you different seats."

"I didn't actually help him," Tal said. "And I don't think changing our seats would be a good idea."

Professor Hedder's face turned red, and he started writing on the board. "All of you will write a paper on the war between the trolls and the goblins under the rule of troll King Azurk. I'll be in my office if anyone needs help." He stomped over to his office and slammed the door.

"I don't think he likes you either," Graham said to Tal.

"Never has," Tal said, pulling a notebook out of his bag, "But he fears my dad, so he rarely bothers to correct me. Plus, I always get an A, so what's he gonna do?"

"Good job, Tal," a boy in the front row said sarcastically, as the class began their assignments. "We would rather listen to a boring lecture over writing a boring paper any day."

Tal started writing. Graham grabbed his pencil and tried to decide how to begin. He wanted to ask why they didn't name their wars, but he was pretty sure that would only make everyone think he was more strange than they already did.

Magical equality was boring. Graham had been looking forward to it, but so far it wasn't anything exciting. Professor Ballina kept talking about how all magic was the same and nobody was any more powerful than anyone else.

Science was fun even if Professor Dovin was evil. He seemed to be a hands-on teacher. Today he showed them how to boil a dragon scale until it became so bright it would light a room. It was cool, but Graham doubted he would ever do it again. He wasn't touching a dragon anytime soon.

If Graham didn't know better, he never would suspect Professor Dovin of anything. He ran his fingers through is blond curls too much, and he had an exaggeratedly smooth voice. He slipped in compliments to himself, but overall, he seemed pleasant enough. Graham watched him and noted anything he said. So far, he hadn't said anything concerning.

"Whoa, watch it," Tal said, shading his eyes. "I think you overdid your scale. That's way too bright." Graham looked at his scale and grimaced. It was pretty bright.

"Rub it between your hands and it will dim," Professor Dovin said as he walked past. Graham rubbed the smooth scale and watched it lose some of its light.

"That's pretty neat," Graham said, looking at the scale.

"Yeah, that's one reason they had to put dragons on the protected species list," Tal said. "Too many people were killing them for their scales. Now it's illegal to buy dragon scales unless it's from a respectable seller."

"So dragons are endangered?"

"No, but it could happen if we aren't careful. There isn't any reason to kill them for their scales. It's easy to take the scales without hurting them because they shed. People are too lazy. It makes me so mad."

"I've seen a dragon before," Graham said, looking at the hand size scale, "But it was tiny. This scale must belong to a much bigger dragon."

"You've seen a dragon before?" Tal asked, raising an eyebrow. "Hasn't everyone?"

"Well, have you ever seen one with scales this big?" Graham asked, hoping Tal would ignore his mistake.

"Sure," Tal said, "Much bigger, in fact. I forget everyone doesn't travel as much as I do. You've probably only seen bantams."

Graham nodded.

"You may all keep your scale," Professor Dovin said. "The light will last as long as you don't rub them too much."

"Sweet," Graham said, putting it in his pocket. Tal was looking at him funny.

"What? Are you going to make fun of me for thinking a dragon scale is cool?"

"No, a dragon scale is cool. I've never had one. You just look more excited than anyone else. You're practically bouncing."

"I'm not bouncing," Graham said, putting all of his things away.

"This is a fantastic class," Tal said. "Professor Dovin is my favorite teacher."

"Really? Don't you think there's something a little ... odd about him?"

"Sure, in fact, sometimes I'm pretty sure he's evil."

"Evil? Why?"

"Not literally," Tal laughed, as he put his bag over his shoulder. "But look at him. Everything about him screams bad guy. He's got the whole sophisticated bad guy look going on. I have a theory regarding it."

"Oh?"

"I'll explain it later. Right now I have to help my dad and he doesn't like to be kept waiting. If you ever see my dad, you'll understand my theory."

"Your dad looks like a bad guy?"

"Totally. See you later."

"Later," Graham said, as Tal dashed off. He wondered if he would ever meet the governor.

CHAPTER 7

The next four weeks flew by. Graham had a few moments where he missed his old life, but for the most part, he liked it better here. School was going well. He had to study a lot for magical equality and history, but everything else was pretty easy. Even geography was easy if you did the homework. This world was a lot smaller than Earth. There wasn't a lot to memorize since they didn't name most things.

Not naming things was really annoying him. It would be so much easier to say the name of a forest or river rather than explain where it is or what happened there. Not having last names was odd, but he hadn't met anyone with the same name. Brake said that in order to prevent doubles, people had to get their baby's names approved.

Tal was right, science was the best class. Professor Dovin was a skilled teacher and was even one of the more supportive ones. Anyone could retake tests until they received full marks. He would let students stay after class and do experiments, and he made everything seem exciting. Graham wondered what his motives were. He hoped he wasn't recruiting anyone for The Dark Cloud.

Morning gym was fun, at least for him. Coach Zalliah was creative. She had them fencing, running, climbing, fighting with clubs, and anything else that popped into her head. One of her requirements was for Wren to do two minutes of pull-ups a day. Wren hated it. The first day she couldn't even do one. Graham and Tal had to help her until she could pull herself up without them. Now she could do eight. Not a lot, but it was an improvement.

It surprised him how fast he had become friends with Wren, Ming Li, and Tal. Ming Li and Wren were warming up to Tal, but he still irritated them. Graham found it all pretty comical.

Brake seemed to enjoy talking to Graham, so Graham hoped that meant he didn't mind having him around. He made sure he kept his room clean and did other chores around the house. Every night, Brake would try to get Graham to do magic, but so far, he hadn't managed anything. He wondered if Wren had given him the light and not realized it.

Brake had seemed intimidating at first, but now he was as friendly and easy to talk to as anyone. Graham volunteered to cook whenever he could, and Brake seemed happy to let him do it. Choking down the food Brake made wasn't easy, but at least dessert was always a thing. Brake was a firm believer in dessert.

Graham sat cross-legged on his bed and tried to remember what he'd done when he made the light. He'd cupped his hands like Wren told him to and thought about how awesome it would be to make a light. Maybe he had been trying too hard since that first time. Cupping his hands, he imagined how cool it would be to hold light. His chest felt tight and his heart pounded as a light appeared in his hands.

"Yessss!" he said out loud. Carefully scooting off his bed, he made his way to the hall. "Brake?" he called. He felt an unexplainable pull between his brain and the light. It was like they were connected.

"What is it?" Brake asked, opening his bedroom door. He saw Graham standing there, cupping the light, and he came into the hall. "You did it!" he said, smiling. "I knew you could. What did you do differently?"

"I thought it would be cool if I could do it, and it happened. I think I was trying too hard."

"Wonderful," Brake said, patting his shoulder. "You didn't give up. I'm proud of you." Graham felt a lump swell in his throat. He wasn't sure if anyone had ever been proud of him before. "Do you want to try something else?"

"Okay," Graham said, letting the light go out. "What should I try?"

"Levitating?" Brake said, rubbing his hands together.

"Alright, how should I do that?"

"I don't think I should tell you anything." He scratched his chin. "That might have been what messed you up last time. Sometimes magic works differently for different people."

"Okay ..." Graham mumbled, looking around. He spotted a small table at the end of the hall with a glass vase on top. Graham put out his hand and imagined the vase going up. He could almost swear he heard a clicking in his brain, like flipping a switch, as the vase raised two feet off the table.

"Ah, ha!" Brake said, slapping his leg. "You have definitely had a breakthrough!" Graham smiled, and the vase fell, hitting the table, and falling to the floor. Graham cringed at the sound of shattering glass.

"Wow, I am so sorry," he said, covering his mouth with his hands, as Brake laughed.

"It's not important," he said, "But next time perhaps you should use something that isn't glass. This calls for one of Mali's cookies, don't you agree?"

"Wren!" Graham called as he pounded on her front door the next day. "Wren! Open up!"

"Where's the fire?" Karlof growled as he opened the front door and glared at him. Graham took a step back. Ming Li had told him that Karlof used to work with trolls and it hadn't ended well. The details weren't clear, but there was a huge fight and Karlof barely escaped alive. That was how he had gotten the huge scar on his face. Ming Li was under the impression Karlof had been in the wrong.

Knowing that he had wronged the trolls didn't make Graham trust him. From everything Graham had read in history, trolls were usually peaceful. That didn't mean they wouldn't fight if necessary, but they rarely caused conflicts. It surprised him that Drew let Karlof live with them. Wren said her uncle was sorry and trying to be a better person, but Graham didn't like to be around him.

"I'm here for Wren," Graham said, clearing his throat and looking away.

"No kidding," Karlof muttered. "WREN!" he yelled, before turning and walking away. Graham stood there feeling uncomfortable until Wren came to the door. She was holding Ben and smiling.

"Hey Graham." She came outside and put the dragon on the ground. "You're early." Ben sniffed Graham's boot. Ignoring him was hard. It was cool to see a dragon, but those teeth still made him nervous.

"I came early to show you something," he said, forgetting Ben. "Watch." Raising his hand, he lifted a large rock off of the ground.

"You learned to levitate!" Wren clapped her hands. "That's awesome, Graham! What happened?"

"I realized I just needed to think that I wanted to do it and I could. I was trying way too hard. Watch," he said, lowering the rock. He cupped his hands, and they filled with light. He felt like a little boy who'd won his first trophy.

"That's such a relief!" she said with a laugh. "Now you won't have to worry people will think you don't belong."

Ming Li came up the walk. "Is that light?"

"Look! Graham can make light, and he can levitate."

"Whoopee," Ming Li said, rolling her eyes. "Can't everyone?"

"I couldn't until now," Graham said, feeling a little hurt that Ming Li didn't seem to care. Not only did she not care, she looked irritated.

"Now you don't have to make excuses when Tal challenges you to some game that requires magic," Ming Li said, stooping to pet Ben. Ben rubbed against her hand and flew to her shoulder. She didn't even flinch.

"Can you do anything else?" Wren asked.

"I haven't tried anything else. I spent most of the night lifting my bed and stuff."

"You can lift your bed?" Wren said, her mouth turning down. "I can't lift anything heavier than that rock." She kicked at the rock Graham had dropped.

"It doesn't seem any harder to lift the bed than the rock," Graham said. "Maybe you're focusing too much on the size. I don't think it matters how big or how little the object is."

"Why don't you use your awesome new magic and get me a glass of water," Ming Li muttered. "It's boiling today."

"I'll try," Graham said. He thought about bringing a glass of water and blew onto his palm the way he had seen Drew get the rag the day he came here. Nothing happened.

"You can't bring something random," Wren explained. "You have to know what you want and where it is. It has to exist. It also can't be in someone's house or business because that's illegal, and people have protection put in place to avoid thieves. You should be able to get something from Brake's house because you live there." Graham nodded. He pictured a glass he had placed in the cupboard at Brake's house. A glass appeared above his fingers as he blew into his palm and he caught it before it dropped.

"FAIL!" Ming Li said, sighing, "It's empty."

"You can go in the house and get a drink," Wren told her friend.

"Nah, let's go," she said, patting Ben's head once more. The dragon jumped to the ground and bounded around Ming Li. "Tal's waiting for us, and I'm not gonna lie. I'm dying to see inside his house. It's the biggest house I've ever seen."

"I still don't see why we keep hanging out with Tal," Wren said, putting Ben in the house and closing the door.

"I think you all misjudged him. He can be annoying, but he's not that bad," said Graham.

"I'm willing to hang out with him if it means I get to look at him," Ming Li said as they began walking down the path. "Unicorns would be nice right now. It's going to take a good forty minutes to walk."

"My dad said I can get an alicorn or a pegasus if I pay for it myself," Wren grinned. "I almost have enough."

Graham shook his head. It still shocked him every time he saw a unicorn. Brake told him that everyone used to have unicorns, but like magic, a lot had died off. People were more aware now, and the numbers were going up again, but they were ridiculously expensive.

"I would prefer a unicorn," Ming Li said. "I enjoy staying on the ground."

"There are some things I definitely miss about my world," Graham admitted as they walked. "Public transportation, phones, TV, radio, fast food, basketball ..." Wren looked at him like he was speaking a different language and Ming Li just frowned. "A place with magic should have faster ways to get around. I've walked more in the last month than I normally walk in a year."

"You can hire a wagon or a carriage," Wren said.

"I haven't seen any wagons or carriages."

"People only use them when they are moving something big or going to a different city."

"So nobody has their own?"

"The governor has one and all the fleet members."

"So your dad has one?"

"Yes, but he only uses it when he is on official business. He doesn't like to stand out if he can help it, and he thinks it's lazy to ride."

"But so much faster."

"They say that before a lot of the magic was lost, you could jump through a portal and go wherever you want," Wren said, smiling. "I bet that's something I would have been able to do."

"I like to walk," Ming Li said, "And I like to run more. Last one to Tal's house is a rotten moakberry!" She smiled and took off running.

Wren's legs were burning when they reached Tal's house. Not as bad as they would have been if Coach Zalliah hadn't been making them run so much. Ming Li had won, but only because Graham didn't know where Tal's house was. He had quickly overtaken her, but had to slow down so she could lead the way. They both had to stop a few times to let Wren catch up.

They walked up the long path to the huge red stone house. The house was similar to Brakes, but bigger. It looked more like a castle than a house. It had large turrets and several balconies. Wren was used to living in a big house, but the size of this house seemed ridiculous. She wondered if the castles on the other continent were even this big.

The door was flung open by an impatient looking Tal. "It's about time you all got here," he said, ushering them inside. A large staircase stood in front of them and a tall man in a perfectly fitted leather jerkin stood at the top by the railing. He had dark brown hair and a goatee. Wren recognized the governor. She had met him several times when she was with her father. His lips turned up in what she assumed was supposed to be a smile, and came down the stairs.

"Ming Li. Wren," he said, nodding, "And this must be Graham. Talon has told me all about you."

"Talon?" Ming Li snorted. Tal glared at his dad.

"Nice to meet you," Graham said politely.

"My wife Valeena has been dying to meet you, but she is unfortunately busy today. How are you finding Akkron?" Governor Briggs asked. "Do you find it much different from Boztoll?"

"I like it fine. It's pretty similar to Boztoll."

"Mmm hmm," the governor murmured. "I always felt the sun shines brighter in Boztoll than Akkron. Don't you agree?"

Wren felt tense inside. What was the governor talking about? Boztoll was lucky to see the sun these days. It was another problem people whispered was caused by The Dark Cloud.

"Yes, very sunny," Graham said, shifting from one foot to the other. Wren closed her eyes.

"Well, we are going to my room to play some games," Tal said, plowing up the stairs. The other three followed. The governor said nothing as he watched them walk past. They walked down a fancy hallway full of golden mirrors, and into Tal's room. He shut the door and locked it. The room was more empty than Wren would have imagined. The bed and wardrobe leaned against the walls, and some clothing was scattered around. A huge bookcase stood across from the bed, and a corner table was buried in papers. The room might only look empty because it was so big.

"I don't want to worry you, Graham," Tal said, looking serious for once. He sat cross-legged on a large blue rug and the other three joined him. "But you need to stay away from my father."

"Why?" Graham asked, shifting on the rug.

"Look," Tal said, putting a hand to his head, "I know this sounds traitorous of me, but I don't trust him, and neither should you."

"Everyone knows that," Ming Li chuckled bitterly.

"My father wants something from you, or wants to know something about you, at least. I told you he wanted me to befriend you. He asks about you every day. It isn't normal. He's never taken an interest in my friends, or in me, and now suddenly he's making me eat dinner with him every night."

"What could he want from me?" Graham asked. "I'm pretty boring."

"Not as boring as you would have us believe, though?" Tal asked, raising an eyebrow. "No one who has been to Boztoll would call it sunny." Wren was panicking. Graham's eyes were wide and Ming Li shook her head. "You don't have to tell me anything. I want you to know my father isn't a good person and you should stay away from him if you can."

"Why did you invite us here?" Wren asked.

"Because my father keeps bugging me about it. I kept putting him off, but he's driving me crazy. He obsessively wanted to meet Graham. I kind of thought he would question him more. I chose a time right before one of his meetings, so he couldn't be too annoying."

A soft knock sounded at the door. Tal stood and opened it. A beautiful woman with long brown hair and a light blue dress stood in the doorway.

"Fleetman Zera," Tal said, bowing gracefully. The others stood and made clumsy bows.

"Tal," she whispered. "May I come in for a moment?" Tal raised his eyebrows, but stood back as she entered. Wren had seen and talked to Zera many times, but was always surprised how beautiful she was up close. Her skin was flawless, and she carried herself with confidence. Everything about her screamed elegance.

"I am here for a meeting with your father," she explained. "I only have a few moments." She glanced at each of them. "I could not believe my luck when I saw you all come in together. The four of you need to be careful. There are some that mean you harm. Do not go anywhere alone and do not tell anyone that I spoke to you. I know that is far from helpful, but keep a watch over each other." With that, she turned to leave the room.

"Wait," Wren said, surprised to hear her own voice. "Who means us harm?"

"It is hard to say," she said over her shoulder. "I overheard some people talking, and I did not recognize their voices. All of your names came up. Be careful who you trust." She left, closing the door behind her.

They all stood still for a moment, looking at one another.

"Why would we be in danger?" Ming Li asked. "I'm pretty sure we only annoy each other ... Well, except Talon. Yes, I'm going to call you Talon," she said, as Tal clenched his jaw.

"Do you think Dovin saw you?" Graham asked, looking at Wren. She shot him a look that she hoped said to be quiet.

"What did Dovin see?" Tal asked.

112

"We can't talk about it," Wren said.

"You can talk about it if it means I'm in danger because of it." Tal frowned, crossing his arms.

"I don't want to be rude, Tal, but we don't know if we can trust you," Wren said, glancing up through her eyelashes. She felt bad saying it, but it was the truth.

"Can't trust me?" he growled. "I just told you my father was evil! I'm on the good side, whatever that is."

"You were never very nice until Graham came," Wren said, and Ming Li nodded.

"When was I mean?" Tal asked, spreading out his arms, "Tell me once?"

Wren thought about it. The more she thought about it, the more she second guessed herself. She couldn't think of a single mean thing Tal had ever done. Sure, he walked around like he was king of the universe, but he hadn't been mean. Heat crept up the back of her neck. A quick glance at Ming Li showed she was equally embarrassed.

"See?" he said. "When I started school, everyone judged me right off. People either wanted to be my friend because of my father, or they decided I was stuck up. I know I've acted snobby, but that's what people expected, and I guess it was easier for me to act that way and pretend I didn't care what people thought." Sighing, he sat on his bed.

"I'm sorry Tal," Wren said, "You're right. We judged you without getting to know you. Solia has always been mean, and I always grouped you with her."

"I'm kind of sorry," Ming Li said, "But you call me Li, so ..." she shrugged.

"Can I please know what Dovin saw?" Tal pleaded. The other three shared a look.

"It's up to you, Graham," Wren said.

"You have as much to lose as I do," Graham told her. "Maybe more."

"I won't tell, I swear," Tal begged.

"I trust him," Wren said, nodding.

"Short version? Wren snuck into Professor Dovin's office and found out he's part of The Dark Cloud and had to make a portal to escape. She came to my world, and I accidentally followed her home, so now I'm stuck here."

That was a lot shorter than Wren had expected. Tal stared at Graham. He looked like he was going to talk, then stopped and started again.

"That was not at all what I expected," he finally said. "You're from a different world?" Graham nodded. "Wow," he said, shaking his head, "Does anyone else know?"

"Only my father and Brake," Wren said. "Oh, and my uncle."

"Why would that put us in danger, though?" Ming Li asked. "Especially me and Tal. We didn't open the portal."

"But if Professor Dovin knows, he could assume you told us he's part of The Dark Cloud," Tal said thoughtfully. "I'm not surprised. Professor Dovin looks evil, you know? Just like my father. Sometimes I wonder why people can't see who the bad guys are. You watch a play and the bad guy is this oily looking, frowning guy with pointy eyebrows and it's like, come on! He even looks bad!" Everyone stared at him. "What?"

"I thought he was your favorite teacher," Graham said.

"He is. But that doesn't mean he can't be evil."

"Professor Dovin doesn't look evil," Wren said. "He looks ... annoying."

Ming Li tapped her chin. "He would probably look better if he didn't put all that junk on his hair. He doesn't have pointy eyebrows either. He's actually good-looking for his age. I heard he's like, seventy."

Graham laughed. "No way. I would guess thirty-five."

"He's way older than thirty-five," Tal said. "He taught my father."

"People here live a lot longer than where you come from," Ming Li said. "Just go with it."

"How long do people live?"

"Usually no longer than two hundred and fifty." Wren said, trying to remember the oldest person she had ever met. Graham looked like he didn't believe her.

"What do we do?" Ming Li asked. "I mean, about being in danger. That seems more important than how old Professor Dovin is."

"I don't believe there's anything we can do," Wren said. "If we don't know where the danger is coming from or why, I guess we just have to be careful."

"Do you think Coach Zalliah figures we're in danger?" Wren wondered. "It seems like she's teaching us self defense." It made sense. Wren had thought herself into a headache a couple of times, trying to figure out why Coach Zalliah was teaching them these things.

"Maybe," Graham said, nodding. "It seems strange to take some random kids and make them do her little program."

"Zalliah seemed shocked when she saw us the first day Graham was at school, though," Wren said, thinking aloud. "It was like she saw something out of the ordinary about us."

"So I'm guessing you come from a world with seven continents and they all have names?" Tal said, with a mischievous-looking smile.

"Yep."

"And you name the oceans?"

"Uh-huh."

"Each person even has more than one name," Wren added. She thought it was adorable, the way Graham wanted everything to have a name.

"You have more than one name?"

"We have a first name and a last name. Some people have a middle name. Everyone in the family has the same last name, so you know they belong together."

"That's super weird," Tal said, shaking his head.

"Ming Li has two names and nobody ever seems to think anything about that."

"It's only one name, it just has a space," Ming Li protested.

"Do you name your house?" Tal asked, cocking his head.

"That would be stupid."

"And naming your ocean isn't?"

"I didn't actually come here to talk about any of this," Ming Li said, yawing. "Do we get a tour of your house or what?"

"Sure," Tal said, grinning. "It's not as impressive as you might imagine, though."

Graham ate dinner that night with Brake and went to his room to finish his homework. There was a desk in his room, which made it convenient to do school work. At least he was sure it would be, if he ever used it for that. Graham sat on his bed and emptied his school bag. He took out his magical equality book and laid on his pillow. It wasn't the best way to study, but it was the most comfortable.

He opened the book and a folded paper fell out. He picked it up and opened it. It said, *Library bookcase 4, second shelf, Prophecies Long Forgotten page 63.*

Graham crumpled the paper and threw it into his trash can. It must have been the previous owner's old bookmark. As far as crazy bookmarks go, that was pretty mild. His cousin Kaylee used to grab whatever was closest to her and stick it in her books. She had used tissues, toys, even a cookie once. Graham shuddered at the thought of a cookie in a book.

It was hard to pay attention to magical equality. It was always more of the same. Magic is the same. Everyone can learn the same things, blah, blah, blah. He looked at the trash can and shook his head and turned to his book. Every few minutes, he looked at the trash.

"Ugh, fine!" he finally said, getting off the bed and retrieving the paper. He didn't know why it was bothering him. He really wanted to know what was on page 63.

Wren opened her lunch and bit into her sandwich. The boys usually beat them to the lunchroom, but they weren't there yet. Ming Li was sitting next to her devouring cookies. Ming Li's mom made the best cookies. No one in Akkron baked like Mali. Wren wasn't sure how she had made it through the first part of her life without Mali's desserts.

"Hey," Tal said, plopping down on the seat across from Ming Li. Graham sat next to him and put a large brown book on the table.

"What's that?" Wren asked, pointing at the book. It looked like it could fall apart any second. It must be old.

"That's why we aren't going to have time to finish our lunch," Tal said, stuffing something in his mouth.

"I found a note in my book last night," Graham explained. He handed the note to Wren. She read it and handed it to Ming Li. "I was curious, so I found the book." He flipped through the book until he came to page 63. He read to himself.

"Come on, I was late for lunch for this. At least tell me what it says," Tal said, through a mouth full of bread.

"It's a poem," Graham said. He passed the book to Wren. She read it out loud.

Five would come when hope was lost,
To save the world, at such a cost.
Five would come to fight the fight,

118

To change the world from wrong to right.

Five would come and raise their voice,
And let all know they had a choice.
Five would come to change the tide,
No longer by the rules abide.

"That's it."

"Not that interesting," Tal said, still eating. "I prefer sonnets."

"Would it be more interesting if I told you I got a note in the same handwriting in my book?" Ming Li said, still looking at the note.

"You did your homework?" Tal asked, smiling, "Weird."

"I don't know why you assume I never do my school-work," Ming Li said, glaring at him.

"What did it say?" Wren asked curiously.

"Um ... I'm trying to remember. I figured someone left it last year, and I threw it away. It said something like, 'Everything you think you know is a lie.' I thought that about summed up my life and threw it out."

"Did you two get a note?" Graham asked Tal and Wren.

"I finished my assignment in class, so I didn't open my book," Wren said. "I left it home since we didn't need it today."

"Same," Tal said, throwing a grape and catching it in his mouth.

"Is someone sending us a message?" Graham wondered.

"It's probably a coincidence," Wren said, feeling a knot in her stomach, "But I won't be able to focus until I see if I have a note."

"Well, let's go," Tal said, grabbing his trash and tossing it into a bin. "We can go to my house first, then to Wren's."

"Wait, my book is in my bag ..." Wren said, feeling confused as she gazed into her bag. She was sure she had left it home. She pulled the thick book out and held it by the spine, shaking it. A piece of paper fell to the floor. The four of them looked at each other. Wren picked it up. It had the same handwriting.

"Well?" Tal said, tapping his foot. "What does it say?"

"The Island of Meegore."

"That's all?" Graham said, frowning. "What is the Island of Meegore?"

"Somewhere I'm not going," Ming Li shuddered.

"It's where the giants live." Tal said, checking his bag to see if his book was there.

"Giants?" Graham asked, with wide eyes.

"Yeah," Wren said, putting her book back in her bag and standing. "It's an island with a cave. A lot of people go there on vacation. There are a lot of old legends about it. The cave is blocked. In front of it, there's a large crystal. It's about five feet across and has five sides. Legend says that anyone who goes inside the cave will receive special powers.

"They say that people used to go in there and get these magic powers, and that they were a gift. People became greedy, trying to have the most powerful magic. They were going into the cave until they were so powerful they couldn't be defeated. It became so bad the island got angry and blocked the cave until five who are worthy come. They place their hands on the crystal, and if they are worthy, the crystal will glow and the cave will open."

"Tons of people visit every year and put their hand on the crystal," Tal added. "It's not even a pretty crystal. I've been there twice and I don't know what all the hype is about."

"And there are giants?" Graham asked, with wide eyes. Wren smiled. He looked cute when he was worried.

"People tried to break into the cave," she explained. "No matter what they tried, they couldn't get in. The giants felt like it should be guarded, so they all moved there. There aren't many giants. They watch over the cave and make sure no one tries to break through."

"How big are they?" Graham asked.

"Not that big," Tal said, scratching his head. "I would say nine to ten feet?"

"It's not their height that's scary," Wren said. "They are super strong. They have huge muscles. I swear their arms are as thick as my whole body."

"Are they violent?" Graham asked.

"Not unless you get on their bad side," Ming Li said. "Although, to be honest, I've never been there."

"We should talk about this somewhere else," Wren said, lowering her voice. "People are staring at us."

"Let's meet at my … er … Brake's house," Graham agreed. "Brake knows a ton of stuff, and he wants us to let him help us. Tal can run home and get his book and meet us later."

"Or we could leave now," Tal offered. "Someone is going through a lot of trouble to warn us about something. School doesn't feel that important."

"We should stay," Wren said. She wasn't in the mood to do make-up assignments.

Tal shrugged. "Okay, you guys finish class and I'll go home and look for my book. We can meet at Brake's after school."

Ming Li sighed. "Oh yay! Look who's coming towards us!"

Wren turned and saw Solia walking confidently in their direction. She frowned. Solia was not her favorite person. The girl had always hated her, and she couldn't figure out why. They didn't know each other and had only talked for the first time when Solia had insulted her in gym class.

"Tal," she said, tossing her long blonde hair over her shoulder. "I know you are going to come crawling back to our group eventually, and since I don't want to be a rotten friend, I thought I would let you know. Professor Dovin has been standing by the wall staring at you all lunch period."

"Staring at me?" Tal asked, pointing to himself.

"Staring at your table. He looks angry, although he could just be wondering why you have come down so low." She looked sideways at Wren. "Remember. Whenever you decide to come back, we will accept you. At least after you do a lot of groveling." She turned and walked away, waving over her shoulder.

"Well, she seems pleasant," Graham joked.

"She's not as nice as she seems," Ming Li muttered. "Don't let her get to you, Wren."

"I don't get why she doesn't like me. I never did anything to her."

"Professor Dovin must have left," Graham said, scanning the room. "And don't feel bad, Wren. Bullies are weak. It's easy to knock someone down. Strong people build others up. Don't let anyone make you feel bad, especially if they are trying to make you feel bad. Don't let them win. They have the problem, not you."

"I keep telling her that," Ming Li said.

"I know it's true, but it's hard."

"Solia only likes herself," Tal said. "She tolerates some people and hates everyone else. Graham's right. Don't waste energy feeling bad about what people like her think."

"Aren't you the one who used to hang out with her?" Ming Li, accused.

"If I'm going to skip, I'm going now," Tal said, ignoring her. "The more we talk here, the more people are looking at us."

CHAPTER 8

I have arrived!" Tal announced as he entered the sitting room at Brake's house. Wren, Ming Li, Graham, and Brake were already sitting.

"Don't worry about knocking," Brake said, with a slight smile. Graham wasn't sure what Brake thought about Tal, but he never seemed thrilled to see him. It was probably because of his father.

"Took you long enough," Ming Li glared. "I'd have thought you would have beaten us here, seeing as you skipped half the school day."

"Hey," Tal said, putting his arms up defensively, "My dad wouldn't let me take an alicorn, so I had to walk."

"You have alicorns?" Wren asked, bouncing up and down, "Why didn't you ever tell us?"

"It's not something I think about," he said, joining the circle.

"So, did you have a note?" Brake asked. "They filled me in while we were waiting."

Tal slumped in his seat. "Not only do I not have a note, my book is gone. I looked everywhere. I always throw it on my bookshelf and it's not there."

Brake rubbed his chin. "Are you sure you did yesterday?"

"No," Tal admitted. "It's a habit, so I'm just assuming I did."

"Who do we think the notes are from?" Graham asked. He had a theory, but it wasn't anything solid. Everyone exchanged glances. This was all odd. Who could get to all of their books?

"Coach Zalliah is my guess," Wren said.

Graham nodded. "That's what I was thinking. The poem in the book repeatedly talks about five people, and when Coach Zalliah was talking to us, she said something about how there should be five of us."

"She said that?" Brake muttered. "Did she say why?"

"No," Tal answered. "She made no sense, which is actually not that different from usual."

"It's possible she has some strange idea that we're part of this five," Wren said. "And the note about The Island of Meegore is referencing a place that's supposed to have five people."

"Or she's crazy," Ming Li shrugged. "Everyone knows all that stuff about being gifted magic isn't true."

"Yeah, if I've learned anything from magical equality," Graham said, "I've learned that you can't be given magic anymore."

"Can't you?" Brake asked, raising his eyebrow.

"Not according to Professor Ballina," said Wren.

"And everyone else," Tal added. "It's the same for everyone."

"Do you know something?" Graham asked Brake.

"I know lots of things," Brake said, lounging back against his chair and putting his hands behind his head. "One thing I know is that our world is magnificent at hiding things we don't want others to know, and things that we don't understand. It's easy to say we are all the same, but are we really?"

"If we practice, then we can be," Wren said, nodding.

"Can we?" Brake asked, raising an eyebrow. "Wren, can you freeze that lamp?" he asked pointing at a tall lamp in the corner.

"No." Wren shook her head. "No one can."

"Graham can you?" Brake asked.

"I don't know." It would be awesome if he could. Stretching out his hand, he thought about freezing the lamp. Graham's body felt cold, and the feeling rushed through him and into his raised arm. Ice blasted from his hand and knocked into the lamp. It didn't freeze the lamp, but it knocked it over. The room was silent for a moment and then Tal clapped slowly.

"You went all Elsa!" Ming Li said, "That is awesome!"

Graham looked at his hand and smiled. "I would say Frozone," he said, looking at Ming Li. Red crept up her neck and onto her face, and she clamped her mouth shut. Graham had some theories about Ming Li, but now wasn't the time.

126

"Freezing things is a lost talent!" Wren said excitedly.

"We aren't all the same," Brake said. "And that isn't bad. It's like I always say, if everyone was the same, it would be boring."

"Everyone is going to go crazy when they find out Graham can shoot ice," Tal said, shaking his head. "He might even become as popular as me."

"I guess you haven't noticed," Ming Li said, coming back to herself, "But he's already as popular as you, or he would be if we were willing to share him. Everyone's always trying to talk to him."

Brake tapped his fingers against his knee. "I think it would be good to keep Graham's gifts quiet for now. I have a feeling we're going to need to have a few surprises up our sleeves in the coming days. What I'm trying to tell you is that everything they have taught you in your magical equality class isn't true. People want to believe it is, but it isn't. A lot of things we call myths and legends are actually true."

"Do you think Graham can do all the lost magic?" Wren wondered.

"I doubt it. The other day, I gave Graham a glass of water and when he put it down, there was ice on the edges of the cup. That's why I had him try that."

"That's pretty awesome," Tal said.

"But this can't be about us," Graham said, holding up the library book.

"Perhaps not," Brake admitted, "But you are a group of kids that want to make a difference. That stands out here. Most people are content to live their lives pretending nothing is wrong."

"We can't be the only ones who want to help," Wren said, shaking her head. "I mean, people have sacrificed themselves to make changes."

"There are others who believe like you do," Brake admitted. "There is a group that's quietly trying to make a difference. I can't say much more about it, but you shouldn't feel alone."

"Others like my mom," Wren said, looking at her hands.

"Yes," Brake said, awkwardly patting Wren's shoulder. "And she didn't die in vain. She discovered things that were incredibly helpful. Still, it shouldn't have happened."

Graham looked at his feet. He felt like a terrible friend. Why had he never even thought to ask Wren about her mom?

"So, you are part of this group?" Tal asked, slowly. "And I'm assuming Wren's dad? It's probably his job to watch my dad."

"Let's not dwell on who is or isn't a part of this now." Brake said, sternly. "The less you know—"

"I know, the less we can tell," Wren sighed. "My dad says that all the time."

"I want you all to know that you don't have to hide things about my dad," Tal said. "I know he's no good, and it won't hurt my feelings or anything if you say things about him. In fact, I can help spy on him if you think he's part of The Dark Cloud."

Brake nodded. "We only have suspicions."

"Where do we start?" Graham wondered. "I'm having a hard time concentrating. I'm not gonna lie. I want to go outside and freeze things."

"That wouldn't be a good idea," Brake said.

"I don't know why you can do everything so easily," Wren said with a lopsided smile. "It doesn't seem fair."

"But it makes him *cooler* than Talon," Ming Li chuckled. "Get it? Cooler?" she laughed at her joke.

"I think we should go to the Island of Meegore," Graham said. "Maybe there's a clue there, or something we're supposed to do." Graham wasn't excited to run into a giant, but it did sound kind of neat.

"I'm not sure there's something we're supposed to do," Tal said, jiggling his leg. "This could all be something crazy that Zalliah dreamed up."

"We don't actually know it was Zalliah," Graham reasoned. "It could be Fleetman Zera."

"Fleetman Zera?" Brake asked, looking up. "Why her?"

"She told us we were in danger." Ming Li said. "She didn't tell us why. That would have been helpful."

"I still think we should go to the island," Graham said again. "If nothing comes of it, at least we would get to see it. It might be fun."

"Been there, seen it, over it," Tal said, sounding bored.

"I've never been there," Wren said. "My dad used to tell me stories about it, though."

"I haven't either," Ming Li said, "And they say the only way to get there is by boat or flight, so if we go, I say boat."

"I'm not sure it's safe," Brake said, scratching his chin. "I don't want to say you can't go, but you need to be careful."

"Can I go too?" said an eager voice from the window. Everyone jumped up and turned to see a skinny blond boy standing at the window. Graham shook his head. They weren't being careful. "Wow, you all look guilty," the boy said, climbing in the window.

"Jaaz, what are you doing here?" Graham asked. Jaaz was in two of Graham's classes. He acted a little strange sometimes, but who around here didn't?

"Do you know him?" Ming Li asked, looking between them with a puzzled expression. "Does he go to our school?"

"We have a door," Brake muttered as he sat back down.

"What do you mean, *does he go to our school*?" Jaaz asked, mimicking Ming Li and looking hurt. "I've been going to school with you since you started."

"Sorry," Ming Li shrugged. "I guess you aren't very memorable." Wren elbowed her friend softly in the side. "What?"

"Not memorable?" Tal laughed. "Do you not remember the rednax in Professor Jissper's classroom?"

"That was you?" Ming Li said, wrinkling her nose. "It smelled forever. Those are the smelliest animals."

"You know me, right Wren?" the boy asked. Graham noticed Wren looked uncomfortable. "Don't you remember when you fell and smashed my head?"

"My favorite memory ever," Tal smiled.

"Remember Wren? Growl, snap, roar! Then ahhh! My face! Then I pretended to eat you?"

"Right," Wren said, looking away.

"We're in the middle of something, Jaaz," Brake said, calmly. "You are going to have to come back later."

"Yeah, you are in the middle of something." He smiled and held up a book. "I found this."

"Is that mine?" Tal asked, taking the book Jaaz offered. He shook the book and nothing came out.

"Oh, did you want this?" Jaaz asked, holding a small piece of paper. Tal snatched it out of his hand. Scanning it he passed it to Graham.

"You have two days. Don't be late."

"It stinks in here," Ming Li said, holding her nose. Wren grinned. You could always count on Ming Li to state the obvious.

Tal rolled his eyes. "It *is* a stable."

"I can't believe I get to ride an alicorn!" Jaaz said, petting the white alicorn in front of him. Wren was still unsure about Jaaz. He was definitely the type to own a wand. She wondered if they could trust him. It was hard to trust someone you met the day before, or that you only remembered from the day before. No one wanted him to come, but he knew too much about what they were up to, and he was very insistent. He just showed up uninvited this morning and nobody knew how to get rid of him.

"You don't know how to ride?" Tal asked, as he led a large black alicorn out of its stall. "We need at least three people who can ride." He looked sideways at Graham, who was staying as far away from the animals as he could.

"I can ride a pegasus," Jaaz stated. "It should be the same, right?"

"Exactly the same." Tal sighed with relief. "I don't dare to take any of the pegasi. My dad would punish me for eternity. He doesn't care about the alicorns as much."

"Why?" Graham wondered. "They look about the same, except the horn."

"The pegasi are purebred," Tal explained, "And the alicorns are mixed. They aren't as valuable. Dad is all about showing off."

Ming Li snorted. "Pegasi sounds super dumb. Are you sure that's what you call them?"

"I brought a bottle of my dad's wine!" Jaaz said, before Tal could answer. "We can celebrate whatever happens today!" He held up a see-through bottle and sloshed around the contents.

"Seriously?" Graham said, rolling his eyes. "I stay far away from alcohol. I'm an athlete and I need all the advantages I can get. Don't you know it does bad stuff to your body? I won't even get started on your brain. You only get one. Take care of it."

"And nobody wants to see you get drunk and act like an idiot," Ming Li said, taking the bottle and dumping it on the ground. "I never understand why anyone thinks it's cool to act stupid and not even remember it the next day. My dad was an alcoholic and drinking never helped him make a smart choice."

"Alright, alright," Jaaz said, putting his hands up in defense. "I've never actually tried it, I just thought ... I don't know what I thought."

"So," interrupted Wren, pointedly changing the subject, "I can fly, Tal, and Jaaz?"

"Can you fly well?" Tal asked, looking nervous.

"I've taken lessons," Wren said for the third time today. "I don't have one, but I'm saving up."

"But can you ride for hours without stopping?" Tal asked.

Wren folded her arms. "Would you rather Graham or Ming Li be in control?"

"No way!" Ming Li said. "That would be a sure way to die. Even worse, Graham. He's probably scared of them."

"I'm not scared," Graham said, still not coming closer. "I'm careful."

"He's terrified of little dragons too," Ming Li said, giggling. Jaaz and Tal laughed.

"Okay, I'm a little nervous around animals," Graham admitted, "Except dogs. Well, some dogs. Goldfish don't really bother me."

"That's okay," Wren assured him. "We're all scared of something."

"Does anyone else think we aren't as prepared as we should be?" Graham asked. "I mean, it might not be that smart to follow some random clues to do something we don't even know what it is."

"All we need to do is answer the question words," Ming Li said confidently. "Who, what, when, where, and how."

"Great Li," Tal said, petting the large alicorn. "That means Graham is right. We aren't ready."

"We know the where," Jaaz said excitedly. "That's enough for me!"

"Let's just call this a quick day trip," Wren suggested. "We can go see the island and the crystal, and if that's all that comes from it, that's okay."

"I'm fine with that," Ming Li said, looking at the bottom of her brown boot. "Let's go soon before I step in anything else." Wren, Tal, and Jaaz led the alicorns out of the stable and into the bright morning sun.

"Who gets to ride with me?" Jaaz asked, mounting the white alicorn. Everyone stared at him.

Ming Li shivered. "Not me, I get to go with Talon."

"I thought you would go with me," Wren said, wondering why her friend would abandon her, and for Tal, of all people.

"Wren, you know I'm terrified of flying," Ming Li said, pushing her hair over her shoulder. "I feel safer with Talon because he has more experience. Plus, the alicorns might like him better because they belong to him."

"And if we crash onto a deserted island, Li gets to spend the rest of her life with me," Tal said with a wink. "Who could resist that?"

"And I'll live longer because I can eat him," Ming Li said, smiling. Tal, Jaaz and Graham laughed. Wren felt nervous. That meant she would end up with Graham.

"So me and you?" Graham asked as Wren quickly mounted the shimmering black alicorn. She nodded. Tal brought a crate over to the side so Graham could get up. Graham sighed and stepped up.

"I feel like a little girl, getting on like this," he muttered, as he clumsily climbed onto the animal. He awkwardly settled himself and put his arms around Wren.

"A little girl?" Wren asked with a small laugh to cover her nerves. "Does that mean I mounted like a big, powerful man?"

"I'm not trying to insult anyone," Graham said nervously. "Are you shaking this thing on purpose? Shouldn't it be more stable?"

"It's not even moving yet," Tal said, the corners of his mouth twitching. "Maybe you should close your eyes until we get there. By the way, her name is Lazreelle." Tal picked up the crate and moved it over to his alicorn. Ming Li walked over with her arms tucked tightly around her waist. "You can mount, right?" he asked. "You said you can ride a unicorn."

"Well, technically ..." Ming Li hesitated. "I've ridden a unicorn, but only once."

"Okay," Tal said, mounting the alicorn with ease. "Stand on the crate and take my hand. I'll help you up." Ming Li stepped onto the crate and sighed. Tal reached his hand out to her, and she awkwardly climbed on behind.

"Ahhhhh!" Ming Li squealed as she slipped sideways and grabbed Tal around the waist to catch herself. She buried her face in his back.

"I would tell you to hold on tight," Tal joked, "But any tighter and I might lose my breakfast."

"And you were teasing me about being scared," Graham laughed nervously.

"Animals don't scare me," Ming Li mumbled into Tal's back, "But, I am terrified of flying."

Tal's eyes crinkled at the corners. "We aren't flying yet."

"I was feeling a little rejected when nobody wanted to ride with me, but now I'm sure I'm the lucky one," Jaaz said, smiling. "I'm going to be surprised if you all make it without falling into the ocean or wetting yourselves."

"Let's go," Wren said, patting Lazreelle. She hoped Graham was too scared to notice that she was sweating. At least she was one of the confident people for once. She didn't want Graham and Ming Li to be scared, but it was nice to know she could do some things better than they could.

"Everyone follow me," Tal said, "Let's go Zeezee," he said to his alicorn.

Zeezee galloped, and Lazrelle followed. Jaaz's alicorn wasn't far behind. Wren closed her eyes as the wind pushed against her face. As Zeezee lifted into the air, Ming Li let out a piercing scream. Wren smiled as Lazrelle lifted off the ground. Take off was the best part. The thrill from the speed and the wind was what drew her to flying. Graham felt stiff behind her, with an iron grasp on her waist. She hoped he wouldn't slide off. If he did, he would take her with him.

Graham was feeling tired. After the first half hour, he stopped feeling scared. It was almost like riding a roller-coaster. Scary, but thrilling. Every time they dipped down, his stomach felt like it was about to jump from his throat. Wren's long locks pelted him in the face, and he couldn't do anything about it, because he didn't dare to let go. He would feel better if there were seat belts.

They had flown over the countryside. There were a few large estates and a lot of forest. They had been flying over the ocean for what seemed like an eternity. Hopefully alicorns didn't get tired easily. Graham wasn't sure if he would be able to walk when this all ended. All of his muscles felt sore. Ming Li looked like she was doing better. In the beginning, she'd screamed every time Zeezee made a move she didn't expect. Graham wondered if Tal had a headache.

"Do you trust everyone?" he asked, leaning in closer to Wren. "For all we know, Jaaz could be spying on us. It seems a little strange that he found Tal's book and came looking for him at my house."

"You said he seems like an okay guy," Wren said, still focused ahead, "So he's probably alright. I'm not saying we should include him in our group or anything."

"He seems okay," Graham said, "But, honestly, Professor Dovin seems alright, and we all know that isn't true. Jaaz is kind of odd. Leaving him behind could have been bad though, since he knew where we were going. Did he ever tell us how he came to have Tal's book?"

"Not that I remember."

"Brake told me not to let Jaaz know anything and not to let him come. He said his dad isn't trustworthy and said we should probably avoid him."

"What?" Wren asked, trying to look back. "Why are we letting him come then?"

"I don't know. I'm not good at confrontation and he seemed so excited to come. We don't have to tell him anything. All he knows is what he overheard at the window."

"If you had doubts about him, you could have told Ming Li. She would've gotten rid of him."

"That's probably true. Sometimes I wonder if we should be trusting Tal. It seems strange he would ditch his former friends to hang out with us."

"Yeah, I've thought about that a bunch of times. I feel like we can trust him, though. Tal told us not to trust his dad, and we have been spending a lot of time with him. It's hard to know what to do. I know we can trust Ming Li."

"I trust Ming Li," Graham said. "At least I trust her to be on our side. I'm not sure I trust her to not do ... or say anything crazy."

"You've been the one to trust everyone," Wren said, not looking back. "Why the change?"

"I do trust everyone, but I'm not so sure that's always a good thing. I'm starting to wonder if we're crazy for following the notes. They could be from anyone. We could be walking into a trap."

"Who would want to trap us? We don't have enemies."

"I'm just thinking about Fleetman Zera's warning. We never figured out what that was all about." They both sat silently. Graham had a wave of panic pass over him. What if this was a trap? Why were they so trusting? Why did they make plans without thinking them through for more than a few hours?

"It's too bad teleporting is lost magic," Wren said. "That would make things a lot easier. We could just teleport to the island and if something was wrong, we could leave. I mean, I can always open a portal, but that would only be the last option."

"Just remember if you do, open the one by your house." Graham wasn't in the mood to fall into a volcano.

"There it is!" Tal called, pointing into the distance. Graham looked at where he was pointing. He could see it ahead. The island was small. The closer they got, the more nervous he felt. He couldn't see any buildings on the island, only trees. Tal and Ming Li touched down on an open spot of land. Right as Wren and Graham landed, a giant stepped out into the clearing.

"Wow," Graham mumbled, sliding stiffly off of the alicorn.

The giant looked to be at least ten feet tall and had long dark hair tied back in a neat ponytail. His brown tunic had seen better days, and he wasn't wearing any shoes. He wasn't frowning, but he wasn't smiling either. Wren had dismounted and was stroking Lazrelle's nose, and Tal was helping Ming Li stand. Her legs were probably as shaky as his were. Jaaz was bouncing with excitement.

"Wow, he's so tall!" Ming Li said, staring at the giant.

"I am Brog," the giant bowed. He had a deep voice, but it was a lot quieter than Graham would have expected. "I will take your alicorns. They will be safe with me." He stepped forward and petted Zeezee's nose. The alicorn rubbed her head against him.

Tal handed Brog some coins. "Thank you."

"If you follow the path behind me into the trees, you will come to the cave of Meegore. Please stick to the path. If you bring any garbage in, take it out with you. Keeping the island clean is difficult if we do not all do our part."

"Of course," Wren said, smiling. "Thank you."

"I can't believe I saw a giant!" Jaaz said, as they walked to the trees. "This is the best day ever!"

"What should we be looking for?" Graham asked. "Do you suppose someone might meet us here? Maybe they wanted us to come to a place where they could talk more freely."

"It's possible," Wren said. "It would make sense if it's Fleetman Zera. It's hard as a fleet member to have any privacy. They have such a tight schedule. The governor knows where they are almost all the time. My dad has to get special permission to do anything."

"The purple crystals are cool," Graham said, pointing to a foot-long crystal that looked like it was growing out of the ground. They were all over the place.

"I just saw a gigantic bird!" Jaaz said, pointing into the trees. Jaaz was definitely making them look like tourists. It might be good to have him along.

Tal pointed ahead. "There it is. The very unimpressive crystal."

"Wow, it's big," Graham said, as they entered a clearing in the trees. A big dull crystal hovered a few inches above the ground. "How is it staying up?"

"Nobody knows," Wren explained. "It looks bigger than I imagined. I wonder why it's so plain when all the other crystals are so pretty."

Thirty feet from the crystal was a grassy hill with a large rock in front of it. Two giants with brown tunics and long brown braids stood by it, holding swords at their sides.

"That's a big rock," Jaaz said, sounding impressed.

"That's the entrance to the cave," Tal told him.

"Or a big rock that the giants decided to guard," Ming Li said, looking unimpressed. "It doesn't even look like there's a place for a door."

"Touch the crystal only once," one giant said. "We have to clean the fingerprints off after and we prefer to only do one swipe."

"Awesome," Jaaz said, putting his hand against the crystal. "Wow, it's slick." He rubbed his hand across the smooth surface. The giant sighed.

"You're smudging it, Jaaz," Tal said, rolling his eyes.

"This is only one touch," Jaaz said, still rubbing it. "I haven't taken my hand off yet."

Tal shook his head. "That sounds like something my father would say. Now they have to take more time to clean. This is one touch," he said, putting his pointer finger on the crystal. Before he could pull away, the side of the crystal glowed bright purple.

CHAPTER 9

D oes everyone see this?" Jaaz exclaimed, backing away from the crystal. Tal stepped back and rubbed his hand on his shirt, but the crystal was still glowing.

"Looks like I broke it," Tal said in a quiet, raspy voice.

"You woke the crystal," one giant said, with wide eyes. Both of the giants walked slowly around the crystal with their mouths gaping open.

"I never thought I would get to see the day," the other giant said in a hushed tone.

"You have been chosen," the first giant said, bowing to Tal. The second one followed his lead.

"It must be a mistake," Tal gulped.

"Your friends must also try," the giant said, gesturing to the crystal. His eyes were shining with excitement.

Wren didn't know how to feel. Part of her wanted to touch the crystal, but she also felt nervous. Graham and Ming Li didn't look like they were going to touch it, so

Wren stepped forward. She reached out a shaky hand and pressed her palm against a side that wasn't glowing. A purple glow sprung up. Wren stared at her hand and the light, and breathed in a shaky breath.

"Awww, why didn't it work for me?" Jaaz complained. Wren could feel herself trembling.

"Because you aren't worthy, or chosen, obviously," Ming Li said from somewhere behind her.

Graham stepped beside her and put his hand against the side, touching hers. More purple light appeared. Three of the five sides were glowing. Wren couldn't seem to pull herself away. The deep purple color made the crystal look more impressive, like something from a legend.

"Now you," a giant gestured to Ming Li.

"No way," said Ming Li, frowning. "I'm pretty sure I'm not chosen."

"That's okay," Jaaz said. "If it doesn't glow, you can still hang out with me."

"Just try Li," Tal said, putting his hand back on the crystal. "If it doesn't glow, it doesn't change anything."

"Fine," Ming Li muttered, looking at the crystal, "But nothing is going to happen." She slunk to one of the dull sides and closed her eyes. She took a deep breath and put her hand out, lightly touching it. Relief washed over Wren as she saw the purple glow reflecting on Ming Li.

"Open your eyes Li," Tal said in a whisper.

Ming Li opened her eyes. "It's glowing!" she said, releasing a breath. "But that doesn't seem possible." Wren wasn't sure how long they all stood there staring at their hands.

"I'm trying again," Jaaz said, putting his hand against the dull side of the crystal. Nothing happened. "I guess I'm not worthy."

"Many worthy people have tried," a giant said, "But they were not chosen."

Wren looked around and noticed they were now surrounded by giants. There were at least thirty.

"We have waited long for this moment," he said. "My name is Tnarg. The T is silent."

"What T?" Jaaz asked.

"The only T in my name," he said, "And this is Mot." He pointed at the other giant. "Do you know who the fifth person could be?"

"No," Wren said as the others shook their heads.

"You may now enter the cave," he said, gesturing to the big rock.

"Even though there aren't five of us?" Wren asked as they walked slowly towards it.

"It will open for even one," Tnarg said.

"How does it open?" Tal muttered as they moved closer. "I thought it was supposed to pop open when the crystal glowed."

"Maybe we do need the fifth person?" Graham wondered out loud. They slowed as they got closer and the cave rumbled. The ground shook and the rock pulled off to the side revealing the cave's opening.

"Wow!" Jaaz said, "This is like seeing something that will go down in history! Can I go in?"

"That would not be wise," said Tnarg, walking behind them. "Only those who made the crystal glow should enter."

They came to the opening in the cave and looked down.

"Oh wow," Ming Li said. "I wasn't expecting it to go down." Stairs carved out of rock descended into the darkness. Wren couldn't see the bottom.

"Who gets to walk into the creepy, dark cave first?" Wren asked, staring into the black abyss.

"I can only imagine the kinds of bugs that must be in there," Tal said, grinning at his friends. "Probably bats too. Anyone want to volunteer to lead?"

"I volunteer you," Ming Li said. "That way, your gigantic head can clear away all the cobwebs."

"I thought we would walk in and get zapped with some power or something," Graham said.

"You haven't come prepared?" Tnarg asked, his bushy eyebrows coming together.

"We weren't expecting this to happen," Wren told him.

"I'll go first," Tal said, making a light appear in his hand. Wren pulled up her own light, and so did Graham. Wren looked at Ming Li and smiled what she hoped was an encouraging smile. They stepped into the cave and the rock slid back over the opening. It was all dark except for the light in their hands.

"That would have been totally creepy," Graham said, "Except I was expecting it. I've seen dozens of horror movies and the door always closes."

"It's still creepy," Ming Li said with a shiver.

Wren shuddered. "Our light doesn't seem big enough. It's hard to see the stairs." They all took slow, even steps and stayed close together.

"Can we make it bigger?" Graham asked.

"I don't know how," Wren admitted, "But I can make two." She made a second light in her free hand.

"Can it be by me?" Ming Li whispered.

"Hold out your hands," Wren said. Ming Li did, and Wren transferred one light to her. She would have to concentrate hard to keep the light going when she didn't have it.

"You know," Tal said from a couple of steps ahead of Wren, "The stories say that people without magic would come here to get magic. That's why everyone used to be magic."

"Really?" Ming Li asked, trying to sound uninterested. Wren could hear the hope in her friend's voice.

"Yep," Tal nodded, still walking. "It wasn't until after the cave was sealed that there were non-magic people around."

"Hm, that's interesting."

"Li, we all know," Tal said gently.

"Know what?" They walked for a moment in silence.

Wren wished they could see better. "This is really deep. Maybe we can shoot some light in and see how deep it is?"

"Do you want to know?" Graham asked. "I don't think I do."

"I'm at the bottom," Tal said, stopping. They all joined him and looked around. They were in a small cavern.

"I forgot," Graham said, digging in his pocket. He pulled out a bright dragon scale. "I always have this with me. Do you want to take it?" he asked, holding it out to Ming Li. She took it and held it up. It was much brighter than the lights they could make.

"This is less impressive than I imagined," Ming Li said, scanning the walls. "Wait, a door," she said, holding up the scale.

"Nice," Tal smiled, getting closer to the door. It looked like a part of the cave wall, but there were hinges. Tal felt around and found a latch. The wide door slowly opened outward.

"Slides?" Ming Li said, frowning. "Really? I am okay with dark stairs, but not with sliding down a dark slide."

Wren peeked over Ming Li and held up her light. Two slides carved from rock disappeared into the darkness. She cringed. She tried not to imagine what might be at the bottom.

"Well, I'm ready," Tal said, sitting at one of the slide's openings, and pulling his cape out from under him. "I'm assuming they'll be slow since rock isn't very slippery."

"I'll go on this side," Ming Li offered, sitting on the open slide next to him. "If we go together, we might have more light."

"Okay. Let's do this!" Tal said, sounding excited. He disappeared into the darkness. Ming Li was only a second after. "Wahooooooooo!" he called, as Ming Li screamed.

Wren's stomach felt tight. "The slides should end at the same place, right?"

Graham looked into the darkness. "I sure hope so."

"Ming Li? Can you hear me?" Wren called into the opening. Ming Li yelled something they couldn't understand.

"What did she say?" Graham asked.

"I don't know," Wren said, sighing. "Let's get down there and make sure they're alright." She sat on the cold rock slide, careful of her light.

Graham sat next to her. "We should have dressed warmer. I can feel a breeze, even with my cape."

"Probably," Wren agreed, trying to smile. "Race you to the bottom!"

The slide was much faster than Graham had expected. It took all his willpower not to scream. He knew Tal would tease him forever if he did. It was steep! The slide turned suddenly and shot off in another direction. A small yell slipped out, but he stopped it. His light had gone out, and with the way he was shooting down this thing, he wasn't able to make another one. When he thought it would never end, he suddenly hit the bottom. On his bottom.

"Ouch," he said, standing up.

"Graham?" Ming Li said from somewhere in the dark. "Where are you?" Graham created a new light. Ming Li slammed into him with a hug. "That was the scariest thing I've ever done! There was no light at the bottom, and Tal wasn't here!"

"I was worried about that," Graham said, awkwardly hugging Ming Li. Hugging had not been a big thing in his life.

"I'm sorry I lost your scale. I dropped it and I don't know where it could have gone."

"It's alright," Graham said, looking around.

"This is ridiculous," Ming Li said, stepping away. "We need more light." As soon as she said it, everything lit up. Graham couldn't tell where the light was coming from, but it was so bright it didn't even look like they were in a cave. He saw the dragon scale on the ground and picked it up. It wasn't shining anymore, but he could always boil it again. A rocky hallway loomed in front of them and stretched out as far as they could see.

"Well, this is kinda awesome," Ming Li said as she looked around. Someone had covered the cave floor in powdery yellow dust. It was sticking to their shoes and the bottom of their pants.

"So, I guess we follow the yellow dust road?" Graham said, raising his eyebrow.

Ming Li glared at him. "What about Wren and Tal?"

"It looks like there are only two ways to go. Down the hall or back up the slide. I don't know about you, but I'm pretty sure I'm not getting up the slide. That thing was steep, and besides, all roads lead to the emerald city, right?" He raised his brow again. Ming Li blinked twice. "I'm hoping we will end up in the same place as Wren and Tal."

"Fine," Ming Li said, rolling her eyes, "But if you say anything about lions, and tigers, and bears, you are on your own." She turned and walked down the path.

Graham grinned. "You are the only one who gets my references," he said, following her.

"I don't know what you are talking about," she said, not looking back.

Graham walked up beside her. "So, are you ever going to tell me where you're from?"

"Nope," she said, staring straight ahead.

"Why not? I know you don't have any magic. It's safe to bet Tal knows, too. I also know you're from Earth."

"What makes you think that?" she asked, glaring at him.

"Well, you didn't make your own light. I've never seen you do magic. You referenced Elsa a while back and I heard you humming *Livin' La Vida Loca* the other day." At least he figured that was what she was humming. It was completely out of tune. He wasn't sure if he should push, but it was the first time they'd been alone for more than a couple of minutes. "Oh yeah, and your mom is the only person around that makes chocolate chunk cookies and cinnamon rolls."

Ming Li sighed. "I haven't even told Wren. She only knows I can't do magic."

"How did you get here?" he asked.

Ming Li stared at the ground. "Brake brought us here."

"Brake?" That wasn't what he expected. "How? Why?"

"You have got to be kidding," Ming Li said, stopping.

Graham stopped. "What do you mean?" Ming Li pointed forward. The path ended at a high rock wall that had an opening at the top.

"I suppose we climb that?" she said, pointing. "How is all of this even fitting under this island? Do you suppose we're under the ocean?"

"Could be," he said, looking up. "I guess we should start. Zalliah has to be the one who sent us here. I just hope there isn't a pit of alligators."

Ming Li looked worried. "I wonder how Wren is doing."

Wren looked at the pit in front of them and sighed. They had not come prepared for this. They should have done a lot more research.

"At least there aren't any alligators," Tal said, looking down. A rope was hanging from the ceiling and wrapped around a rock on the ground in front of them. They had walked about fifteen minutes down a rocky yellow path and come to this. She was just glad the cave was so well lit.

"So, instead of getting eaten by alligators, I can fall and break something," Wren said, feeling discouraged.

"We can climb down and back up the other side," Tal suggested.

"That will take too long," Wren said. "I'll feel better once we find the others."

"Okay," Tal said, tapping his lip in thought, "I'll go first. I'll throw the rope back. You grab it and when you get to the other side, I'll grab you so you don't go back. You made it far enough last time, you just didn't let go. I'm not the best at levitating, but if you fall, I can make you fall slower."

"Why are you smiling like that?" Wren asked, crossing her arms and glaring.

"Sorry," he chuckled. "I laugh every time I remember you falling on Jaaz's head. You would laugh too, if you had seen the whole thing. And he came into math class bragging about it."

"Bragging that I fell on his head?"

"Bragging that he saved you," he said, grabbing the rope. "Okay, here I go." He stood back as far as he could, took three fast steps and jumped over the pit. He made it look easy. "Ready?" She nodded as he swung the rope back.

After just barely catching it, she tied a knot in the rope and anchored her hands above it. The rope was prickly and uncomfortable, but it felt sturdy. "This rope has to be ancient. What if it breaks?"

"It's probably magic. It feels sturdy enough. Ready?" he put his arms up ready to catch her.

"Alright," she sighed. "One, two, three!" she sprang forward. Her arms burned with the strain of holding on as she flew over the pit. Tal grabbed her around the waist and pulled so she would have to let go. They both fell to the ground in a heap, and Wren's head smacked against something hard. She hoped it wasn't his head. "Are you okay?" she asked, scrambling up, brushing yellow dust off her backside.

"Fine," Tal said, rubbing his shoulder.

"Thanks," she said, looking down the cave. "This is ridiculous. Why would people come here multiple times? They must have been crazy. I would have stopped after that crazy slide if there'd been a way out."

Tal nodded. "Yeah, well, people do crazy things for power. Believe me, my dad would be here every day if he could get in. I'm going to levitate the rope and send it back to the other side."

"Coach Zalliah has to have been the one to send us here," Wren said as they started walking again. "She must have known what types of things we would have to do."

"It makes sense," Tal agreed. "Do you hear water?"

Wren stopped and listened. She could hear running water in the distance. "I hope we don't have to cross it or anything," she said. "It's already freezing here."

"I bet we do. It's that kind of day."

"I hope it's not deep," she said.

"Can you swim?"

"Yes. I'm pretty good at swimming. It's one thing I can do better than Ming Li."

"You're better than her at a lot of things."

"Not active things."

"You are way better at school than she is. Minus gym."

"I might not be if she tried. I feel like I have to try hard with everything."

"It's more impressive if you accomplish something because you try hard than if you're just naturally good at it."

Wren shrugged. That was easy for him to say. He had good grades, he was athletic, and he didn't seem to try that hard. But she was judging again. She didn't know how much he studied or practiced sports.

The water was getting louder. They turned the corner and saw a stream crossing their path. Actually, it seemed more like a small river. It was about twenty feet across and it looked filthy.

"I wish we could see the bottom," Tal said, walking to the murky water.

"Do you think it's deep?" Wren asked, trying to see to the bottom.

"I can't tell. I wish there was a stick or something I could poke in there," Tal said, scanning the ground.

"What if there are alligators?" Wren asked, shivering. "Coach Zalliah went through some effort to have alligators in the obstacle course."

"I doubt it," Tal said, bending and sticking his finger in the water. "If alligators could get in, then people could get in. If people haven't been able to get in, then it's safe. The water is freezing." He wiped his finger on his cape.

"So what do we do?"

"I guess one of us is going to have to step in," Tal said, with the lopsided grin that always came with his teasing. "Hopefully we won't have to swim it. I'm guessing it's only a foot or two. So me or you?"

"I'm considering going back and climbing the slide," Wren said, only half joking.

His eyes twinkled. "If we can walk across this and not swim, I don't see any reason for both of us to get wet. So, do you think you can carry me?"

Wren laughed. "Not a chance."

Tal squatted and stuck his arm into the water. He pushed it down until it was almost to his shoulder. "There's the bottom."

"That's not too bad."

"It's soooo cold," he said, pulling his arm out. "Seriously though, it would be stupid for both of us to get wet. We don't know what else might be in front of us. Jump on my back."

"That will make it harder for you," she said, shaking her head.

"It doesn't matter. You can do the next crazy thing we come to. You can't carry me, so this is the only thing that makes sense." He unfastened his cape and handed it to her. "Can you try to keep this dry?"

Wren took the cape and rolled it around her arm. She felt ridiculous climbing on Tal's back. She put her arms around his neck and tried to keep the cape out of his face. He had a good grip on her legs. She pulled her cape up so it wouldn't drag in the water. She wished his arm wasn't wet, but as soon as the thought crossed her mind, she felt guilty. Touching his wet arm wasn't anywhere near as bad as what he must be feeling.

"Ready?" he asked, stepping into the water. He sucked in a breath as the water rose past his knees. "Wow, that's cold," he said, shivering. He took a few steps forward before the water became deeper.

"I can walk," Wren offered.

"No," he said through clenched teeth. "You're keeping me warmer." He walked faster. If the water kept going up, she might end up getting wet.

"What's wrong?" Wren asked when Tal stopped and stiffened. He didn't answer, but trudged forward at greater speed. They passed the middle without the water reaching Wren and soon it started going down. She could tell he was moving as fast as he could. He stepped out on the other side and ran a few feet away from the water before putting Wren down.

"Come on," he said, grabbing her hand and pulling her forward.

"What's wrong?" she asked, trying not to trip.

"Something touched my leg in there," he said, not slowing. Wren could hear his teeth chattering.

"At least stop and put your cape on," she said, pulling him to a stop. He grabbed the cape and wrapped it around himself. He was shaking too hard to clasp it. "Let me help you," she said, fastening it for him.

"Thanks. Let's get away from whatever is in that water."

"Do you suppose it was an alligator?"

"No, it was probably a fish or something. It freaked me out, though."

"I wonder if we have to come back the same way." Wren said, rubbing the goosebumps on her arms. The thought of going through the water knowing something was in there was way too freaky.

"I hope not."

"Thanks for carrying me."

"Anytime," he said, keeping his eyes forward. She hoped he wouldn't get sick or anything.

They turned a corner and instead of being met with more hallway; they were in an enormous cavern. The walls

156

were shimmering with a silvery glow. It was bright and there were colorful bubbles floating everywhere. A round platform sat in the middle. It was about a foot high and about four feet wide.

"Well, this is interesting," Tal said, looking around.

"What are these things?" Wren wondered, stretching out her arm to catch a pink bubble.

"Whoa," Tal said, grabbing Wren's arm. "We're in a strange magical cave. It might not be safe to go grabbing the first shiny thing we see. What if they're dangerous?"

Wren pulled her arm in. "I didn't think of that. They look like bubbles."

"If you look close, they're thicker," Tal said, pointing to one that was close to her head. "And it looks like there's liquid inside."

"One bumped the back of your head and nothing bad happened."

"Could this be the magic?" he wondered. "I remember something about choosing the magic. Maybe each color is a different kind."

"If so, I'm assuming we can only take one. That must be why people used to come back so much." Wren was upset with herself for not researching more. She hadn't thought to, since it seemed impossible to believe that the cave would open after thousands of years, and for her. She was still having trouble believing it.

"I hope we find Li and Graham," he said, pulling his cape tighter. "Should we wait for them?"

Wren bit her lip. "I don't know. What if they don't come to the same place? There could be more than one cavern."

"I don't see any other ways out," he said, with chattering teeth. "I'm not sure if I'll be able to make it out unless I dry off. My legs are feeling stiff."

They walked around, looking at the bubbles. Wren wasn't sure what to do. She looked at the raised platform. "There's writing on here!"

Tal came closer. "What does it say?"

"In the cavern where you stand, take the power in your hand. When you find the one that's right, stand up straight, embrace the light."

"Huh," Tal said. "That's not vague or anything."

"I don't see any reason to wait," Wren said. "Since we don't know what the colors mean, I guess we hope for the best."

"You don't suppose there's terrible magic, do you?" Tal asked, watching the bubbles float around. "Not like evil, but like something stupid?"

"I don't know. I hope Ming Li gets something good."

"Yeah, then she won't have to pretend anymore."

"Wait, you know she doesn't have magic?" Wren thought she was the only one who knew.

"Everyone knows," Tal said, grabbing a blue bubble. "Wow, it feels thick and solid."

"I don't think everyone can know," Wren said, remembering the tricks they'd done to make it look like Ming Li had magic.

"Maybe everyone doesn't know, but it's a rumor at school," Tal said, looking at the bubble. "How do you think this works? I hope we don't have to eat it or something."

"I bet it happens when we stand on the platform."

"Hurry and choose and we can try."

"What if we don't like what we get? I wonder if we can get rid of it."

"I don't know, but I'm willing to risk it. What about you?"

"Okay," she said, looking around. "Green seems safe, right?" she grabbed a green bubble out of the air. "So now we stand on the platform?" They looked at the platform. Wren's heart was beating almost as fast as when she flew down that awful slide.

"Let's do this," Tal said, smiling. He took Wren's hand, and they stepped onto the platform.

"Did you see that?" Graham asked, as they watched Tal and Wren disappear in a swirl of color. He pulled his cape tighter to stop the shivering. His legs felt numb. That water had been so cold! After climbing the wall, they'd followed a path at a gradual decline and ended up at a river.

"Nice of them to wait for us," Ming Li said through her chattering teeth.

"They both had one of these bubbles in their hand," he said, grabbing a red bubble out of the air. "So I guess we choose one."

"I'm not sure it will work for me," Ming Li said, watching the bubbles bounce around.

"It should. That's why everyone used to be magic here, right?"

"I guess."

"And the crystal chose you."

"Don't you think it's strange the crystal chose us when we aren't from here?" Ming Li said, looking at her wet boots. Graham shook his head. He had offered to carry her across the water, but she was stubborn and had refused. Now they were both freezing.

"Maybe we ended up here because we were chosen," Graham said thoughtfully. It was strange to think that he had been chosen, a poor boy from the inner city. It almost blew his mind. He wondered if that's how Ming Li felt. "Are you going to tell me how you got here?"

"We should choose a bubble and leave." She grabbed a pink bubble. "Let's get on the platform and hope we swirl away to wherever the others are."

"Do we hold hands?" Graham said, scratching his head. "Tal and Wren were. If we do, we won't get separated."

"You don't have to ask me twice," Ming Li said, smiling as she grabbed his hand. Her hand was freezing. Graham took a deep breath, and they stepped onto the platform. A rainbow of colors swirled around them and they lifted off the ground. Graham wasn't sure what was happening. All he could see were colors. The breeze against his wet pants was making everything colder.

They hit the ground and landed on their feet. They were outside. He still had Ming Li's hand, but the bubble was gone, and he was dry. Before he could speak, something hit him in the head and everything went dark.

CHAPTER 10

T hey should be back by now. It's been at least a half hour," Wren said, looking around. After the swirling colors had dropped them back outside the cave, giants swarmed them, wanting to know what the cave was like. Tal told them everything that happened, but when the giants asked where the bubbles were, they realized they didn't have them.

"They could have had a longer path," Tal said, gazing into the trees. "I'm still wondering where the bubbles disappeared to. I thought I had a good hold on mine. It's crazy the way my britches dried. Not that I'm complaining."

The giants were all looking for Graham and Ming Li. No one was sure whether they would appear in the same place.

"How big do you suppose this island is?"

161

"Five, maybe six miles across," Tal said. "If we don't find them after the search, I can go back through the cave really fast."

"I do not believe they are still in the cave," Brog, the giant who took their alicorns said, coming up to them. "When you two appeared, your sides of the crystal became dull, but the other two sides were still shining. Now the whole crystal is dull."

"So they're out here?" Wren said, motioning at all the trees and crystals.

"It shouldn't take long to search," Brog said. "Giants are fast."

"Hey, where's Jaaz?" Tal asked.

Wren felt awful. She hadn't thought about Jaaz since they'd left him.

"He was annoying everyone with his constant questions," Brog said, "So we suggested he go explore the island."

"Ugh, now we have to find him as well," Tal sighed. "Or we could leave him here with an alicorn."

"That would be rude," Wren said, even though it sounded tempting. "You better never leave me somewhere."

"Nah," Tal said, smiling. "You're part of the team. Jaaz is like the crazy neighbor kid you can't get rid of."

"I wish they would let us search." She hated waiting when they could be helping.

"I can see why they want us to wait. If we get lost, it will take longer."

"That's true," Brog agreed, "And we have better things to do than look for lost teenagers. Even chosen, lost teenagers."

"We aren't very good at being chosen," Wren said. "It was pointless going into the cave since we lost the bubbles."

"Not lost," said a feeble voice behind them. They turned and saw an old giant. She had long gray hair and a leather dress that hung past her knees. "When you leave the cave, the magic absorbs into you."

"I've never heard that before, Haltina," Brog said, looking surprised.

"Yes, well, the fewer people know about everything, the safer things can be. I've been around for a long time. An incredibly long time."

"If we absorbed the magic, how do we know what it is?" Wren asked.

"You will know soon enough. You should be feeling different already."

"I feel kind of off," Tal said. "But I figured it was because we haven't eaten in a while. I feel like there's something itching in my head."

"I feel that too," Wren said.

"If we touch the crystal, will it glow again?" Tal asked.

Wren shrugged. "Why didn't it glow the last time you came here? Didn't you say you came twice?"

"Yeah, well, maybe I wasn't worthy back in those days," Tal said, flashing his lopsided smile. "Or it's possible I didn't touch it because my parents made me come and I was being rebellious."

Wren cocked her head. "Maybe both."

"Once you find the fifth person, you can go through all together. If you come out of the cave at the same time, you will be bound together," Haltina said.

"Bound how?" Tal asked. "I'm feeling more relieved that Jaaz wasn't part of this."

"I do not know exactly, but time will tell." She smiled and waddled away.

"Haltina is one of the oldest giants," Brog said. "She knows many things."

"I can't just stand here," Wren said, walking back and forth in front of Tal and Brog. "Can we walk to the ocean?"

"I'm sure that would be fine."

Wren and Tal walked through the trees and headed for the water.

Wren sighed. "This is all so overwhelming. I thought someone would be here to give us a message. I never thought the crystal would glow."

"Neither did I. And what does it mean, anyway? Does that mean the poem is about us? And if so, what do we do now?"

"I don't know," Wren said, feeling tired. "All I know is that we need to plan better."

"Graham, wake up!" Ming Li hissed. Graham groaned and tried to touch his head, but someone had tied his hands behind him. He opened his eyes slowly. He was lying in the dirt. Ming Li was sitting next to Jaaz. Their hands and feet had also been tied. All the trees were slightly out of focus.

"It's about time," a deep voice said from behind him. Graham pulled himself into a sitting position and looked at the black-cloaked figure. The man wore a gray mask obscuring his face. He reminded Graham of the Phantom of the Opera. Three other figures dressed the same stood behind him.

"If you were in such a hurry, you shouldn't have knocked me out," he said, glaring at the man. He wondered if his head was bleeding. "Are you two okay?" he asked Ming Li and Jaaz. They nodded. Ming Li looked serious, but Jaaz looked excited.

"This is the first time someone has kidnapped me," Jaaz said, "I can't wait to tell people at school!"

"If you return to school," the figure laughed. "We can make this easy. You give us the magic, and we let you go."

"We didn't get it," Graham said. "It disappeared."

"Don't make me angry," the man said. "We don't have time for this. The giants will find us at any moment. If you don't give us the magic—"

One of the other cloaked figures touched his arm, and he stopped.

She said something Graham couldn't understand. It was a different language.

"She wants to know if any of us speak Flordillian," Jaaz told them.

"Hello? Jaaz?" Ming Li said, glaring at the boy, "You obviously speak it, so maybe you could, oh I don't know, say I speak Flordillian?"

"Oh right," said Jaaz, beaming. "I speak Flordillian. I knew I would be useful!"

"Great," Ming Li said, rolling her eyes. "Now say it in Flordillian."

"Ohhhhh," Jaaz smiled again. "It's good you're here, Ming Li."

"So good," she said, gritting her teeth.

Jaaz and the woman spoke back and forth. She sounded irritated and Jaaz sounded, well, like Jaaz.

"What did she say?" Graham asked.

"She said if you lost the magic, you need to open the cave again so they can go in." The two remaining cloaked figures sliced the ropes on their feet and helped them stand.

"No one is by the crystal," the first man said, "We can hurry over there, you touch the crystal and we let you go." Someone pushed Graham, and he began walking. Their hands were still tied, and it was rubbing painfully against his wrists.

"Graham, we can't let them in," Ming Li said. "They won't let us go. As soon as we open it, they'll kill us, so we can't tell anyone."

"Probably."

"That's their plan."

"What are you saying?" the man with the deep voice said.

"Wouldn't you like to know?" Ming Li said, glaring at the man.

"She wasn't talking quietly," Graham muttered, trying to come up with a plan.

"I'm speaking English," Ming Li said. "They can't understand us. Just make sure you talk fast so they don't catch any of it."

"We're always speaking English," Graham said, wondering if he could freeze everyone. Maybe if he could get his hands free.

"I've never heard you speak English," Ming Li said. "Well, until now."

"What?"

"We don't have time," Ming Li said. "I speak Flordillian. It's the troll language. She told Jaaz he was supposed to block the cave door so they could get in. He said it shut too fast. Now they are planning on killing us and going in before we know what happens."

"So we shouldn't have trusted Jaaz."

"Stop talking," the man said. They were almost to the crystal.

"Be ready," Ming Li muttered.

"I said no talking," the man barked, smacking Ming Li in the back of the head. She looked ready to hurt someone.

They stopped in front of the crystal. Graham's brain felt overloaded. He tried to come up with a plan, but he had nothing. The ropes on his wrists slipped off. Without warning, Ming Li stomped her boot against the leader's toe and spun around and punched him in the chest. She was probably too short to hit him in the face. He grunted. Her hands were untied.

"You will regret—" the man began, as Graham lifted his hand and blasted him with ice. It knocked the man over. The other three must have been shocked because they still hadn't reacted. One of them lifted their hand, and a rock lifted off the ground and he hurled it at Graham. He ducked and raised his hand and shot ice and then shot more at the other two before they could react.

He turned to see Ming Li sitting on top of Jaaz, pushing his face into the dirt. Graham wished he had seen her take him down. Jaaz was so much taller than she was. A group of giants came running in from different directions. Wren and Tal weren't far behind.

"What is going on?" a giant asked.

"These people," Graham pointed, "Were trying to force us to let them in the cave."

"People in masks are not to be trusted," Brog said as four giants grabbed the four cloaked figures off the ground. Their capes were torn from the ice shards.

"Did a giant really just tell us not to trust people in masks?" Graham said, his lip twitching. "Best thing ever."

"Why is that funny?" Ming Li said, narrowing her eyes. Graham shrugged. It wasn't funny if he had to explain it.

"Take off their masks," Tal said, with authority.

"Not today," the one with the deep voice said, and they all disappeared.

"How did they do that?" Tal asked. Wren was wondering the same thing.

"We didn't see any of their faces," Graham said, shaking his head. "They might try something again."

"I've never seen anyone disappear before," Wren said. "I thought that was lost magic."

Tal nodded. "It is, or was. How will we ever find out who they were?"

"Hello?" said Ming Li, still sitting on Jaaz. "We still have him."

"We brought him."

"He's working with them."

Wren frowned. They shouldn't have let Jaaz come. They were making too many mistakes. Her stomach growled, reminding her they hadn't even packed food.

"But they left him behind," Graham said. "My guess is he doesn't know much." Wren was sure he was right. If he knew anything, it would have been careless to leave him.

"Let me up!" Jaaz said, squirming. Brog nodded at Ming Li. She let him stand and Brog grabbed both of his arms so he couldn't do any magic. His hands were still tied, but it was comforting to know Brog had him.

"Who were they?" Tal asked Jaaz.

"I don't know," Jaaz said. "They always had masks. You can't blame me. They threatened me."

"You were speaking Flordillian, and you were smiling," Ming Li said, getting in his face. "Who were they?"

"I don't know," he shrugged. "But I want to be on your side. You guys are much more fun. When they got me to help them, I didn't know you very well."

"But ... you still helped them," Wren said, frowning. "And you still don't know us that well."

"I speak Flordillian," Ming Li said. "You were in on enough of the plan, and you were going to let them kill us!"

"I wouldn't have ... mmhhmm," his mouth clamped shut.

"That's right," Ming Li said. "Ming Li has magic now."

Tal frowned. "We need to take him back with us."

"Of course," Brog said, bowing.

"You know what your magic is?" Wren asked.

"Sure," Ming Li nodded. "Don't you?"

"No," Wren said, and the boys shook their heads.

"It's hard to say exactly, but I can do some cool stuff. I untied my hands and Graham's, and I shut that traitor's mouth. I might be able to do something with the wind as well."

"How did you know you could do that?" Graham asked.

"I don't know," Ming Li said, "I just knew. Maybe it's easier for me because I couldn't do magic before? All I know is, it was totally awesome!"

Brog dropped Jaaz in the dirt in front of them.

"Ouch!" Jaaz complained. "You could at least try to be soft."

"Traitors don't get soft," Ming Li hissed, trying to kick him.

Tal pulled her back, "Calm yourself, little Li." Wren was pretty sure he shouldn't have said that.

"Little Li? Are you serious?" she said, shoving his shoulder. "It's easy for you to say calm down. You weren't the one captured and tied up!"

"True," Tal agreed, "But we have more important things to do than kick our captive."

"What do we do now?" Wren wondered. "It's not like we can turn him over to the authorities. If we suspect ..." she trailed off, looking at Tal.

"My dad. You can say it. I know what we're dealing with here."

"Okay," Wren said, still feeling bad, "If we suspect Governor Briggs, we can't turn Jaaz over to him."

"Yeah," Graham agreed, "But we also can't take him home and lock him in our basement."

"Let's not plan in front of him." Wren said, looking at Jaaz.

"I can help with that," Brog said, pulling a small brown pouch out of his pocket. He untied the cord that held it shut and took out a handful of gray powder.

"You better not do anything creepy to me!" Jaaz warned. "I'm sure The Dark Cloud will come back for me!"

"I thought you said you didn't want to work with them anymore?" Tal said, raising an eyebrow.

"That doesn't mean they won't come back for me!"

Brog kneeled by Jaaz and held the powder out in his hand. "It will only make you sleep," he said as he blew some in Jaaz's face.

Jaaz sneezed, "I ..." His eyes rolled back in his head and he immediately started snoring.

"I need some of that," Tal said.

"It is helpful from time to time," Brog said. "You should leave soon, unless you want a lot of attention. Word of the cave opening will spread like fire. People will swarm the island, hoping to get in."

Brog picked Jaaz up and flung him over his shoulder. "Follow me and I will take you back to your alicorns." They all followed him back through the trees.

"I didn't think about people finding out about this," Wren said, looking at the others. "And where do we go? Where do we take Jaaz?"

"To Brake maybe?" Graham suggested, rubbing the back of his head.

Tal shook his head. "That seems a little obvious."

"Well, where do you think?"

"I have an idea. I'm not sure if it's a good one, though."

"Just say it," Ming Li said, rolling her eyes.

"Fleetman Zera."

"Why her?" Wren asked.

"We can trust her," Tal said. "She warned us we were in danger. She also votes opposite of my father almost every time."

"Why is it fleetman? Why not fleetwoman?" Ming Li wondered.

"The fleet used to be only men," Tal explained. "I'm not sure why they didn't change it once women joined."

"I can't see a better idea," Wren said. She knew her dad trusted Zera. "I'm not sure what she would do with Jaaz, but she might have an idea. It would be convenient to go to my dad, but he only wants to focus on the governor and be ignorant of everything else. It's getting annoying."

"You must be careful who you trust," Brog said. "But you also must trust. If you do not trust anyone, everyone will become your enemy."

They all nodded.

"I say we go to Zera," Graham said. "If she can't help us, we'll figure something else out. I could use some Tylenol. It's difficult to think with my head pounding like this."

"What's Tylenol?" Wren asked. There were some strange words in Graham's world.

"It's pain medicine. It won't take away the bump, though."

"This should help some," Brog said, pulling a bottle out of his pouch. Graham took it and held it in front of his face.

"It doesn't have directions."

"Pour some in your hand and rub it into the area that hurts."

Graham poured something that looked like lotion onto his hand and rubbed it onto the back of his head. Wren frowned as she saw him grimace. Nothing had prepared them for today.

"Now it's all over in my hair," he said, trying to rub it out, "But it feels a lot better. So Zera's house?"

"Do we have time to change first?" Tal asked as they came to the shore where the alicorns were waiting. Brog had given them food and water and they seemed to enjoy the sun and the sand.

"We should go straight there." Wren said. "We need to take care of this fast. We don't want Jaaz to wake up."

"Don't even try to tell me you guys didn't rip enormous holes in the backside of your britches going down that rock slide," Tal said, grinning.

Ming Li burst out laughing, and Graham chuckled. Wren didn't say anything. She had noticed a hole in her pants after the slide. She had never been more grateful for a cape in her life.

"You can't slide down rock like that and not wear out your pants. You can only laugh at me if you show me yours aren't ripped."

"Fine," Ming Li said, smiling. She turned around and lifted her cape. Her pants were still intact. Filthy dirty, but no holes.

"I guess it's only you," Graham laughed, lifting his cape. Tal burst out laughing, and Wren tried not to smile. Graham's pants had an immense hole and his bright green underwear showed through.

"How can you not feel a breeze?" Tal laughed, "That's a bigger hole than mine!" Graham frowned and dropped his cape. "I won't ask Wren. Her face says enough."

Wren glared at him, but a giggle slipped out. She was embarrassed, but it was kind of funny. Brog slung Jaaz over one of the alicorn's backs.

"Uh, we have a problem guys," Ming Li said, looking at Jaaz. "Who's going to fly? Graham and I don't know how." They all looked at each other.

"Zeezee can carry three," Tal said, frowning. "Tanta will probably follow me when we leave. Alicorns can usually find their way home, but I'm not sure if she can do it from this far."

"I also want to warn you," Brog said, fiddling with his hands. "I do not wish to offend you, but you are much too trusting. You do not know me, but you speak freely around me. You can trust me, but you do not know that. When I said you need to trust, I did not mean someone you do not know."

"You're right," Wren agreed. "If we had been more careful, Jaaz wouldn't have overheard us. I mean, he obviously knew something, but we didn't even shut the window."

"It is expected that you would make mistakes. I will give you some of my ailam powder in case he wakes up before you get there. This destiny you have discovered is new to you. You will learn as you do the best you can. The giants know more than people suspect. Things are about to get very complicated. When it calms, you are welcome to come back and Haltina would be happy to tell you what she can."

"Destiny is a heavy word," Wren said, feeling a chill.

"Extremely heavy," Graham agreed.

CHAPTER 11

G raham sighed with relief as the alicorns touched down in a large courtyard. The ride back had been a lot more uncomfortable than the ride there. He wouldn't be able to sit comfortably for a few days. His head felt a lot better, but there was still a dull throb, and his vision was a little off.

The house in front of them wasn't huge, but it was big. It looked like it was made of white and black marble. Two large columns stood by the tall mahogany door. It was an interesting house, but Graham liked it.

The front door opened and Fleetman Zera came out. She was wearing a long pink dress and her long brown hair was flowing down her back. She was frowning.

"What is going on?" she asked as Tal pulled Jaaz off the alicorn and let him crumble to the ground. "Is he okay?" she asked, coming forward.

"He's fine, just sleeping," Graham said, lifting him over his shoulder.

"Come in quickly," she said, holding the door open. "I don't want anyone to see you."

Tal whispered something to the alicorns, and they flew off. "They'll go home. Don't worry," he said in response to Wren's concerned look. They all filed into the house, careful to wipe their dirty shoes on the spotless white mat.

For looking so thin, Jaaz sure felt heavy. Inside the house matched the outside. Graham couldn't imagine living in a house with so much marble. It seemed like it would all be cold and slippery. Fleetman Zera led them into a front parlor. The furniture was black and white and looked stiff and uncomfortable.

"Put him on the sofa," she said, "And the rest of you come have a seat at the table." Graham put Jaaz on the sofa and joined the others at a mahogany table that had six matching chairs. The chairs were a lot more comfortable than they looked.

"We are sorry to bother you, Fleetman Zera," Tal said.

"Please, call me Zera," she said, waving her hand and making four glasses of water appear in front of them.

"We didn't know where to go," Wren said, looking at her glass.

"You can trust me. I will do what I can to help. Why is he tied up?" she asked, gesturing to Jaaz. "That is Notic's son, if I remember correctly."

"Yes," Tal answered as Graham shrugged.

"Did you send us the messages in our books?" Graham asked.

"What messages?"

"That means no," Ming Li said, taking a sip of her water.

"We all got a piece of paper in our school books that convinced us to go to the Island of Meegore," Graham explained. "We kind of thought it could have been you. Either you or Coach Zalliah."

"You were at the Island of Meegore today?" Zera asked, standing and pacing near the table. "You were the four that opened the cave?"

"How do you know about that?" Tal asked, looking surprised. "We just got back."

"You will find it difficult to find anyone who does not know about that by tomorrow," Zera said, sounding worried. "I only returned home five minutes before you came. I was having an emergency meeting with the governor about this. The giants let the governor know what happened. They did not give names, though. They only said it was four youths."

"How did the giants get to the governor so fast?" Wren asked.

"They sent a message," she explained. "The giants have their own magic. Tell me what happened and we will decide what to do." She looked back at Jaaz and her mouth turned down. They told her what the notes in their books said and all the things that had happened on Meegore. She stopped them occasionally to ask a question, but for the most part, she listened.

"We didn't know what to do, so we came here," Graham said, when they finished.

"I am a little surprised you came to me," Zera said, sitting. "So he has been given ailam powder. It will not last very long. Perhaps a dose of ellebasi will be in order. It has more side effects, but it lasts longer."

"We thought about telling Brake," Graham said, "But we thought that might be obvious since he's my uncle."

"And we couldn't tell my dad," Wren said, rolling her eyes. "He probably wouldn't want to know."

Zera smiled, "I am sure you are right. Drew is a great man, but he only likes to focus on one thing at a time."

"We aren't sure if we can trust you, but we don't have a lot of options," Ming Li said. "Why are you kicking me, Wren?"

Wren's face turned red and Tal laughed. Graham smiled, and Ming Li glared at all of them.

"It is hard to know who to trust," Zera said. "I believe I can trust you, because the cave opened for you. I am a member of a group that is trying to fight The Dark Cloud."

"The same group as Brake?" Graham asked.

"Yes," Zera nodded. "You can verify with him if you like."

"What's the group called?" Graham asked.

"It does not have a name."

"You don't name your world or your rebel groups?" Graham said, shaking his head. "It's really confusing."

"What do you mean when you say, 'your world?'" Zera asked, eyes narrowing as she studied Graham.

"Weren't you the one saying we needed to be more careful?" Ming Li said, playfully punching him in the arm. Graham sighed. He needed to stop messing up like this.

"We need to name things is all I'm saying," Graham said, hoping she would forget his slip.

"We are not a rebel group," Zera said. "We are a group of people trying to do the right thing."

"By going against the law and the governor? In secret?" Graham asked. "That sounds like a rebel group to me."

"I can come up with the name to make Graham happy," Tal said, raising his hand. "We're going to end up joining if we're fighting for the same thing. We don't want to be stuck with a lame name."

"We have more important things to deal with at the moment," Zera said, motioning to Jaaz. "We have a place where we can keep prisoners. It is far away, out in the jungle."

"Can you zap him there or something?" Graham asked. "The Dark Cloud members all disappeared from the island when we caught them."

"Except Jaaz," Ming Li added. "He's kind of pathetic."

"We don't know how to do that."

"Wouldn't it be like the way you made the glasses appear?" Graham asked.

"It's not the same. It could be dangerous to try on a person."

Ming Li shrugged. "Well, Jaaz is a bad guy, so maybe it would be okay to experiment."

"I am not willing to try on him," Zera said, "He is still young, and we do not know what his involvement is."

"I came as soon as you summoned me," Brake said, entering the room smiling. His eyes sparkled as he looked at Zera. Graham figured she probably got that look a lot. She was one of the prettiest women he had ever seen. "And I made sure no one followed me." Brake looked at Graham, Wren, Ming Li, and Tal and his smile faded away. "What are you four doing here? And what did you do to Jaaz? Ming Li?"

"I didn't do it," Ming Li said, pushing her long hair over her shoulder. "Well, I knocked him to the ground and sat on him, but I didn't knock him out."

"It's ailam powder," Wren explained. "Jaaz betrayed us."

Brake let out a slow breath and sat in the empty chair. "Why did you take Jaaz? I warned you against it."

Graham shrugged. "He showed up, and I didn't know how to leave him behind."

"It's not surprising, considering his parents."

"You suspect his parents?" Tal asked. Graham looked at the floor. Zera shook her head and Brake sighed.

"I don't know if we have time to get into that," he said. "I heard a rumor that four teenagers opened the cave at Meegore."

"Not a rumor," Ming Li said. "Watch," she said, as she put out her hand and made her glass scoot across the table.

"You have magic!" Brake exclaimed, with a tired smile. "I wondered if it would open for all of you. I was worried it would and worried it wouldn't."

"Why worried?" Graham asked.

"Because now you all have a lot of responsibility. You will also have many people trying to get you to take them into the cave. You are going to have to be careful."

Jaaz was stirring. "We need to get him to the jungle prison." Zera said. "They can tell you the story later."

"I can do it," Brake said, "I won't be missed like you will. People are used to me disappearing."

"So are we all going to be part of the Piranhas of Akkron?" Graham asked, smiling.

"Ugh, no, that's a terrible name," Ming Li said.

"What's wrong with it? You step in the water and a piranha bites you before you even knew it was there!" Graham said. "It's awesome. No? Fine. I'll keep brain storming."

"Do I even want to know?" Brake asked, and everyone shook their heads.

"I keep having a funny feeling that I can make a portal to where I want," Wren said, looking at nothing. "Ever since we came out of the cave, I just feel like I can."

"But you aren't allowed to make portals," Graham said.

"But if I can do it and go to a certain destination, it wouldn't be as dangerous."

"Can she try?" Tal asked. "We could get Jaaz to the prison a lot faster."

Brake and Zera looked at each other for a moment. Zera nodded.

"Alright," Brake said, "But I don't want everyone jumping through. I'll go first and if it works, I'll send word to Zera. Deal?" They all nodded.

Zera took out a map and pointed to a spot in the jungle. "It's right here." Wren took a deep breath and put her thumb and pointer fingers together. She pulled them apart and a large silvery portal opened. It rippled like silver water. Graham was amazed at how beautiful it was. How had he missed it last time?

Wren smiled and let a small giggle escape. "You don't need to go through first, Brake. I can see what's on the other side."

Wren was so excited. This was the best thing that could have happened to her. Now she could go anywhere without worrying she was leaping into danger. As soon as she opened the portal, she could see the jungle.

"What do you see?" Zera asked.

"Just trees and vines."

"This could change so many things," Brake said, awe and emotion evident in his voice. His eyes were watering. Wren wondered why. It was a neat thing, but nothing to get watery eyed about.

"Now is not the time," Zera said, placing a gentle hand on Brake's arm. Her eyes looked a little misty as well. Wren looked away, unsure of what to make of it.

"Should we all go?" Graham asked.

"I'm going," Tal said. "I'm pretty sure I'm not ready to face my father yet."

"Me too," Ming Li chimed in. "I told my mom I would be gone all day."

"I better stay behind," Zera said. "If the governor tries to summon me, I don't want to explain why I am in the middle of the jungle."

"That's probably best," Brake said, looking at the ground. Zera smiled at him, but the smile didn't reach her eyes.

"Wren and I are going," Graham said. "I'm pretty sure if Wren doesn't come, we're all in for a long walk home."

Wren nodded. "Can we go soon? I'm feeling a bit shaky keeping this open."

"Grab Jaaz and we'll go," Brake said. Graham picked Jaaz up off the couch. Jaaz muttered something as they stepped through the portal after Brake. Ming Li and Tal followed and Wren brought up the rear. She stepped through the portal and was surprised to land on her feet on the other side. It was the first time she hadn't crashed painfully to the ground. Ming Li, Tal, Graham, and Jaaz were all in a pile on the dirt. Brake was watching with amusement.

"When you go through a portal and people are behind you, it would be wise to hurry out of the way," he said.

Ming Li got to her feet, and Graham and Tal stood. Jaaz was still asleep, sprawled out on the ground.

"Well, that was exhilarating," Tal said. "I've never been through a portal before."

"You have a hole in your pants," Brake said to Tal. "You might want to keep your cape over it."

"Yeah," Tal said, unbothered, "It was one of our cave souvenirs, right Graham? Wren?" Graham ignored him and Wren frowned.

"Where's the prison?" Wren asked, looking around. All she could see were a lot of trees. It felt humid and hot, and it sounded like there were birds everywhere.

"It's not exactly a prison," Brake said, looking at the ground. He walked around, searching for something. "It's a place we meet, but it has a few cells ... well, they are more like high security rooms. We lined them with rednax venom so that no one can use magic to escape. Follow me. We're close."

"I hope it doesn't smell like rednax," Ming Li said, shuddering. Wren hoped so, too. Rednax smelled worse than anything she had ever smelled before. Graham picked Jaaz up, and they followed.

"What types of animals do you think they have here?" Graham asked, scanning the trees.

"Probably lots," Ming Li said. "I bet there are scary little dragons."

"I don't know how you can be afraid of dragons," Tal said, hopping over a root. "Dragons are usually pretty sweet. At least bantams."

"There are a lot of bugs," Wren said, waving her hand in front of her face. There were a lot of large roots and, if she wasn't careful, she might land on her face. The hole in her pants was embarrassing enough.

"Here we are," Brake said, spreading out his arms.

"It looks the same as everywhere else," Tal said, looking around.

"Of course it does. We can't let anyone find it by accident."

They were standing in front of an enormous tree. "Let me guess, there's a secret door in the tree?" Tal said.

"No, we need to climb the tree."

"Great," Ming Li said, looking up. "Your meeting place is in a tree? There isn't even a treehouse up there."

"Follow me," Brake smiled. He seemed to enjoy their confusion.

"I can't climb a tree and carry Jaaz," Graham said. "My arms are already burning."

"Can you levitate him up?" Wren asked.

"I can try. I'm not sure how stable I am."

Brake was already making good progress up the tree. "Try levitating him to this branch and I'll take care of the rest."

Graham put Jaaz down and looked serious. "Here goes nothing," he muttered. He stretched out his arms and raised them. Jaaz lifted effortlessly off the ground. Graham lifted him higher and higher, avoiding the branches on the way up. By the time Jaaz was to the branch Brake was pointing at, Graham was sweating.

"Hold him steady," Brake instructed. He reached out and carefully grabbed Jaaz's arm and pulled him up so he was sitting on the branch, slumped over. "Okay, you can let him go." Graham lowered his arms and rubbed his shoulder.

"Alright, so now Jaaz is unconscious in the tree," Ming Li said, "I don't see what that accomplished."

Brake smiled and pushed Jaaz over the tree branch.

Everyone screamed as Jaaz fell backwards and disappeared. "Relax," Brake said, "I pushed him into our meeting house. Climb to this branch and fall over it. It's an illusion."

Tal put his hand against the tree and frowned. "You could have at least warned us."

"Where is the fun in that?" Brake winked. Wren shook her head. Brake was turning out to be a lot more interesting than she ever would have ever imagined.

"Seriously, Uncle Brake," Ming Li lectured, "I don't even like Jaaz, but you almost gave me a heart attack!"

"That's ridiculously high," Wren said, "Way scarier than going through a portal." They all climbed the tree. There were a lot of sturdy branches, so it was easy, even for Wren. That was a tremendous relief.

When they reached Brake, he pointed to the branch he had tossed Jaaz over. "Drop over that branch. I'll go first." He climbed up, so he was sitting on the branch. "Don't worry. It's a soft landing." He fell over backwards and disappeared.

"It better be soft. This day has been exhausting," Tal said, taking the spot Brake had vacated. "See you on the other side," he said, falling over the branch.

"Let me go next," Wren said, trying to feel brave. "If I don't go now, I might chicken out." She climbed to the branch and sat on it. She didn't want to go backwards, so she turned around so she could go feet first.

"Careful," Graham said, as she struggled.

"I can't," she said, after looking down through the branches. This was scary high. "Someone is going to have to push me." Ming Li climbed onto the branch with her and linked their arms.

"Let's go together," she said, smiling at Wren. Wren nodded and swallowed. Her throat felt dry. "One, two," Ming Li pulled her and they fell. Wren closed her eyes and screamed. Before she knew what happened, they landed on a soft, bouncy cushion. Tal grabbed both of them by the hand and pulled them off right as Graham fell through.

"Thanks," Wren said with a shaky voice.

"Anyone else ready for this day to end?" Graham asked, getting off the cushion. "I don't remember the last time I was so tired and sore." Wren nodded. She could sleep right then and there.

Tal yawned as he looked around. "Check this place out." They were in a large white room. It had no windows and only one door. Wren wondered where the door led. There were a bunch of large, round cushions sitting on the floor, along with several comfortable looking chairs, arranged in a messy circle. Brake had pulled Jaaz onto the floor. The door opened and a short, balding man came in. He stopped and stared at all of them, blinking a few times.

"Hamble," Brake said, nodding at the man.

"I received Zera's message," Hamble said, still studying them. "I was the only one here. It's hard to believe the crystal has chosen."

"Whatsgoinon?" Jaaz mumbled, sitting up. His hands were still tied.

"And that must be the traitor?"

"Yes," Brake said, grabbing Jaaz and standing him up.

"Let's take him to the cell," Hamble said, holding the door open.

"You can't put me in a cell!" Jaaz protested.

"It's more of a room," Brake said, guiding Jaaz towards the door.

Hamble laughed, "A room you can't leave."

"You four sit and rest, and you can tell us about today," Brake said, closing the door behind them.

Tal flopped onto a large red cushion. "Wow, this is soft," he said, closing his eyes. Graham sat on a blue one and did the same. Ming Li flopped onto a red one and bounced a few times. Wren chose a chair so she could stay awake.

"How do you suppose the adults all keep sending messages to each other?" Ming Li wondered. Wren wasn't sure if anyone answered. She had fallen asleep.

CHAPTER 12

The smell of cinnamon filled Graham's nose. After opening his eyes, he grabbed his head and fell back to his cushion. He was sitting in the meeting room. How long had he been asleep?

Ming Li chuckled as she walked towards him. "You look confused." She handed him a plate with a cinnamon roll on top.

"How long have I been asleep?" he asked, biting into the warm pastry with vigor. He was starving. Next time they planned an all day adventure, they needed to remember to pack food.

"All night," Wren said, taking a bite of her own roll. She was sitting on a chair across from him. "But don't worry. We all fell asleep."

"You slept way longer than the rest of us, though," Ming Li said, sitting cross-legged on the floor.

"You didn't even wake up when Wren fell off her chair," Tal smirked. Wren ignored him.

Ming Li was also smiling at Wren. "Wren opened a portal outside and Brake went and got us some cinnamon rolls from my mom. This place is bigger than I expected. It has a kitchen and stuff. There's actually a door to go outside. You don't end up in the tree or anything. I don't know why you can't come in through it. I mean, you can't actually see it once it closes, so that might be one reason. Brake somehow sent messages to our families last night, letting them know we were all okay, so she made them for us."

"I wonder if people are going to know we're the ones who opened the cave," Tal said, licking frosting off his finger. He was sitting in a chair near Wren. Graham figured this must be where the group met together to discuss things. He found it hard to imagine Brake and Zera sitting on cushions.

"It's likely people will know it was at least some of us," Wren said. "We don't know who The Dark Cloud members were on the island. There's a good chance they recognized some of us."

"Probably not Graham," Ming Li said. "He's still pretty new."

Tal frowned. "There's not a lot of chance they didn't recognize me. Especially if they're from Akkron. I wonder if my father knows. I bet most people would recognize Wren. She goes to all the fleet events with her dad."

"I hate the thought of people talking about us," Wren said, scrunching her forehead.

"People were already talking about us," Tal said, his frown changing to a mischievous smile.

"What? Who?" Wren asked.

"Everyone at school, of course."

"Why? We're pretty boring."

"We aren't boring anymore," Graham said. "I bet everyone's talking about us."

"What were people saying about us at school?" Ming Li asked Tal.

"Well," he smiled, raising an eyebrow, "They're talking about our love square, of course." There was an exaggerated gagging noise from Ming Li's direction.

Graham rolled his eyes. "And what is a love square?"

"It's like a love triangle, but a square."

Wren coughed and Ming Li snorted. Graham shook his head.

"You know how it goes. I'm in love with Wren, who is in love with Graham, who is in love with Li, who is in love with me. That's what they're all saying."

"Nobody is saying that," Graham said, biting his roll.

"Well, they should be. Right Li?"

"I am not in love with you," she said, glaring.

He winked. "I'm not saying you are. I'm just saying what people are saying about us."

"Nobody would say I was in love with you. Everyone knows you drive me crazy."

"Exactly."

"We have more to talk about than Tal's fantasies," Graham said. "Like, did the giants get our names? Yesterday was all a blur to me."

"I don't remember," Tal said, standing. His smug grin had morphed back into a frown. He put his plate on his chair and started pacing. "If my dad knows, I can't go home."

"I'm not sure if any of you should go home," Brake said, entering the room with another plate of cinnamon rolls. "You'll all be targets now. All a person has to do is take any of you to the Island of Meegore and they can get into the cave. I'm meeting with the rest of our group later today, and we will try to figure out the best way to proceed."

"Our group," Graham muttered, "I need to work harder on the name."

"Tal should go home to tell his parents," Brake said. "Tell them what happened and come back here when you're done. Don't tell them where you are, only tell them it's a safe place until we figure out what to do."

"If I go tell my father I have access to a ton of magic, there's no way he'll let me come back," Tal said, swallowing an immense piece of his roll. "I don't know if he's a member of The Dark Cloud or not, but he will use me for his own personal gain either way."

"Why aren't there windows in here?" Wren asked. "It feels claustrophobic to not have windows."

"Yeah," Ming Li agreed. "It's just white walls and crazy colored chairs. It's kinda depressing."

"No windows means nobody is looking in," Brake said. "Tal, I think you need to talk to your father. You can't just disappear. We don't need everyone in Akkron searching for you."

"I can go with you," Wren offered. "If it looks like he isn't going to let you leave, I can open a portal."

"That's what I was hoping for," Brake admitted. "Thank you Wren." He held the plate of cinnamon rolls out to her. She shook her head.

"Ming Li, do you want me to put something on that goose egg?" Brake asked. "I have something that will take care of it."

Ming Li touched the bluish green bump on her forehead. Graham didn't remember her having it at Meegore. He had been staring at it off and on all morning. Something in the back of his mind was itching to come out, but he wasn't sure what it was.

"I guess," Ming Li said. "It's really not that bad." Brake nodded and moved to the door.

"Wait," Graham said, standing and walking towards Ming Li. He squatted beside her.

"Quit looking at me like that," Ming Li said, leaning away. "What are you doing?"

"Can I try something?" he asked. Ming Li raised an eyebrow and shrugged. Graham reached out and put his hand across Ming Li's forehead. He felt something flow through his body and down his arm. He didn't know how to describe it.

"I don't have a fever," Ming Li said, pulling away and shivering.

"And you don't have a goose egg anymore," Graham said, sitting down hard. Ming Li put a hand to her forehead.

"Whoa," she whispered. "Does that mean you can heal people?"

"That was amazing," Brake said, with wide eyes.

Graham felt dizzy and a little sick to his stomach. He put his head between his knees. He couldn't believe it. All his life he had wanted to help heal people, and now he could. He wondered if he would get sick every time.

Ming Li leaned forward and touched his shoulder. "Are you okay?"

"Fine," he said, looking up and trying to smile. "Just a little dizzy."

"Now we only need to figure out Tal's magic," Wren said, giving him a speculative glance.

"I have a bit of an idea, but it's confusing," Tal said, frowning. "Is there some type of magic that involves plants?"

"I've never heard of any," Wren said.

Brake shook his head. "Neither have I."

"I don't know what it is," Tal said. "I felt different when we were walking through the jungle. It was almost like I could feel the trees thinking."

"Trees think?" Ming Li asked, cocking her head.

"Not thinking exactly. Maybe feeling? I don't know how to describe it."

"I'm sure it will come to you," Brake said. "Don't rush it."

Graham looked around at his friends. Everything was going to be so different. They were going to have to rely on each other a lot more. If they were going to be hiding, school was out. He had only been there for four weeks.

"Wren and Tal, you should probably go talk to Tal's parents," Brake told them.

"Might as well," Tal said, kicking at the ground. Graham felt for him. He knew what it was like to have a hard family.

Wren and Tal stood outside the large tree. Tal looked nervous. "Are you ready for this?" she asked him.

He grimaced and stared into the treetops. "Is anyone ever ready for their life to change?" he asked. "I've been wanting to get away from my father forever, so I guess I should be excited."

"It's hard to make changes," Wren said, quietly. "Even when the change might be good."

"I guess so," he said, running his hand across the tree bark. "Can't you feel that?"

"What?"

"It feels like the whole jungle is pulsing."

"I don't feel anything."

"I feel like I could tell it something and it would obey me," he said, in awe. "I probably sound crazy."

"No ... Well maybe a little," Wren smiled.

He smiled back. "I'm ready."

"Alright," Wren said, taking a deep breath. "Here it goes." She opened a portal. She could see Tal's house. "You can hold my hand. It might make it easier for you. I used to crash through, but last night when I stepped through it was smooth. Being able to see makes a tremendous difference."

"You don't have to make up excuses to hold my hand," Tal smirked, his sassy smile back.

Wren was sure she was red. "Fine, fall on your head."

He grabbed her hand, "I would rather not. You know that bump on Ming Li's head was from falling through the portal, not from The Dark Cloud. It's unnerving stepping into something you can't see."

"Okay, ready?" she asked. He nodded. They stepped through the portal and into Akkron. Tal stumbled but didn't fall.

"That was much better," he said, staring at his house. "It's good you didn't take us right to the door. I'm not sure I'm ready." They still needed to go up the long path to the house. Wren didn't want to jump out and run right into the governor.

"Are you nervous or worried?" she asked.

"Isn't that the same thing?"

"Not exactly."

"I don't know what I am," he admitted. "I'm ready to leave. Ready to do something better with my life. I'm a little worried my father will stop me."

"He doesn't know I can make portals," Wren assured him. "If it goes badly, I'll open one and pull you through. You don't have to be nervous."

"You're the one still holding my hand, and pretty tightly," Tal grinned.

Wren tried to pull her hand away, but Tal held on. She was nervous. Governor Briggs wasn't a man to take lightly. He was powerful, and likely evil.

"Don't worry. I won't let my father get you. Come on," he said motioning to the house with his head.

"Do you suppose the color of the bubbles on the island mattered?" Wren wondered.

"What do you mean?"

"I thought that each color was a different type of magic. Now that we're figuring out what our magic is, I'm wondering if the color didn't matter. I received what I needed to help with what I already had. Graham has always wanted to heal people and now he can."

"Maybe," Tal said, thoughtfully. "I've always had a fascination with nature and animals. I still don't know what I can do, but I know it's related. It's hard to know with Ming Li. What has she wanted?"

"She's just always wanted to fit in."

"Is she from the same place as Graham?"

"I don't know," Wren said. "It's always been a sore spot for her. She wouldn't ever talk about it."

"How long has she been in Akkron? Fiveish years?"

"That sounds about right."

Ming Li never wanted to talk about her life before she came here. They had become friends quickly. Wren had even helped teach her their language. Ming Li's language was similar, but the pronunciation was a lot different. Usually only Trolls and occasionally goblins spoke a different language. Wren had quickly learned what Ming Li would talk about, and what she wouldn't.

"Well, this is interesting," a voice said to the side of them. Tal dropped Wren's hand, and they both spun to see Governor Briggs walking out of the trees. He had a pair of gardening shears. Wren remembered the governor liked to garden. Her father said it was the one thing he liked to do when he was stressed.

Wren swallowed hard. Why did he make her so nervous? He had a strange gleam in his eye. He was smiling like a little kid who had gotten an entire cake to themselves.

"It took you long enough," Briggs said to Tal. "Brake sent a message that they had detained you for the night, but I thought you would be here first thing this morning."

"It's still morning," Tal said.

"So are you going to tell me about your little adventure?"

"Weren't you there?"

"What are you talking about?" he asked, looking surprised. "Why would I be there?"

"I don't know. Why would you?"

"You are being very confusing Talon," his dad said, shaking his head. "What was it like? In the cave? Don't look surprised. Who would have thought, my son would be one of the first to go back into the cave at Meegore?" He laughed. "Things are finally coming together."

"I don't know what you think is coming together," Tal said, "I just came to tell you goodbye."

"Goodbye?" he said, raising one eyebrow.

"It isn't safe for us here right now."

"You don't have to worry. I've already taken that into consideration. I have plans to hide you."

"I bet you do," Tal muttered.

"What do you mean by that?"

"I'm sure you have plans for me, now that I could actually be of some use to you." Tal said.

The governor's eyes narrowed. "Are you trying to play a victim here? I have always given you whatever you wanted. I'm even willing to overlook the fact that you took alicorns without permission."

"Great, thanks," Tal said, "But I'm not staying here."

"I believe you are." Briggs said, coming a step closer. Wren's eyes moved to the shears. He wouldn't hurt his son, would he?

"I can help all of your friends. You won't have to worry."

"I can't trust you," Tal said, stepping back.

His eyes narrowed. "What have I ever done to make you distrust me?"

"What have you ever done to make me trust you? When have you ever cared? Never, that's when." Tal said. Wren was shocked at how calm he seemed.

Wren put a hand to his arm. "Let's go," she mumbled.

"This is unexpected, and it could cause problems." Briggs said, pointing from Tal to Wren.

"It's not a thing," Tal said. "Friends help each other. I know you don't understand things like that."

"I can't let you go," Briggs said. "You are much too valuable to me."

"Yeah, valuable, because now you know you can use me. If I left last week, you wouldn't even care."

Governor Briggs clenched his teeth. "I don't know why you would say that. Why are you talking this way?"

"Because I can now," Tal said. "I'm not staying here anymore. You don't care. You have never cared. Buying tons of junk for your kid doesn't mean you care. It means you want to impress your public. I get it and I will not fight you on it. I have better things to do than hold a grudge. That doesn't mean I'm going to stay here, though."

"Will you give me a moment to explain my vision?" Governor Briggs asked, his eyes pleading with his son. "If you hear what I have to say, I'm sure you'll be happy to join me."

Tal looked at Wren, and she nodded at him.

"I'll listen," Tal finally said, "But I'm not promising anything else."

The governor smiled, "That's all I ask." He dropped the shears near his feet. "I want you both to imagine a world with no conflict. A world where no one has to worry about who they are or what they can do. Wouldn't that be magnificent?"

"Go on," Wren said. She couldn't figure out where he was going with this. If he belonged to The Dark Cloud, that was *not* their goal.

"I believe this vision can be a reality. If power is placed into the right hands, the world can be governed and peace can fall over the entire world."

"Who is to say who the right hands are?" Wren questioned, as Tal shuffled his feet around. He was looking at the ground, not at his father.

"Is it not obvious?" Briggs said, pointing at himself.

"So you should have all the power and control over the world?" she asked.

"Of course not," he said. "I would only be part of it. It would be me and the fleet and the two of you and your other two friends. We would work together for the greater good. If we had the use of Meegore, we would be unstoppable. We would start with Akkron. We would make sure we moved all the people in Akkron who are not magic to Boztoll. Once they were there, they would be easier to take care of."

"You want to send them all to Boztoll so you can take care of them?" Tal asked, looking up. "That doesn't make sense. They don't need to be cared for, they only need to fit in."

"They aren't safe in Akkron. If they are all in one place, we can put people over them to watch them. Boztoll is a very fertile land. They can all have jobs growing the crops we need and in return, we will protect them."

"Boztoll isn't growing much of anything these days," Wren said, trying not to roll her eyes. This sounded a lot more like The Dark Cloud.

"But that won't be forever," Briggs said.

"So they grow all of our food in exchange for safety?" Tal said, narrowing his eyes.

"Yes," he smiled, "It's a good idea all around. It will give them all purpose. Everyone wants purpose."

"What if they don't want to be farmers?" Wren challenged.

"They don't all have to be farmers, of course," he said, looking at the sky and stroking his goatee. "There are people like Mali. I'm fairly certain she has no magic, but her baking is amazing."

"Leave Li's mom out of it. If you bother her in any way …" Tal threatened. He clenched his fists, and a vein was poking out on his forehead.

The governor laughed. "Why would anyone bother her? I have her watched at all times. We can't lose her talent."

Wren's eyes narrowed. "So you want all the non-magical people to be your servants?"

"Not servants. They will be a joyous part of my kingdom. Everyone will live in peace and harmony."

Tal snorted. "Kingdom? Are you making yourself king?"

Brigg's eyes sparkled. "That's a good idea. I would make you part of the king's council. Think of all the good you and your friends could do."

"Unbelievable," Tal said. "I really think you believe this is a good idea."

"It's a fantastic idea. No one will harm non-magical people anymore. There will be a total separation, unless exchanging goods. Of course Mali can stay in Akkron. I'm sure Ming Li will want to take her mother to the cave, so that will solve that problem. Imagine Mali's cooking if she has magic!"

"I don't know what to say," Tal said, looking at Wren. "This is all so ridiculous."

"Wouldn't it be better to take the people from Boztoll to Meegore so everyone has magic?" Wren asked.

His eyebrows came together. "Goodness no. That would be a disaster. They would be so far behind. They would never be happy. I forbid you from ever taking anyone to Meegore without my permission. Mali is an exception."

Tal's eye twitched. "We aren't working for you."

Wren decided it was time to go. Nothing good was coming from this. She grabbed Tal's hand and pulled him farther from his father.

"What are you doing?" Briggs asked, frowning.

Before he could follow, Wren opened a portal and pulled Tal through. They didn't land too hard, but they both ended up on the ground. Tal was breathing hard and didn't seem in any hurry to get up. Wren didn't get up either. She watched the emotions play across Tal's face. He was mad.

"Maybe we should have tried to talk to your mom," she said.

"Nah," Tal said, standing up. He put a hand out and pulled her to her feet.

"She can't be as bad as your dad ... Sorry," Wren said, looking away.

"It's fine. My mom is nothing like my dad. She's really nice, but mostly absent."

"What do you mean?" Wren asked, brushing dirt off her pants. She needed some clean clothes, preferably without a hole in the backside.

"My dad married my mom because she's beautiful. My mom married my dad because he's rich. They're both happy with the arrangement. She spends most of her time traveling and spending money. If she is home, she's pleasant. She's more like an aunt that pops in every once in a while to say hi and bring presents."

"I'm sorry," Wren said, not knowing what to say.

"Don't feel bad for me," he said, running his hand against a tree. "My father has an awesome mother. I don't know how he turned out so bad. My grandma raised me. She lived at our house until she got sick and had to go live somewhere warmer. She was always kind. I never felt bad about having my parents because I had her."

Wren heard something. She jumped and turned. "Did you hear that?"

"It's a flock of naverbs." Tal said, looking into the trees. "They're birds that live all over the jungle."

"I don't see them," Wren said, looking above them.

"Me either," he said, "But I feel them in my head."

"That sounds kind of creepy."

"It is," Tal smiled, "But it might come in handy if we ever need a bird army."

"Are you going to be okay?" Wren asked as they walked to the meeting tree.

"Yes. I'm not angry because Briggs is my dad. I would be angry even if he wasn't. People like him shouldn't be in power. Even if he isn't part of The Dark Cloud, he needs to be taken out of office. His ideas are so wrong."

"So what do we do?"

"I don't know. Don't worry. The four of us will figure it out."

Wren hoped it was true. Everything seemed so much more real today. Was there really anything four teenagers could do?

CHAPTER 13

Brake showed Graham and Ming Li around the jungle house. It was a lot bigger than Graham had imagined. The room they had been in was one of two meeting rooms. A kitchen, two bathrooms, and a few bedrooms made up the rest of the main floor. There were also rooms for prisoners, but he didn't take them to the place Jaaz was staying. The bedrooms were there in case anyone ever had to go into hiding. It looked like they would be staying.

Brake left them in the kitchen to go to his meeting with the other members of his group. They really needed a name. Some members weren't ready to reveal themselves, so they didn't invite Graham and Ming Li to the meeting. The kitchen had a table with ten chairs and an island with stools. There wasn't much to it. The walls were white and so were the appliances. It wasn't very big. Ming Li sat at the island and doodled on a paper Brake had given her.

Graham sat by her. "So, are you ever going to tell me why Brake brought you here? And why did you say that I've never spoken English until yesterday?"

Ming Li sighed and kept doodling. "My dad was a pretty lame guy. He was from California. My mom came from Taiwan to go to college. They met and fell in love. He was okay at first, but he liked to drink." She frowned, not looking up. "One day he got into a fight. He lost."

"I'm sorry," Graham said.

She shrugged. "After he died, my mom found out he had a lot of debt. She started a bakery when I was little, and it did alright, but not enough to take care of the debt. She ended up selling it. It covered the debt, but left us with nothing. She thought about taking me back to Taiwan. The night we turned the bakery over to the new owners was crazy. We were walking. It was dark. We heard someone calling for help."

"Please tell me you didn't go into some dark alley," Graham said.

Ming Li smiled, but still looked at her paper. "No, but we followed the voice. We found Brake. He was hurt. Really bad. He didn't want to go to the hospital. We had nowhere to take him. We had lived above the bakery. My mom told him we didn't have a home anymore and tried to get him to go to a hospital. My mom helped him stand. He looked like he might collapse. Brake threw open his arms and threw some type of dust into the air and made a portal. He pulled us through with him. We ended up at his house. He was unconscious."

"Wow," Graham said, taking it in. "He didn't even ask if you wanted to come?"

"No," Ming Li said. A tear escaped her eye, and she brushed it away. "But we will forever be grateful to him. Our lives have been so much happier since we came here. My mom tried to find help for Brake, but since she didn't know where we were, she was afraid she would get lost in the woods. She came back and nursed Brake back to health. When he recovered, he helped her build a bakery with a house. He wouldn't let us pay him back."

"Why was Brake in California?"

"He was looking for someone. He never explained more than that. If he doesn't want to talk about it, I figure that's his business."

"Hmm. And what were you saying about not speaking English yesterday?"

"When I came here, I didn't speak the language. I'm talented at language, so I picked it up super fast. My mom still struggles even after five years. I guess it makes more sense to say I didn't speak the way people here do. It's not exactly a unique language."

"But I didn't learn a language."

"We're speaking English now," Ming Li said, "But most of the time we speak the same way everyone else does. I call it Akkronese in my head. I guess that doesn't make sense because it's the language most people in this world speak."

"How could I speak a language I don't know?"

"No clue," Ming Li said, "Although my guess is that your parents were from here. When Wren goes through a portal, she speaks whatever language the people there do. She doesn't even realize. I've seen her do it a few times. Don't tell anyone. We weren't supposed to be going through portals."

"So we can naturally speak languages?"

"Not always," Ming Li said. "It only works for Wren if she goes through a portal. She can't speak the language later, only while she's there. I guess it's the same for you."

"That's hard to comprehend."

"Yeah, Wren thinks I'm joking when I tell her she was speaking a different language. The weird thing is—when I came out of the cave, I could understand everything better than before. I mean, I speak Akkronese well. I even think in it as much as I can, but now it feels more natural."

"I can read and write at school with no trouble."

"Yeah, they have the same alphabet here and they write numbers the same way. I asked Brake about it once and he said that this world and Earth used to have a strong connection. That made learning the language a lot easier. I guess there were portals anyone could go through for a while that were hidden somewhere in England and California. There could be more."

"How did you communicate with Brake when you first came here?"

Ming Li laughed. "It was ridiculously hard and kind of funny. Brake can speak a bit of English. We did a lot of charades and drew pictures. We could also write and almost understand each other that way. Spelling was a little tricky. I'm explaining this wrong. My mom says I like to brag and she might be right.

"I'm good at languages, but Akkronese is mostly English with a strong accent. Like a super duper strong accent. That's probably why I learned it so fast. It's usually the same word, but you would never know when you hear it. Once you know both, you can tell it's the same. Does any of this make sense?"

"Kind of," Graham said, nodding, "But if the languages are so similar, why can't your mom learn it?"

"She can get by. She can understand most things now, but she's terrible at the accent. English is her second language, so that makes it harder. She already had a strong accent before we came here."

"So, do you have a last name?"

"Sure, but it doesn't matter anymore, right?"

"I guess not. It's nice to know someone here has something in common with me, though."

"It's Hansen."

"Hansen?" Graham chuckled. "That's not what I would have guessed."

"Hey, my dad was from California, remember?" she smiled. "My mom's last name is Liu. Is that more of what you were expecting?"

"Maybe."

"Well, I enjoy having a boring last name. It surprises people. It also surprises people when they find out I'm half Asian and I can't do math. I'm good at languages and I speak English, Akkronese, Flordillian, and Spanish. Do I speak Chinese? I can count to ten and say hello, goodbye, and where is the bathroom. That's me, ruining stereotypes since I was born."

"You don't speak Chinese?" Graham asked, raising his eyebrow.

"Nope," she said. "My dad was against it. He said Spanish was more useful, so I was in a Spanish immersion school. I was going to learn Chinese to spite him, but there isn't a lot of reason here. Plus, my mom would have to teach me and she doesn't have the patience."

"I wonder if my parents were from here," Graham said. "Maybe only one of them was. I'm pretty sure my aunt isn't magic."

"I guess it's possible."

"Hey guys," Tal said as he entered the kitchen with Wren. "Are you sitting here trying to come up with a name for the group?"

"How about The Chameleons?" Graham suggested. "Chameleons can turn their eyes backwards and stuff. It would tell our enemies that we're watching everything."

"Give up on the name," Wren said, laughing.

"Do you have any better ideas?"

"How about The Winners," Ming Li said, "Because we're going to win."

"That sounds kind of dorky," Tal said. "It would be like, 'Hey, we're going to go have a secret meeting with The Winners,' kind of lame."

"Should it have something about light in it?" Wren asked. "Since we are the opposite of The Dark Cloud."

"The Light Chameleons," Graham said, nodding.

"Noooo," Ming Li protested, going back to her drawing.

"The Light Piranhas?"

"Nope."

"Does it have to be an animal?" Wren asked.

"Too bad The Fleet is taken. It sounds professional."

"It sounds stuffy," Tal said. "And their slogan? We are the Fleet! Because we are all moving in the same direction!"

Graham smiled, and Wren and Ming Li giggled.

"The fleet isn't even going in two directions," Tal said. "I think they are all going in different directions."

"Probably," Wren agreed. "Well, except my dad and Zera are on the same side."

"The Initiative? The Matrix? The Jedi?" Graham spouted.

Ming Li rolled her eyes. "So original."

"Actually, they sound pretty good," Tal said.

"They sound like you stole them from Hollywood."

"What's Hollywood?" Wren asked.

"A place in the world where me and Graham are from," Ming Li said, looking at Wren.

"Okay, I say no more secrets," Graham said. "Since we all have absolutely nowhere to go right now, we are going to sit and tell each other our origin stories."

Wren nodded. "I agree. If we all understand each other, we will be more connected."

"Does it have to be right now?" Tal asked. "I feel like I've already been through enough these last two days. Plus, we already know Graham's and Wren's. Wren doesn't have secrets. I have wondered about Li's though."

Ming Li sighed. "Might as well get it over with. I'm not usually in the mood to talk about my past, but since I've already told Graham today, I might as well tell it again."

"You told Graham before me?" Wren asked, sounding hurt.

"He kept bugging me about it and it came out." She gave Wren and Tal a quick story about her past.

"Are there seriously as many worlds and dimensions as people say there are?" Tal wondered. "Isn't it kind of unbelievable to think that if there are so many of them, Graham and Ming Li would both be from the same one? What are the odds?"

"It could be that there are some places that are easier to open a portal to than others," Graham said. It made sense to him. Or maybe some worlds were tied together somehow, like Brake had told Ming Li. He was curious about Brake. Brake had been so against Wren opening portals, but from what Ming Li said, Brake had opened at least one himself.

"I know there are a lot," Wren said. "I can feel them pulling at me sometimes."

"Before we believed how dangerous portal jumping could be, we traveled to a few places," Ming Li admitted. "But one unpleasant experience made us change our minds about that kind of fun."

"That's for sure." Wren shuddered.

"What happened?" Tal asked.

"Nuh-uh," Ming Li frowned. "Tal's backstory next."

"Uggggh!" Tal said, rubbing his temples and sitting on a stool. "It's not a great story. Dad's evil, Mom likes money, grandma raised me. Grandma is good. That's all you're getting from me. I'm tired."

Ming Li rolled her eyes. "Okay. I guess we've made some progress."

"The Honey Badgers," Graham said. Why hadn't he thought of it before?

"What are you talking about?" Tal asked.

"We could be called The Honey Badgers."

"What is a honey badger?"

"It's a fierce little animal," Graham explained. "They have been known to attack animals much larger than themselves. Even lions. They're fearless."

"Anything with honey in it sounds kind of weak," Tal said, shaking his head.

"It sounds like a cub scout group," Ming Li said, frowning.

"Do we need a name?" Wren wondered.

"It would be way more convenient to say, 'We are joining with The Honey Badgers' than saying, 'We are joining with the group that's opposed to The Dark Cloud.'"

"It doesn't sound very threatening," Wren said, shrugging apologetically. Graham sighed. They were right. It did sound lame, but if they ever saw a honey badger in action, they might change their minds.

"We outvoted you," Tal said, smiling. "How about The Talons?"

"I thought you hated that name?" Wren said.

"I do," Tal said. "That doesn't mean it wouldn't make a noble name for a group, though."

"I like it," Ming Li said, her legs swinging under her stool. "Better than Tal. I thought your name was Towel for, like, two years."

"We finished with our meeting," Brake said, poking his head in the doorway. "A few of the members have stayed and we would like to talk to you."

They followed Brake into the second meeting room. It looked like the first one. Drew stood and opened his arms to Wren. She went and gave him a hug. Zera sat in a chair next to a tall woman with olive skin and black wavy hair. She wore a bright red dress that came past her ankles. She was studying them intently. Graham tried not to fidget. In another chair across from them was Hamble, and he was sitting next to a smiling Brog. Graham wondered how the chair wasn't breaking under him. This wasn't too bad. The only one they didn't know was the woman in the red dress.

"You know Zera, and Brog," Brake said, "And you met Hamble last night. This is Austra," he said, nodding towards the woman in red. "Austra, this is Graham, Wren, Ming Li, and Tal." She nodded slightly and Wren gave a little wave.

Tal plopped down on a cushion. Graham, Ming Li, and Wren did the same. As soon as he sat, Graham regretted it. They should have used chairs because now the adults looked even bigger and more intimidating.

The door opened and Professor Hedder came in. "Sorry I had to step out," he said, sitting. Graham sighed. He could have done without his history/geography teacher.

"Professor Hedder is a good guy?" Ming Li said. "I guess that blows your theory, Tal."

"What theory? Of course I'm a good guy," Hedder said, through squinted eyes.

"Why would you think otherwise?"

"Tal has a theory about what bad guys look like," she said, grinning. "You fit the description."

"Come on Li," Tal muttered, as he rubbed the back of his neck. "Can't you keep anything to yourself?"

"Maybe if I try."

"Please try."

"No, I want to know," Hedder said, glaring at Ming Li. "Why do I look like a bad guy?"

"It's a combination of the ponytail and the weak facial hair."

Hedder's eyes narrowed, and he shook his head.

"Are we finished?" Brake asked. Ming Li nodded. Graham wanted to smile, but he didn't need Professor Hedder to hate him more than he already seemed to.

"We have been discussing your visit to Meegore," Brake told them, as he sat on a big blue chair.

"I'm shocked to find that the cave opened for children," Austra said with a thick, crisp accent.

Ming Li shifted in her seat. "We aren't children."

Austra sighed. "I don't work well with children."

"We don't work well with people who call us children," Ming Li said, crossing her arms and trying to look tough. Graham smiled. It was hard to take Ming Li seriously, the way she was awkwardly sitting on the cushion.

"This conversation is going in the wrong direction," Zera said, her voice commanding authority. "What we need to do now is figure out our next step. Yesterday we never would have dreamed the cave at Meegore would open. Things are changing and this is our opportunity."

"We shouldn't do anything hasty," Brake added. "These four need to learn how to use their new magic before we act."

"Hasty?" Austra laughed. "You talk of hasty? You are the one who let these children run off to the cave with little to no preparation. If we had met with them first, we could have warned them of the dangers in the cave and helped them prepare."

"We didn't know the cave would open. If I had brought four teenagers here and told everyone that we needed to get them ready to go to Meegore, everyone would have thought I was crazy."

Austra opened her mouth to argue and then shut it. She must have realized he was right.

"I know a lot about Meegore," she said, glaring at Brake. "I could have been beneficial."

"It wasn't that dangerous," Wren said. "There were some hard spots, and it was kind of scary, but it didn't feel dangerous."

Tal grimaced. "Speak for yourself. There was no 'kind of' scary. I almost wet myself when that thing touched my leg in the water."

"Should we go to Meegore again?" Graham wondered. "Should we be trying to get more magic?"

"We need to be careful," Wren said. "The whole reason the cave closed was from people going in and getting too much magic. We don't want to become like them."

Zera nodded. "That is smart. We should avoid Meegore for now."

"I agree," Brog added. "It would be dangerous for you to be there right now."

"Why did the cave have all of those pointless obstacles?" Ming Li asked. "Wren's right. They weren't that hard. It was more of an annoyance."

"They were not placed there as a challenge," Austra told her. "That is just the way the cave was, though it was said the path could change. At least that's my understanding of it."

"Can we take someone to the cave?" Ming Li asked. Graham wondered if she was thinking of her mom.

"Perhaps sometime," Zera said, "But not right now. And you would need to be careful of who and when."

"And why," Drew added. He had been silent until now. "Make sure you are taking them for the right reason. Power can be a dangerous thing."

"What's your goal?" Graham asked. "We want to take down The Dark Cloud."

"That's our goal at the moment as well," Brake said, and Zera and Austra nodded.

"Our goal is to capture The Dark Cloud and help the people in Boztoll," Zera explained. "Boztoll is full of people without magic. More and more end up there every year. About one third of Boztoll doesn't have magic. Clouds have been hovering over the city for a long time. The people are having a hard time growing crops because there is no sun getting through. There are a few of our people there trying to help. We have figured out a way to part the clouds for short periods of time."

"Whatever magic The Dark Cloud is using, it's strong. We should be able to get rid of the clouds completely, but we can't," Brake said, frowning.

"Why don't they move to another city?" Graham asked.

"Everyone's scared," Brake explained. "They don't know who to trust."

"Some people have left," Austra added, "Some go to Flordillia and live by the trolls. That's not the best solution, as trolls don't enjoy living near people."

"Should we go to Boztoll?" Tal asked.

"I am not sure we can help them until we find out who belongs to The Dark Cloud," Zera said. "Anything we can do in Boztoll now is only temporary."

"Do we know who any of The Dark Cloud members are besides my dad?"

"We don't know that your dad is involved," Drew said, shaking his head. "I've tried to get any type of proof against him and I have failed."

"You haven't failed," Brake said. "You have to keep trying."

"It shouldn't be that hard to find proof my father is corrupt," Tal said, looking unconvinced.

"I can prove he's corrupt, but not that he's in The Dark Cloud," Drew clarified.

"Oh," Tal said, leaning back on his cushion.

"Should we tell them about our conversation with your dad?" Wren asked, tilting her head and looking at Tal.

"Might as well."

"Governor Briggs wants the four of us to join him and take over the world."

"What?" Graham said, sitting straighter.

"That's what he told us," Wren said, glancing at Tal. "He wants to send all non-magic people to Boztoll and make himself King. He also wants all the people in Boztoll to farm for everyone else."

"He better leave my mom alone," Ming Li said, clenching her fists.

"Briggs said he has your mom watched to make sure nobody bothers her. He adores her baking. I'm not so sure the governor is part of The Dark Cloud. He might have his own agenda."

Zera nodded. "It would be wise to keep you all away from the governor."

"So what do we do?" Wren asked. "I feel like we don't have a lot to go on."

"We don't," Zera admitted. "We have more hope though, since the cave opened."

"Is Coach Zalliah part of this group?" Graham asked.

"No, why?" Zera asked.

"She's been making us do extra gym time," Graham explained. "She made us all learn to do some things we needed in the cave."

"Zalliah can see auras around people," Zera said, tapping her chin. "Maybe she saw something about you and realized you needed to be prepared."

"I attended school with Zalliah," Hamble pipped in. "All she cared about was trying to get better at seeing auras. She used to give herself migraines all the time."

"Seeing auras is difficult," Austra said. "I tried, but decided it wasn't worth the pain."

"Brake told us that Graham can heal with a touch," Brog said. "That will be very useful."

"I don't think I can heal everything, probably only small things. I only did it once, and it made me want to hurl."

"Wren can open portals," Brog continued, "And Ming Li can untie knots?"

Ming Li frowned. "When you say it like that, it sounds totally lame. I can use my mind to control the air. I pushed the air into our ropes to free us, and I can move things. It feels like a powerful wind, but more controlled. I need to experiment more."

"And Tal doesn't know what he can do?" Austra asked, raising an eyebrow at Tal.

"I think I can control plants," Tal said, "And possibly animals."

"Really?" Drew exclaimed, leaning forward. "That hasn't been done in a thousand years."

"I've never heard of it," Brake said, turning to Drew.

"There are stories about people who could cause animals to attack, and plants to block their enemy's path. There aren't a lot of references to it. It's something I tried when I was younger, but it never worked out."

"How do we learn our magic when there isn't anyone to teach us?" Graham wondered.

"Yeah, Hogwarts would be helpful right about now," Ming Li smiled.

"I don't see how warts on a hog could help anything," Wren said, giving her friends a pointed look.

"Nobody lives in this jungle," Zera said. "You can practice without fear of anyone seeing you. We have other security measures. Just be careful."

"It doesn't seem like a solid plan." Wren frowned.

"It's not," Brake admitted. "We didn't expect this to happen, so we don't have a perfect answer to anything."

"We are going to hope we figure something out before anyone else gets hurt." Zera said.

"What do you mean, anyone else? Who's hurt?" Graham asked. The group all shared a look.

"A house collapsed in Akkron yesterday. Everyone inside was non-magical." Zera said, "Two people were seriously hurt. They said they had been getting threats, telling them they would regret it if they did not move."

"I need to take my mom to Meegore," Ming Li said. "I'm going to do it soon, with or without anyone's permission."

Wren laid in her new bed and stared into the dark. Ming Li was across the room from her in another bed. Wren wondered what she was thinking. These last two days had been hard. She felt a little better after she took a shower and put on a clean pair of pajamas.

"Do you want to play *Would You Rather*?" Ming Li asked from the dark.

Wren sighed. She hated that game. Especially with Ming Li. Ming Li came up with the weirdest things. It was funny the first few times they played, but now it was just annoying. "Not really," she admitted.

"Okay, I'll go first," Ming Li said, ignoring her. "Would you rather kiss Graham or Tal?"

"Ming Li!" Wren exclaimed, shaking her tired head. "I don't want to think about that right now. I'm too tired. My last yawn almost broke my face."

"We're best friends. Best friends tell each other these kinds of things."

"Until the best friend tells the entire math class who their friend has a crush on."

"Oh, come on. That was like two years ago. You can't bring up stuff that happened that long ago."

"That was so embarrassing."

"Just pick one," Ming Li said. "I won't tell. And you can't say you wouldn't kiss either of them, or you automatically have to kiss Jaaz."

"Since it's all pretend, I don't have to kiss anyone," Wren said, rolling her eyes. The last thing she wanted was to be stuck in here with one of the boys, thinking she wanted to kiss them. She didn't trust Ming Li to not bring it up by accident.

"Don't be boring," Ming Li complained. "I'll give you three minutes to decide and then you are kissing Jaaz."

Wren frowned. Ming Li didn't know that she thought Graham was cute. She had always thought Tal was attractive, but until recently, she hadn't liked him. Now that she knew him better, she noticed a little more often how cute he was. He had been helpful inside the cave. She was as bad as Ming Li, thinking all the boys were cute. The thought of kissing either of them made her face burn.

"Well? Who is it?" Ming Li asked. "And if you don't pick, or you say you don't want to kiss any of them, you lose, and I'll tease you forever about wanting to kiss Jaaz."

"If I say then you have to," Wren said.

"Fine," Ming Li agreed. "I've already thought about it a lot."

Wren was sure she had. Ming Li never kept her thoughts secret and Wren had a long list of boys Ming Li had crushed on in the last five years.

"The only problem," Ming Li said, "Is the germs."

"What are you talking about?" Wren giggled.

"If you kiss someone, you get their germs in your mouth," Ming Li said. "That's super nasty. The thought of it makes me want to gag."

Wren laughed and paused when she heard a laugh and a thud on the other side of the door. She bounced up and threw the door open. Ming Li was at her side, holding a big stick. Where had she gotten a stick? The two boys were wrestling on the floor. Graham had Tal in a headlock and was covering his mouth. Graham looked guilty and Tal's eyes were smiling.

"Were you spying on us?" Ming Li asked, pointing the stick at them.

Wren felt like she might die of embarrassment. She was glad she hadn't made a choice. The last month was turning out to be one embarrassing moment after another.

"Of course not," Graham said, jumping up. Tal was still on the floor and he burst out laughing.

"You were!" Wren said, horrified.

"I want to know the answer, Wren," Tal said, sitting up.

"If you were better at being quiet, you would have heard," Ming Li said, lowering her stick.

"And my germs aren't gross," Tal said, winking at Ming Li.

"But his are grosser than mine, because he only brushes his teeth for like forty seconds," Graham said.

"I expect this out of Tal, but not Graham," Wren muttered. She couldn't believe Ming Li was still getting her into these situations.

"So I guess Wren chooses Graham," Ming Li said, shrugging.

"I didn't say that!" Wren gasped.

"So she chooses me," Tal smiled, standing up.

"I didn't say that!" Wren protested.

"I would probably kiss either of you," Ming Li admitted, drawing the attention away from Wren. "If you didn't have germs, anyway."

Graham and Tal laughed.

"Come on Wren," Tal baited. "You have to choose."

"Can't I choose Brog?" Wren joked.

"He looks like a gigantic version of Thor," Ming Li said, pausing, "But no. You have to choose one of them."

"I'm going with Jaaz," Wren said as she slammed the door. She smiled when she heard the boys laughing in the hall.

"Dude, why couldn't you keep quiet?" Graham asked as he and Tal entered their room. "Not cool man." Graham took off his cape and tossed it onto his bed.

"Sorry," Tal said, looking unrepentant. He sat on his bed and pulled off his boot. "Ming Li is so funny. She's the most boy crazy girl at school and she's scared of germs. Don't you think that's funny?"

"Yeah," Graham admitted, "But if you had kept quiet, we could have heard more."

"Do you actually want to know their answers?" Tal asked, taking off his other boot and tossing it on the floor.

"Yes. No. I don't know," Graham said, sinking into his bed.

"Besides, they were both going to choose me," Tal said, lying on his pillow with his hands behind his head.

"It would sure be nice to have some clean clothes," Graham said, yawning.

"I could do without the breeze in the backside too," Tal said, waving his hand and turning out the light. Graham was going to have to ask him how to do that sometime.

"Maybe tomorrow Wren can make a portal and get us something. We're probably all starting to smell. Taking a shower and putting on dirty clothes isn't very fulfilling."

"Hey," Tal said, sitting up in the dark, "The girls were wearing pajamas!"

"They were," Graham nodded. "Did they go get them while we were outside?"

"They must have," Tal said, lying back down. "Way to help the team girls!" he called, pounding on the wall between their rooms.

After dinner, Tal and Graham had gone out to work on their magic. Graham practiced hitting things with ice. He couldn't coat anything in ice, no matter how hard he tried, but he could sure hit things hard. There were a lot of rocks out there that wouldn't be messing with him anytime soon. Tal hadn't let him hit any trees, so he had to focus on non-living things.

"This room is so small," Tal complained. "I've never shared a room before."

"It's way bigger than mine back home," Graham said. His room back home had been about the size of a bathroom. A small bathroom. He had felt lucky to have his own room and not sleep on the floor, the way Aunt Temper had treated him.

"I thought Brake's house was pretty big," Tal said.

"I meant my room from Earth. My room at Brake's house is pretty big."

"I wonder if Wren can make a portal into my room. That way, I could grab all of my clothes."

"She probably can," Graham said, thoughtfully. "If I could get my stuff from Earth, I wouldn't have to run around looking like I stepped out of a Shakespear play." Graham pictured himself walking around in his basketball shorts and a cape. That might draw more attention than he wanted.

"What's a Shakespear play?" Tal asked. "Actually, don't tell me. I'm pretty sure there's a boring explanation, and in the end, you are making fun of our clothes."

"Yeah, pretty much," Graham said, smiling into the darkness.

"I can make anything look good, so I won't take offense this time."

"I wonder if my aunt has thrown away all of my stuff yet," Graham said, feeling a little sad. He had little that mattered, but his books could come in handy.

"You know," Tal said thoughtfully, "now that Wren can open portals anywhere, you could go back home if you wanted."

Graham suddenly felt wide awake. He hadn't thought of that. "I don't want to go back," he said, with no feeling of hesitation. "I miss my friends sometimes and our dog a little, but I like it here. It's nice to do things without someone getting angry every second."

"You probably should go back and tell your aunt you're okay," Tal suggested. "I mean, they made me go tell my dad, and he's evil. Your aunt just sounds mean."

"Maybe," Graham said, shaking his head. "If she were to see me, she would probably yell about how many times I've missed cleaning the house. She would probably hand me a mop and walk away."

"Well, if she did, you could leave and you wouldn't have to feel guilty about leaving everyone wondering."

"I don't feel guilty. I didn't do it on purpose and they probably don't care."

"You can tell yourself that," Tal said, "But from what I've gotten to know about you, I think you care."

"Maybe a little."

"We can ask the girls their opinion tomorrow. If they want to go, we go. Deal?"

"We?"

"I've never been to another world. You have to take me."

"I'll think about it."

CHAPTER 14

G raham looked around his delapidated old neighborhood. It felt like he'd been gone for an eternity, even
though it hadn't been much time at all. They had stopped
by Wren's house and gotten some gold coins and some
real money. Drew had a bunch of money from the United
States and had no intention of telling them how he got it.
It was enough to buy anything they wanted, but Wren still
took some gold to be safe.

"Wow, it feels weird to see graffiti again," Ming Li said,
looking around.

"It sure does," Graham agreed. "Akkron has its problems, but it's meticulously clean."

"Why would someone do that?" Tal asked. "Why make
your city look like that?"

Graham didn't have an answer. He had spent plenty
of his time painting over graffiti on his aunt's fence. It
looked like it was about noon. If they were lucky, his aunt

wouldn't be home and he could change and leave a note. A note sounded a lot better than a confrontation. There were no people around, so they weren't drawing any attention yet.

"Let's get to my house and hope nobody sees us," Graham said, leading the way. They left the park and walked across the street to Aunt Temperance's broken-down house. The brown paint was peeling, and the white door hung a little crooked. The pink azalea bush was the only thing that made the place look happy. He knocked on the door, not wanting to scare anyone. When no one answered, he opened it and led them all in.

"I haven't seen a house like this since I visited Boztoll," Tal said, looking around at the worn furniture. It was bizarre to hear Tal and Wren speak English. Now that he was aware, he could hear the difference.

"You've been to Boztoll?" Wren asked, surprised.

"Sure, I've been about everywhere."

"What's going on here?" Aunt Temperance growled, coming up behind them. Graham turned around and saw his aunt glaring at him. She looked thinner and her short black hair wasn't fixed. That wasn't normal for her. She might live in a dump, but she always looked perfect. Her fingernails weren't even polished. Guilt surged through him. She didn't look like this because of him, did she?

"Aunt Temperance," Graham said, stepping forward.

"Don't you Aunt Temperance me!" she said, snarling. "Where have you been? Who are these people?"

"I came back to tell you I'm safe," he said. "I'm going to grab my things and go."

She pulled a cell phone out of her pocket. "You aren't going anywhere. The police have been searching for you for weeks!"

"Don't call them!" Graham pleaded. "If you do, we'll just leave."

"Well, at least they'll know where to look. Kaylee came home talking about how you were out conversing with invisible people, and you never came home. What is everyone supposed to think? And now you come home filthy and dressed like that."

"If I tell you what happened, you won't believe me," Graham said. He looked at his friends. They all looked uncomfortable.

"He was talking to me," Wren said. "Kaylee couldn't see me." Temperance glanced at Wren and the color drained from her face. Graham was sure they looked odd. Tal and Graham hadn't ditched their capes because of the holes in their pants. The girls could almost fit in if they weren't both wearing shirts that seemed to change colors every time you didn't focus on them. Why had they worn those, anyway?

"Graham, you're okay!" Kaylee said, entering the house with a smile that quickly slipped into a frown. "Not that I care. What are you wearing? You look like a dork! And who are your dorky friends? Next time you run away, take Walter. I'm sick of doing your jobs."

"Kaylee, go to your room!" Aunt Temperance yelled. She never yelled at Kaylee. Kaylee's black eyes widened, and she ran up the stairs as fast as she could. Temperance put a hand to her forehead and closed her eyes.

"I'm not trying to cause a problem, Aunt Temperance," Graham said. "Just let me grab my things and I'll be gone."

"I knew something like this would happen someday," she muttered. "And I'm not your aunt." She sank onto the tattered brown sofa.

"What do you mean?" Graham asked, sitting next to her. The other three sat awkwardly on the stairs and tried to pretend to be interested in anything but them.

"Lance came home one day," she began, staring at her hands in her lap. "He said a man he worked with was going on vacation and needed someone to watch his baby, but they were leaving that very day. I didn't want to do it at first, but he offered a lot of money. We took you, and then your parents died. Lance was too much of a softy. He talked me into adopting you."

Graham had always thought that his life would have been better if his Uncle Lance hadn't died. He remembered him as a nice, friendly person. He was always laughing. Lance died when Graham was six and Kaylee was a baby. That was when Temperance had gotten overly bossy and mean.

"Why did you tell me you were my aunt?" Graham asked.

"Because being an aunt isn't as stressful as a mom. Taking in your nephew sounded a lot better to me."

"So you didn't even know my parents?" Things made a lot more sense. She would never talk about his parents when he asked about them.

"Not at all," she said, glaring at him. "I saw your parents for about one minute when they passed you over to me.

I came in the house and looked out the window. Your parents walked to a car and looked around like they were trying to see if anyone was watching. Your dad raised his hands into the air and tossed some dust and this huge silvery, glistening thing popped up. They jumped through it and they disappeared!"

"Wait, so they didn't die?" Graham asked, feeling a lump in his throat.

"I don't know what happened," Temperance said, looking exhausted. "Lance said I imagined it, but I know what I saw. We got a call a few weeks later telling us that their ship had capsized and they weren't found. They had boarded the boat, though."

"And their names were John and Mary Dryson?" Graham asked. His mind was spinning. His parents had to be from Akkron. Or at least that world. Could they be alive? Probably not if someone had seen them on the boat. If they used a portal to save themselves, they would have come back for him.

"All I know is they left me in a mess and I've had to deal with you all these years," she said, shaking her head. "They didn't even tell us your name. They were in such a hurry. All we knew was Dryson. And your parents were dressed like you are now. Lance said that John didn't usually dress like that. He thought it was funny. Now here you come back like nothing happened with these people," she said, gesturing at the others on the stairs. "And now you want to get your stuff and leave again?"

"Why do you care?" Wren asked from the stairs. "If he has been such a problem to you, what does it matter if he leaves?"

"If I leave, she has to clean her own house," Graham said, his mind still spinning.

"How dare you?" Temperance huffed. "You have two minutes to grab your things before I call the police. Your friends stay here where I can see them."

"Fine," Graham said, getting off the couch. He had come here hoping to get his stuff, but now he had so many questions.

Wren watched Temperance. The woman sat on the couch, looking distressed. It made her mad that this woman had treated Graham so poorly, but she still felt bad for her. It must have been hard losing her husband and having no money and two kids.

"Why do you all keep staring at me?" Temperance snapped. "If you're looking for a show, it's over."

Tal and Ming Li looked away. Wren stood and walked over to the couch and sat by Temperance. "Graham is one of my best friends," she said, startling the woman. "He is also one of the best people I've ever met. He wants to make a difference."

"Yes, with his medicine," Temperance said, rolling her eyes. "He isn't smart enough to know that he's never going to have the money to go to college."

"He is smart," Ming Li added. "And he doesn't have to go to college to heal people. He has mrff—" Ming Li mumbled as Tal covered her mouth from the stair above her.

"I'm sorry you can't see what we see in him," Wren continued. "Graham believes college is an important thing in this world. Take this." Wren handed Temperance a handful of gold coins.

"I know this is a great deal of wealth here," Wren said. Temperance's eyes were enormous as she looked at the gold. Her hand was shaking. "I want you to take this and get a better house. Preferably in a place that doesn't write words all over the neighborhood. I want you to raise that little girl upstairs to be polite and smart. Send her to college. You don't need money to be smart and polite, but she needs some lessons."

"This can't be real," Temperance whispered.

"It is," Wren said. "Now make a better life for your family. And I want you to promise that you will always talk to Graham if he has questions."

"You should go to college too," Graham added, coming down the stairs. He had two backpacks full of something. "That's a lot of gold, Aunt Temperance. You can do a lot of good with that. I want you to let me borrow the Ford. You can pick it up later at the mall." Temperance nodded, still staring at the gold in her hands. Graham grabbed a key off a hook by the door and motioned for his friends to follow him.

"Your mother had brown hair," Temperance said, looking at Graham. "She was pale. Almost looked sick. Your father looked more like you. He was tall. He looked tired, but strong. That's all I remember."

"Thank you," Graham said as they walked out the door. He led them over to an old, beat up rusty metal thing on wheels and Graham opened a door. "This was my uncle's truck. It's kind of old."

"That was intense in there," Tal said, "Not to mention awkward. What is this thing?" Ming Li climbed into the questionable looking contraption.

"We can't go jumping through portals to get everywhere," Graham explained. "The more we do that, the more chance someone will see us. Climb in." Tal nodded and climbed next to Ming Li.

"What's it going to do?" Wren asked wearily.

"It's a truck, and it's going to take us to the mall. It's how we get around on Earth. We don't have flying horses or magic."

Wren climbed onto the seat. She wondered where the animals were. How would they make it move?

"Sorry it's squishy. It's only meant for three. Two of you are going to have to share a seat belt."

"That's not legal," Ming Li protested.

"I don't know what else to do," Graham said, shutting the door and heading to the other side. Wren climbed over Tal to be closer to Ming Li.

"If someone has to share, it's going to be me and Wren," Ming Li said, pulling the seat belt around the two of them.

"Is this safe?" Tal asked, pulling on the seat belt. "I mean, it doesn't seem safe if we have to tie ourselves in."

"It's usually safe," Ming Li said, reaching over and taking Tal's seat belt. She clipped it in and smiled. "There you go, all safe."

Graham put the keys into a lock and let out a breath.

"You know how to drive, right?" Ming Li asked, "You look kind of nervous."

"Of course I do," Graham said, moving a lever. They jerked backwards a few feet and Graham stopped a little too hard.

"Sure you do," Ming Li said, giving him a sideways glance.

"It's been a while," Graham said, trying again. "There, see?" he said, as he backed down the driveway and into the street. "No problem."

"I want to see your license," Ming Li protested.

"Yeah, well, I don't exactly have a license, but I have a permit. I would have gotten my license by now if I hadn't left. I would've taken the test two weeks ago on my birthday."

Wren felt awful. "Your birthday was two weeks ago? Why didn't you tell us?"

"Birthdays aren't that exciting. Well, I turned sixteen, so that's exciting ... or it was when I thought I would get to drive. Now it doesn't change anything since there aren't any cars in Akkron."

"That means you're, like, a month older than me," Tal said, looking out the window. "Can we get moving? This is exciting!"

They started moving, and Wren was terrified. Once they turned onto a wider road, other people driving these things surrounded them. They seemed to come in a lot of shapes and colors. How had anyone ever invented such a terrible way to get around?

"This is so awesome!" Tal said. "I want to move here so I can do this all the time." He pressed his face against the glass. Wren was glad she hadn't stayed by the window. Everything looked so different.

"It's surreal to see everything after five years," Ming Li said, looking out. "It almost seems like something from a dream. This is a super green place. A lot greener than California."

"How long will this take?" Wren asked, as they stopped. A green light in front of them turned off and a red one lit up.

"Only a couple minutes," Graham said. "It's pretty close."

"I was hoping it would take a lot longer," Tal complained. The light turned green and Graham started again. The lights must be some sort of code.

"You sure took charge with Graham's aunt in there," Ming Li told Wren. "I was proud of you."

Wren rolled her eyes. "I know how to do things."

"But it was sure cute the way you made the mean woman indebted to you," Tal laughed. "She's probably still in there staring at the gold. I was proud of Graham, too. It's usually me and Ming Li that have to tell everyone what's what."

"I don't know why everyone assumes I'm shy," Wren muttered. "When people think I'm shy, I feel dumb and then I act shy. It's annoying. Are we going too fast?" Graham turned into a place full of vehicles that were all sitting in rows. There was a long brick building that people were walking back and forth to.

"Yay a mall!" Ming Li said, clapping, "It's been so long!" Wren sure hoped this mall was as awesome as Ming Li seemed to think it was. It felt like they'd risked their lives in this thing to get here. Shopping with Ming Li could be horrible. She had the habit of scanning every item in every store she shopped in. It could take forever.

Graham hoped the others couldn't see he was sweating. Remembering how to drive was more stressful than he had expected. Definitely not like riding a bike. He leaped out of the truck and bounded to the otherside to help the others get out. He opened the passenger door. Tal was pulling on his seat belt. Graham reached over and pushed the button. The seat belt retracted and Tal jumped.

"Woah!" Tal said, jumping out of the pickup. "That was so fun!"

"Yeah, great," Wren said, sliding out. She looked pale. "I prefer alicorns." Graham shook his head. How could someone prefer being on an unreliable animal? They walked through the parking lot and into the mall.

Wren looked around with wide eyes. "Wow. There are a lot of people here."

"And a lot of shops," Tal said. "This is so awesome."

"Why is everyone staring at us?" Ming Li asked.

"Ugh!" Graham exclaimed. "We didn't change our clothes."

"Let's hurry and get some and ask if we can change in the store. I'm sure they'll let us," Ming Li said, pushing her hair over her shoulder.

"There must be a lot of poor people," Tal said, looking around. "Look at how many people have holes in their pants."

"We should offer to help some of them," Wren suggested.

Graham laughed, "It's the style," he told them. "They buy pants with holes in them."

"That's the oddest thing I've ever heard." Tal frowned. "That doesn't make any sense. Why would you buy worn-out clothes?"

"I never got it," Graham admitted, "But it seems to be a fashion that doesn't want to die."

"It could be cooler," Wren said, not looking convinced. "I would prefer something without holes, though. They have them, right?"

"There are tons of different styles," Ming Li assured her. "Of course, I was only nine when I lived here and styles change fast, so I'm not the one to give advice." They walked into the first store that sold clothes.

"Find something you like and you can try it on over there," Graham said, pointing to a dressing room. They all separated and looked around. Graham quickly found a blue t-shirt and a pair of jeans. He tried them on and waited for his friends to finish. It felt like an eternity. They all kept grabbing things and trying them on and grabbing more. When they were all ready, Graham looked skeptically at the pile of clothes they were all holding.

"Why are you getting so much? We're only going to be here for one day."

"Yeah, but it's not like we can come back whenever we want," Ming Li said, grabbing a pair of earrings from the counter. "Yay earrings! I wonder if I can still get them in my ears."

"You are going to put those in your ears?" Wren asked, looking doubtful.

"Yes. See these little holes?" she said, pointing to her earlobe. "They go in that hole. See, look at her," she said, pointing at the cashier. "She has earrings." They all looked at the teenager behind the counter. She was wearing long blue and white leather earrings. She was also looking at them like they were crazy.

"Grab some more clothes," Ming Li told Graham as she put her pile on the counter. "We have plenty of money, and you might want it later. I remembered to get a pair for Jaaz." Graham sighed and grabbed a few more shirts and a couple of pairs of jeans.

"Aren't you going to try those on?" Wren asked.

"Nah, they should fit," he said. One time in a dressing room was enough for him. The cashier rang up their purchase. Graham took the money from Wren when she looked confused with all the bills.

"Thanks, Emma," Graham said, reading the girl's name tag. "Would it be possible for us to change into some of these clothes before we leave?"

"I guess," she shrugged.

They all headed back to the dressing room. Graham put on the blue shirt and jeans. He threw the filthy clothes he was wearing in the trash. When he came out, he burst out laughing. Tal was wearing blue swimming trunks with flamingos on them and a bright purple button-up shirt with lightning going across the front.

"What's so funny?" he asked. "There are lots of people wearing these short pants."

"You're wearing a swimming suit. And that shirt does *not* go with it," Graham said, laughing.

"It looks good to me," Tal said, holding out his arms and turning. Ming Li came out in a pink shirt with light blue skinny jeans. As soon as she saw Tal, she started laughing.

"I told you," Graham smirked. Tal just smiled and crossed his arms. Wren came out in a green t-shirt and pants that matched Ming Li's. Only a lot longer. It was almost funny to see them all in normal clothes.

"I bet if we wore pants like this at Meegore, they wouldn't have torn so easily," Wren said. "These feel so thick!"

"Now we blend in?" Tal asked as they gathered their bags and left the store.

"Well, most of us do," Graham smiled.

"Tal looks like the Jaaz of this world," Ming Li giggled. She was wearing the dangling heart earrings. Her earlobes looked red. She must have had to push them in pretty hard.

"Oh, man!" Tal said, "Really, I'm Jaaz?"

"Yup," Graham said, leading them to the food court.

"At least I'm so good looking nobody will notice, right?"

"Keep telling yourself that," Ming Li smiled.

"Where should we eat?" Graham asked.

"Chinese!" Ming Li said, pointing at an Asian restaurant. They walked over and Ming Li breathed in slowly through her nose, "Ahhhh! I've missed that smell."

"I'm pretty sure that's not the smell of something I want to eat," Tal said, fanning his hand in front of his face.

"You can go eat a boring burger or something," Ming Li said. "Mall food isn't that great wherever you go, but this is definitely better than any other place."

"I'll give everyone some money and we can meet back at one of those tables by the wall," Graham said, pointing. He passed out some money. He wondered if it was okay to be spending it like this. Especially Wren's money. Wren and Tal walked around looking at all the pictures of food, trying to decide what to try.

Graham didn't even need to think. Food in Akkron was good. Some of it was superb, but tacos were something he'd missed. He grabbed a few beef tacos and a water bottle and sat with Ming Li. She was eating some type of noodle with chopsticks. Tal joined them, placing a huge cookie, a donut, and chocolate milk on the table.

"You're going to get diabetes," Ming Li said, shaking her head.

"I was going by smell, and these smell the best," he smiled, taking a bite of the donut. "Wow," he said, with his mouth full, "Does your mom know how to make these things?"

"She makes something similar, but they don't taste exactly the same."

"What did I get?" Wren asked, sitting her tray in front of her. "I told them to give me the best thing, and this is what they gave me."

"That's a huge hotdog, not made of dog," Graham clarified quickly. You could almost see the hotdog through all the toppings. "And those are french fries," he said, pointing to the fries. "That's enough for five people."

"At least," Wren said, taking a small bite of a french fry.

"Dip it in the ketchup," Ming Li suggested. "The red stuff there."

"That sounds gross," Wren said, eyeing the ketchup. She dipped it in and bit it. "Maybe it gets better as you go."

Graham felt normal for the first time in a long time. Just sitting with friends at the mall with no worries and a taco. He wondered if he should be feeling this relaxed. Why were they here, anyway? The plan was to save Akkron, yet here they were in another world, buying clothes and eating like they had no cares at all.

"Should we be here?" He asked, "I mean, there isn't any reason for us to be here. It's like we're off playing when we should be doing something bigger."

"I would agree," Wren said, "But have you ever tasted one of these things?" She held up her hotdog. "This is amazing."

"I wonder how hard it is to get some ADHD meds without a prescription," Ming Li said, taking a drink.

"You have ADHD?" Graham asked.

"Of course I do," Ming Li said, rolling her eyes. "Isn't it obvious?"

Graham shrugged. "I just thought you didn't like school."

˙ "I don't like school," she admitted. "You should try going to school when your mind wants to be somewhere else. I did pretty well after I started taking medication, but then we moved to Akkron. My mom asked around and nobody had a clue what she was talking about. I guess it's not a recognized thing there. Since we couldn't get anything for it, she made me be super active and meditate all the time."

"I can't picture you meditating," Tal said, smiling, "And what are you talking about? ADBT?

"ADHD," Ming Li said." It means I have a hard time focusing on certain things and I get hyper sometimes."

"And you take medicine for that?"

"I used to. Before we moved to Akkron."

"Is it magic or something? It makes you focus and not be hyper?" Tal asked, raising his eyebrow.

"It's not magic, but it helped a lot," Ming Li said, crossing her arms.

"Just trying to understand," Tal said. "I'm not trying to be rude. I'm still trying to picture you meditating, though."

"Yeah, well, I'm not great at the mediating part of my mom's program. The active part is more of my thing. I used to run back and forth across our house and bump into the walls. I did it when I was thinking. After I made a hole in the wall, my mom got me into running. That was before Akkron."

"You're faster than I am," Tal admitted, stuffing the rest of his donut in his mouth.

Ming Li smiled. "I'm WAY faster than you."

"We should hurry and get back soon," Graham said, taking a huge bite of his taco.

"Graham! Graham!" He turned his head and saw Kaylee running at him. She had Walter on a leash.

"What are you doing?" Graham asked, as Kaylee stopped in front of him. Walter jumped on him and wagged his tail. Graham rubbed his head. "You can't bring dogs in here."

She was out of breath, but smiling. "Graham, you'll never guess!" she said. "You and your friends are my favorite people ever!" Her black braids bounced with her. Graham smiled. It reminded him that Kaylee hadn't always been a brat. There had been a time when they got along well. Before Temperance had turned her into her little clone.

"Oh, yeah?" Graham asked.

"We're getting a new house and a new car!" she giggled. "And the best part? We're going to Disneyland! Can you believe it?"

"It sounds fun, Kaylee," Graham said, as she handed him Walter's leash.

"You have to take Walter. You know me and mom don't know how to deal with his mood swings."

"A dog with mood swings?" Tal laughed, bending over to pet Walter. Walter licked his face.

"He gets insulted pretty easily," Graham said.

Kaylee threw her arms around Graham. "I'm sorry I've been such a brat the last few years. When you didn't come home, I was so scared. I cried and cried. Mom says you aren't coming back, but I feel better knowing you're okay."

Graham hugged her back. "Have fun at Disneyland."

"I will! Mom's waiting. I have to go." She waved and bounced off.

"That was unexpected," Ming Li said, patting Walter.

"It sure was," Graham admitted.

"Guys," Wren said, looking nervously around. "Have you noticed all the people in cloaks and masks sitting around in here?" Graham looked around. She was right. There were six people he could see, spread throughout the food court, wearing cloaks and masks. People near them were getting uncomfortable and leaving or moving away.

"We better leave," Tal said, pointing to the exit. Ming Li and Wren stood and grabbed their bags. They walked casually, but quickly, towards the door.

"As soon as we get outside, open a portal, Wren," Graham said, pulling Walter along. It was hard, since he was also carrying his backpacks and clothing bags. A cloaked figure walked in front of the door and blocked them. They turned, but all six of the figures were surrounding them.

"Really?" Tal said. "In front of all these people?" Most of the people in the food court were watching.

"It doesn't matter what these people see," said one figure. The voice matched the large man from Meegore. "It's not like they can tell anyone who matters."

"You can come with us and no one will get hurt," said another one.

"Yeah, right," Wren said, ready to make a portal.

"Anytime, Wren," Graham said as the cloaked figures moved in closer.

"I can't move my arms," Wren said in a panic. "They're stuck to my side!"

"The only way you get to go home is with us," a woman's voice said. Graham was pretty sure she had also been at Meegore. She sounded like the woman who spoke Flordillian.

"I don't think so," Ming Li said, pushing out both of her arms and aiming the palms of her hands at the two cloaked figures nearest her. A fierce wind came out of them and blew both of them over.

"I still can't move," Wren said, struggling. Graham had already dropped Walter's leash and dropped his bags. He shot a bolt of ice at the leader. At least, the person he assumed was the leader. The man jumped unnaturally high, and the ice blasted the wall. People in the food court cheered.

"Great, they think this is a show," Graham muttered, shooting more ice at the man. It hit him and knocked him over.

Behind him Ming Li was keeping the two figures she had blown over on the floor with wind. Tal had picked up a food tray and was smacking one of them with it. Under different circumstances, it would have been funny to see Tal attacking people with a tray in his flamingo swimming suit. Graham didn't want to shoot too much ice and risk hitting someone innocent.

The leader must have been keeping Wren bound because now she was free and was levitating small objects like napkin dispensers and throwing them at The Dark Cloud members. A few of them were flinging things back at her. Something was wrong. The Dark Cloud didn't seem to be trying very hard. Six experienced adults should fight better than four teenagers.

One figure grabbed Ming Li from behind, pulling her arms to her sides. The two people she had been keeping secured hopped up and disappeared. Ming Li stomped on the figure's toe and spun around when they let go and punched them in the face. The mask broke, and the person spun around to cover their face and disappeared.

Graham levitated a table and threw it at the two figures that were throwing things at Wren. They both disappeared before it could hit them, along with the one fighting Tal. The remaining member of The Dark Cloud turned and laughed. Blood ran from his arm. Graham figured it was from the ice.

"We were worried you might be a danger to our organization," the man laughed. "You have proven here that you hold little to no threat to us." Walter ran up and bit the man's leg. He yelled out in pain and disappeared. Graham turned to his friends. Tal dropped the tray. Ming Li looked like she had been in a tornado. Her hair was windblown, and she was breathing hard. Wren had a cut under her eye that was bleeding.

The food court erupted into applause. "Bad acting, but wonderful effects!" a man called out. Ming Li smiled and blew a kiss at the audience.

"Time to go," Graham said, as a security guard rounded the corner into the food court.

Wren opened a portal. The crowd cheered again. They grabbed their bags and Tal grabbed Walter's leash, and they all hurried through.

CHAPTER 15

"I guess we should have held hands," Wren said, pushing Graham off of her, and rolling off of Ming Li.

"Sorry," Graham apologized, jumping up. They had been in such a hurry to leave, they'd landed in a heap. Tal and Ming Li stood up. Walter was bouncing around as far as Tal and the leash would let him. Their new clothes were all over the ground. They picked them up and stuffed them back into the bags.

"Next time we get into a fight, I vote it's in the jungle," Tal said. "I felt pretty stupid hitting people with food trays."

"What would you have done in the jungle?" Graham asked. Tal threw his arm out to its full length and pulled it back in with lightning speed. A vine wrapped around Graham's leg and pulled him upside down. He yelled and Ming Li screamed. At least Wren thought Ming Li screamed. It was hard to hear over her own scream. It took her a second to realize Tal had done it. Walter was barking and looking at Graham.

"That's what I would have done." He lowered his arm slowly and gently dropped Graham.

"That was not cool, bro," Graham said, standing and brushing the dirt off his pants.

"But it was impressive, right?" Tal asked, smiling. "I wasn't sure it would work as well as it did. It was a great first practice."

"It would have been more impressive if you weren't wearing the flamingo swimsuit," Ming Li said, tossing her messy hair over her shoulder.

Graham frowned. "I wish you wouldn't test things out on me."

"I don't get why everyone is against flamingos," Tal said, looking at his shorts.

"Did anyone hear that?" Wren asked, looking around. "I think I heard an animal."

Graham looked around nervously. "Give me Walter's leash," he said, taking it from Tal.

Tal laughed, "If you knew how many animals are super close to us right now, you wouldn't be here." They all looked around. "Just the amount of snakes alone ..." He laughed as Ming Li and Wren linked arms.

"Let's go," Wren said. "How are we going to get Walter up the tree?"

"I'll have to carry him," Graham said. "He isn't that heavy. Can someone take my bags, though?"

They all took one. Wren grabbed a branch and pulled herself into the tree. It was a lot harder with the bags.

She liked animals, but she didn't want any popping up to surprise her. She even liked snakes, but she wasn't in the mood to run into a poisonous one. Looking down, she saw that Ming Li and Tal were already climbing. Wren reached the secret branch and plunged over it. After doing it a couple of times, it didn't feel as scary. Falling into the meeting room and bouncing off the cushion was fun if you knew what was coming.

"Where have you been?" Brake asked. Wren hopped off the cushion and looked at him. He had his arms crossed, and he looked angry. "Where are the others?"

Wren set the bags down and opened her mouth to speak, but closed it as Ming Li fell into the room. She rolled off and narrowly missed being hit by Tal.

"Where's Graham?" Brake asked.

"He's coming. He's slow because he's carrying a dog," Wren explained.

"A dog?" Brake asked, shaking his head. Graham fell in, holding Walter against him like a baby. He fell onto his back so Walter wouldn't get hurt. "Why is there a dog? Nevermind," he muttered. "Drew said you all went to Earth. What were you thinking?"

They all looked at each other. Brake sighed and sat in a blue chair. He put his elbows on his knees and steepled his fingers together.

"We wanted to tell Graham's aunt he was okay," Ming Li said. "Oh, and we went shopping," she said when she noticed Brake was staring at the bags she had in her hands.

"That explains the bags, but not the gash on Wren's face." He pointed, and Wren looked away. "I'm uncertain, but it looks like Tal's getting a black eye. And why does Ming Li look like she was in a fight with a hurricane?" he raised his eyebrows and sat waiting for answers.

"The Dark Cloud found us," Wren admitted.

"What?" Brake said, looking up in alarm. "That shouldn't be possible. What happened?"

"We fought them," Wren said, "And they disappeared."

"How many of them were there?"

"Six."

"I think they were testing us," said Graham. "The leader said that we proved we were not a threat or something like that."

Tal slumped on a cushion. "I'm pretty sure they look worse than us." Walter bounced over and sat on his lap.

"That was reckless," Brake said. "We brought you here to keep you safe. We can't do that if you go wandering off without permission."

"Wait ..." Ming Li said, crossing her arms, "We have to have permission to leave?"

Brake rubbed his temples. "It's better if we know where you are going so we can see if there is any danger. We can all talk about it and see if it's a good decision."

"Our life sure sounds exciting," Tal said.

"No need to be sarcastic. I can't believe Drew let you go. And he told me how much money he gave you. That was enough to get into a lot of trouble."

"I'm a little worried about that," Graham said. "We gave a lot to my aunt. I don't know how we'll pay Drew back."

"He doesn't want you to pay him back," Wren said, surprised he would be worried about that. "He has a lot of money. That wasn't enough money to even be missed."

"How did your dad have Earth money?" Tal wondered.

"I gave it to him," Brake said. "Not for this purpose, of course. I didn't need it anymore, and he collects things."

"That's for sure," Wren said, sitting on a red chair. Her dad liked to collect things from faraway places. He had one room in their house that he kept it in. He didn't let Wren go in there often, but when she did, it always amazed her when she looked over his collection.

"Who knew where you were going? The Dark Cloud shouldn't have any way to track you."

"Only my dad and Brog," Wren answered.

"Brog wouldn't tell," Graham said, "Would he?"

"No," Brake said, "And neither would Drew."

"Well, they definitely knew," said Ming Li. "And we put up a pretty good fight ... although I was so busy concentrating on holding my two down I didn't see what the rest of you were doing."

"Why did you have that money?" Graham asked Brake. "And why were you on Earth the time you brought Ming Li here?"

"That doesn't matter right now."

"You never told us why you were there," Ming Li said. "You must have had a reason. And you opened a portal. You used some type of dust though, not like Wren."

Brake sighed. "I was in California hunting some criminals from Akkron. They had escaped and were living there.

I had to make a deal with the goblins. They sold me some dust that can open portals."

"You can get dust that opens portals?" Tal asked.

"Not anymore," Brake said. "I was able to bring in all the criminals but one. He was too strong. I was so hurt when I brought Ming Li and Mali back, I wasn't thinking clearly. I had no more dust, so I couldn't take them back."

"We didn't want to go back anyway," Ming Li said. Brake nodded.

"Were the criminals from The Dark Cloud?" Wren asked.

"No, well, I suppose they could have been, but that isn't why we were after them. Near the end, we were looking for The Dark Cloud. We don't know when they started."

"Who is we?"

"I was waiting here to question you four, not the other way around. I don't like to talk about my time on Earth. It cost me more than I ever thought I would have to pay."

Tal narrowed his eyes. "So, one criminal is still on Earth? Maybe we could help you find him."

Brake frowned. "Believe me, I have more reasons to want to go to Earth than you can imagine, but now isn't the time. I'm going to summon the rest of our people and tell them what happened," he said, standing. "I would suggest Graham practice his healing on the rest of you. And Tal? Your outfit looks ridiculous."

"Okay, hold still," Graham said, kneeling beside Wren's chair. He felt nervous. What if he actually threw up this time? Tal would never let him live it down.

"It's not bad," Wren said, cringing. "It doesn't need to be healed."

"Maybe not, but I need to practice," he said, trying to sound confident.

"Alright," she said, sighing.

"Okay, I can do this," he muttered, reaching out his hand. He placed it on Wren's cut and felt the heat going through his body and coming out his hand. Bile rose in his throat. He pulled away and groaned. The cut was gone.

"You look kinda pale," Tal said.

"Not just a little," Ming Li said, shaking her head. "I'm not sure how useful this talent is going to be if it makes you sick. You should ask for a refund."

"Hilarious," Graham mumbled, moving over to Tal. "Let me fix your eye."

"I don't want you puking on my shoes," Tal protested, "Or worse, on my stylish flamingos."

"Puke on the flamingos," Wren smiled. "It will be a service to us all." Wren and Ming Li giggled.

Graham sighed and put his hand over Tal's eye. Everything was spinning. He sat on the floor and held his throbbing head.

"That felt creepy, weird," Tal said, moving away from Graham.

"Are you okay?" Wren asked.

"I will be," Graham said.

"You can't do it all from within," Zera said from the doorway. Graham looked at the fleet member. She was wearing a long blue dress and her brown hair was hanging over her shoulder. She looked concerned.

"You got here fast," Ming Li said. "Did you learn to make portals?"

"No," she said, shaking her head. "I was already on my way here. Wren, Brake was wondering if you could make portals for the others. We should not be wasting your talent when it saves so much time."

"Sure," Wren said, leaving the room. Ming Li followed her.

"Stay sitting," Zera commanded, sitting on the ground in front of Graham. She blew into her hand and a glass of water appeared. She handed it to him and he sipped it. The cool water calmed his stomach.

"Most magic doesn't come free," Zera explained, arranging her dress around her as she spoke. "Healing is one of those."

"So he's going to get sick every time he heals someone?" Tal asked.

"If he keeps it up like this, then yes," she warned. "I did a lot of research in my younger days about healing because I thought I might want to be a healer. I ended up changing my mind."

"So a person can learn to be a healer?"

"Yes, and no. They can learn how to heal with herbs and knowledge, but it's been over two thousand years since anyone has healed with magic. Records show that people with magic would use herbs to enhance their healing. When they made medicine, it worked better because of the magic. We still have ways of mixing medicines that are very good, but they are nothing compared to what someone with your power can do."

"So, you're saying that I need to learn to do something that no one can teach me to do?"

"I'm afraid so."

"Medical school was always my dream, but I kind of figured I would have a bunch of people to teach me."

"I have a book," Zera said, holding out her hand and blowing on it. A thick, old, leather book appeared in her hand. She gave it to him. He carefully opened it. It looked like a recipe book. "It has the ingredients for different medicines. They should work better for you than anyone else."

"So do I mix it in a cauldron or something?" Graham joked.

"I suppose you could if you wanted to. I would use a mixing bowl, but whatever you feel comfortable with."

"This is overwhelming."

"I imagine so. It would be helpful to find a healer that can guide you." She tapped her fingers on her chin. "I will have to think about it. There are quite a few healers in Akkron. I need to think of who would be the most trustworthy."

"Not Gorbel," Tal said. "That guy is terrible. He's our family's healer. He's incredibly snooty."

"No, not Gorbel. He is on the governor's payroll, which means he is not suitable."

The door opened and with it, a flood of people. It was all the people from the night before, Karlof and a man they didn't know. Graham and Zera stood up and sat on chairs. Graham smiled to himself when he saw Professor Hedder's haircut and clean shave. Brake caught them all up on what had happened on Earth. Most of them were frowning.

"This shows that they are too young to make their own decisions," Austra said.

"I agree," added the man they hadn't met. He was heavyset, with a black comb-over that was poking out in all directions.

"Maybe we were careless, but we will not agree to be bossed around by you guys," Wren said. Graham nodded in agreement and he noticed Tal and Ming Li did as well.

"We can't let you go off getting into danger," Drew told his daughter. "I made a poor decision when I let you go today."

"We can't hide forever," Tal said. "The cave didn't open for us so we could spend the rest of our time in the jungle in an invisible house."

"We don't mean for you to hide forever," Brake said. "Everyone here is under a great deal of stress, and we don't want to be hasty. We would appreciate it if you would all cooperate until we can figure out what steps we need to take."

"I can cooperate for a short amount of time," Graham said.

"A very short amount," Ming Li agreed.

"Will you please agree to tell us before you go off on your own?" Brake asked.

"Only if you'll let us go if we all decide its best," Wren said.

"I can agree to that if you agree to listen if we have concerns," Brake said, raising his eyebrow.

"That sounds fair," Graham said, and the other three nodded.

"For now, you should stay here and work more on your magic. That's only until we all decide what to do," Brake said.

"This is all so troubling," Austra sighed. "It's too bad we don't live in the days of the silver eclipse. That would have solved some things."

"What's the silver eclipse?" Graham asked.

"A powerful magic," Zera explained. "Only a few people could summon the silver eclipse. It was a powerful silver mist or cloud. We aren't sure which. They would send some type of magic up to the moon, and there was an enormous boom and the world would shake. It would reset the weather. We do not know a lot about it."

"They only used it when things got out of hand. Too much magic affecting the air, that sort of thing," Brake added. "It made everything right again. There are only records of it ever being done three times."

"YEEEES!" Graham said, jumping up and punching the air. Everyone stared at him. "We are The Silver Eclipse!"

"What are you talking about?" Austra asked.

"That is the name of this group. We are now officially The Silver Eclipse." He dabbed. Some people groaned. Graham just smiled.

Austra shook her head. "That sounds ridiculous. And why do you get to say what is official?"

"You have all been meeting forever without a name. Someone needed to come up with something," Graham said, feeling smug.

"I can't believe you dabbed," Ming Li said, shaking her head. "I'm pretty sure that stopped being popular before I came here."

"How about this?" Graham said, flossing. He knew he was doing the dance move wrong, but he was excited. It was the perfect name. "Do you wanna see me moonwalk?"

Ming Li shook her head. "Nope, but later I'll teach you to floss correctly."

"I'm up for it," Graham said, sitting back down. Everyone was looking at him like he was crazy.

"It figures he needs to name us," said Professor Hedder. "He has an unhealthy obsession with naming things. Before long, he will name everyone's legs. Left and right won't be good enough for him. He will worry we will get confused and not know which is which."

"Nice haircut," Ming Li said, smiling. Professor Hedder glared at her and stopped talking.

"I have a question for the portal maker," the messy haired man said, turning to Wren. "There are records about secret portals that could be made and hidden. They wouldn't open without a password. Have you ever heard of this?"

"It sounds familiar," Wren said. "But I don't know anything about it."

"If you could figure out how to do that, imagine how convenient that would be for our group," he said.

"You mean convenient for The Silver Eclipse," Graham interrupted.

The man ignored him. "If you could make a secret portal between all of our houses and our meeting place here, we could all come at a moment's notice. We wouldn't have to fly here or wait for you to make individual portals."

"Tram has a point," Brake said, tapping on his leg. "It would make things a lot easier. Especially for people who don't want to be missed," he muttered, glancing at Drew and Zera.

"I agree," said Austra. "Should we vote?"

"Wait," Wren said, looking concerned, "I don't even know how to do it."

"It might be dangerous," Graham added. He had a feeling they were going to have a hard time getting a fair voice in this group. Everyone was still going to see them as kids.

"Dangerous how?" Brake asked.

"It would leave a portal for anyone to find."

"No one could find them except a person with a password," Tram explained. "It won't open without it or show up to anyone until they say it."

"Doesn't it feel like another way to make us vulnerable?" Graham didn't want to be the negative one, but he already had to stay hidden so people wouldn't use him to get into the cave. The portal sounded like another reason for people to want to find them. People would pay to have a portal.

"It seems like it would make things a lot easier, though," Tal said. "I mean, think about it. If we get split up or something, Wren is the only one who can get back without flying."

"I guess that's true," Graham said, nodding. "But it only takes one person to betray us and they can lead anyone here."

"That's also true," Brake agreed.

"Maybe there's a way to only let certain people in?" Ming Li added. "Like you need a password and something else? A fingerprint?"

"A password should be enough," Karlof spoke, in his gravelly voice. "This is a great idea."

"We need to remember that Wren doesn't even know how to do this," Graham said, watching Wren. She looked stressed.

"It's only an idea," said Tram. "I can send some books to her about portals. I have some old ones in my library. I've never studied them, so I don't know what's inside them."

"That would be great," Wren said, looking excited. "Can you summon them?"

"Sorry no," Tram apologized. "I haven't looked enough at them to know where they are exactly or what they look like. I just remember they're there."

"Okay, thanks. If we're going to be stuck here, can all of you can send us books that can help us with our magic?"

"It might take a while, but we can try," Zera said. "A lot of the valuable old books will not be hidden in a public library. We will have to search our own family books and ask around."

"I'll search my books," Austra said, "But not now. I'm about to be late for an important meeting."

"Let's all meet back in three days," Brake said. "Can you send everyone home, Wren? And in three days, bring them back?" Wren nodded.

"This meeting of The Silver Eclipse is officially over!" Graham said, slapping his leg.

Wren followed the adults out of the room. It might be nice for Wren to not have to open portals all the time. A permanent one would be good.

"How are we going to get this whole 'Silver Eclipse' name out?" Tal asked.

"Does it need to get out?" Graham asked. "I mean, it is a secret group."

"Yeah," Tal agreed, "But people will eventually assign us a name, if we don't do it ourselves."

"That's true," Ming Li said, "And they might come up with something way worse."

"Does anyone think Karlof is evil?" Tal asked, changing the subject. "He kept looking at me funny."

"He was probably staring at your clothes," Graham smiled. "I think everyone was looking at you funny."

"Fine, I'll go change," Tal sighed. "I'm telling you, though. I could make this style take off."

Tram was good to his word. Within an hour of leaving, he had sent a message to Brake, and Wren opened a portal so he could give her his books. He had three old books on portal making. They were large and boring, but some of the information was helpful. Wren had been studying them for two days. A lot of it was history and stories about people and what they accomplished with portals.

"You know you are super boring today, right?" Ming Li said from across their bedroom. She was painting her toenails bright orange. Wren was propped up on a bunch of pillows, reading.

"I know," she admitted, "But the faster we get a good grip on our magic, the faster we can do something."

"I guess," Ming Li said, blowing on her wet toenails. "The book Austra sent me is so boring. It's called *Controlling Your Inner Wind*," she said, rolling her eyes. "When Tal and Graham saw it, they laughed for a solid five minutes."

Wren smiled. Ming Li was not a fan of reading. No matter how many books Wren recommended to her, she never finished one. She would learn better from an actual person.

Brog cleared his throat from the doorway. "Sorry to bother you."

"You aren't a bother," Ming Li said, hopping off her bed.

"What do you need?" Wren smiled. She should have figured her friend would have a crush on a giant.

"Jaaz keeps asking to speak to one of you," he said, looking uncertain. "I keep telling him he cannot, but he is tiring me."

"Did he say why?" Wren asked. She didn't want to talk to Jaaz. Graham and Zera had talked to him. Even Austra had gone down there for a few minutes and then stomped back, muttering something about kids and the education system.

"No," Brog admitted, "Although I assume he wants to tell you he is innocent. He has been telling me since I have been guarding him. I have become an expert at blocking him out."

"We'll talk to him," Ming Li assured him, "And we will tell him to stop annoying you."

"It is my job to watch him," Brog said. "It does not bother me too much. Come when you are ready." He bowed his head and walked away.

"Do you have to have a crush on everyone?" Wren asked, putting a paper in her book to mark her place.

"What?" Ming Li said, looking shocked. "You think I have a crush on Brog? He's like a million times bigger than me. I mean, sure, he has that whole Thor thing going on."

Wren raised her eyebrow. She wasn't convinced. She knew her friend too well.

"Okay fine. But he isn't my crush," Ming Li said, making air quotes. "He's like my backup crush. Not even that, he's like my backup, backup crush."

Wren laughed. "It's good you're prepared." She stood and stretched.

"I guess we should go talk to Jaaz since you volunteered us. Should we take the boys?"

"Nah," Ming Li said. "They went outside to practice and I hope this doesn't take long. Do the stairs have carpet? I don't want to put boots on and ruin my toes."

"I don't know," Wren said, stepping into her boots. They left the room and walked down the hall to the door that led to the cells. Wren opened the door and smiled when she saw the carpet. They tramped down the stairs and entered a small white room. There were four closed doors. Brog was sitting on the floor reading a book. When they came in, he stood.

"Don't you get bored here?" Ming Li asked.

"No," Brog said, "I have spent my life training to be a guard. I can entertain myself."

"Were you training to be a guard at Meegore?" Wren asked.

"Yes, I wanted to help guard the crystal. When Brake told me about the mission to stop The Dark Cloud, I wanted to be a part of it. It sounds more helpful than standing outside a cave no one can enter. By keeping you safe, I am in a way guarding the crystal. If you four are safe, so is the cave."

"That makes sense," Ming Li said, smiling at him. "That's brave of you."

Wren shook her head. "Where's Jaaz?"

"He is in this room," Brog said, pointing at a white door. "You can go in, but you cannot pass the black line on the floor. He can't pass it either, so you are safe. You cannot use magic in there because of the rednax venom." He opened the door, and they squeezed past.

"It's about time!" Jaaz said, hopping off his bed.

The room looked like the one they were staying in. It had a bed and a wardrobe. A bookcase full of books took up one wall. It didn't look a thing like a prison ... unless you were Ming Li, of course. Jaaz didn't look like a prisoner. He was wearing a blue shirt and black pants that Ming Li had picked up when they were at the mall. He had some bedhead going on, but that was to be expected when you couldn't leave a room.

"What do you want?" Ming Li asked him, hands on hips. "We have better things to do than sit around talking to you."

"It's so boring here!" Jaaz moaned, "And that big giant guy won't listen to me. He nods and pretends to listen, but I can tell he isn't."

"You're a prisoner. It's not our priority to entertain you."

"Don't you think you are all being harsh? I mean, I didn't actually do anything wrong, I mean, besides listening to those bad guys. I didn't get to know anything, and I didn't know they were bad. They told me you could lead them to something that they lost."

"You knew they were planning to kill us," Wren said, eyes narrowed.

"I didn't," he protested. "I don't even speak that language. What was it called again?" They both looked at him. "They taught me what to say and told me what it meant, but they didn't tell me what they were saying, except the part they wanted me to tell you."

"So you did all this crazy stuff for some people that you didn't know?" Wren asked, raising her eyebrow.

"Well, yeah. It didn't sound like anything bad was going to happen. Plus, they made me believe I could go into the cave and get some super powers or something. It sounded pretty epic to me. I didn't think they might be bad guys. Besides, my dad was the one who told me I should help them, so I didn't dwell on it much."

"Your dad must be part of them," Wren said.

"Score," Ming Li said. "Now we know another member of The Dark Cloud."

"You think my dad is part of The Dark Cloud?" Jaaz laughed.

"It sure sounds like it," Wren said. "Why else would he have you help them?"

Ming Li rolled her eyes. "Are you really this dumb?"

"You might be right," Jaaz said, with wide eyes, "He is always disappearing at night and he won't ever say why!"

"I would reevaluate my life choices if I were you," Ming Li said. "You can't blindly follow any creepy person who wants you to."

"Do you believe me?"

"I do," Ming Li said, looking at Wren. Wren nodded. The Dark Cloud might have tricked Jaaz, but he had gone into it much too willingly. Believing him didn't make him innocent.

"So do I get to leave?"

"I doubt it," Wren said. "You still could have gotten us killed."

"And you know where we are. You could lead people here."

"I have no idea where we are. I haven't seen anything but this room." He waved his arms around. "I was knocked out when you brought me here, remember?"

"Right," Wren said, still thinking. She wasn't ready to believe him. Still, it wouldn't be nice to keep someone captive if they were innocent. "We can't just let you go because you say you're innocent. We're going to have to look into it some more."

"I could help you by spying on my dad," he said hopefully.

"Are you always ready to flip sides so easily?" Wren asked. "You trust whoever tells you anything? You trust your dad, The Dark Cloud, and us, and now you are ready to turn on your dad?"

"Well ... I am pretty trusting," he said, scratching his head. "It's gotten me into trouble a few times. Turning on my dad isn't hard, though. He isn't that nice of a guy. I should have known he was a bad guy."

"We'll bring all of this up to The Silver Eclipse tomorrow when we all meet," Wren said, "But I can't promise you anything."

"They might still want to keep you here even if you are innocent," Ming Li said. "You are a lot less annoying when you can't talk to anyone."

CHAPTER 16

I'm not ready to trust him," Brake said, as The Silver Eclipse met the next day. They all sat on the mismatched chairs, eating cookies that Ming Li's mom had sent with Brake. "Even if he's telling the truth, he made some awful decisions."

"I agree," said Zera and Austra at the same time.

"We should keep him locked up until we can prove it one way or another," Tram said, stuffing a whole cookie into his mouth.

"It worries me you are so easy to convince," Karlof grunted. "He shouldn't talk to any of them."

Graham wasn't sure what to think. Ming Li and Wren had told him and Tal about their conversation with Jaaz. They seemed to believe him. Graham thought it was likely he was telling the truth, but he was still a wild card.

"He isn't the brightest," Tal said, "But is it fair to lock him up for that?"

Drew shrugged. "It's not like he's suffering. He has a comfortable room and plenty of food."

"If we were sure he was guilty, we would have taken him to our real prison," said Brake.

"What do you mean, your real prison?" Tal asked, "I thought this was the real prison."

"No," Tram laughed, brushing cookie crumbs onto the floor. "The real prison is a lot more prison-y."

"Prison-y?" Wren asked, tilting her head. "Like with bars and stuff?"

"Yes," Brake admitted, "But it isn't a place for you four to worry about."

"I feel like we're supposed to be the superheroes here," Ming Li said, glaring. "So, shouldn't we get to know about all the prisons and stuff?"

"Superheros?" Brake asked, shaking his head.

Austra sighed. "This is why we shouldn't be putting the fate of our world in children's hands."

"Maybe not superheroes," Graham said, "But we are into this as deep as we can be. We can't walk away from whatever's happening, so we should get to know things."

"We have a prison that is heavily guarded. It's also hard to find," Zera told them.

"Zera," Brake shook his head.

"No Brake, they should know. They are as much a part of this as any of us."

Graham liked Zera more and more. She kept her eyes locked with Brake. He didn't look happy, but he finally nodded.

"We have other meeting places as well," she explained. "It would be careless of us to only have one. If one is discovered, we don't want to be without resources."

"That sounds smart," Graham said. "So, do we get to know where these other places are?"

"Eventually," Brake promised, "It isn't important right now though. We have a lot more pressing matters to deal with."

"Who's in the prison?" Ming Li asked, narrowing her eyes. "You told us you hadn't ever caught any Dark Cloud members before?"

"Is it the people you captured on Earth?" Graham asked Brake.

"We might have captured some of their members, but we aren't sure." Brake rubbed his forehead. "We aren't talking about that now."

"Wren, have you learned anything about the portals?" Karlof asked.

"I've learned a lot, but not how to make the ones you guys want."

"Have you read the books?" Tram asked, reaching for another cookie.

"Not all of them. I finished one and I'm halfway through the second."

"We had hoped you would make that a priority," Austra muttered.

"It's only been a few days," Wren protested.

"And she's been reading nonstop," Ming Li complained. "She has been totally boring."

"That's true," Tal said. "She's even been reading during meals."

"Those are enormous books to get through," Graham added. "Plus, she probably has to read some things twice to make sense of them. I know I do when I'm reading the books you all sent to me."

"I am happy to see the loyalty you have cultivated within your little group," Zera said, smiling. "It will be an advantage in the coming days."

"Wait!" Graham said, remembering something. "Jaaz has to be lying. He told you he didn't speak Flordillian, but when the plan didn't go as expected, The Dark Cloud told him things that couldn't have been rehearsed."

"That's true," Ming Li frowned. "Why didn't I remember that? And his Flordillian was perfect. He didn't have an accent."

"Alright," Brake sighed, "No more talking about releasing Jaaz."

"Should we have these four attend the Governor's speech tomorrow?" Tram asked.

"Absolutely not," Austra protested. "They cannot be out in public."

"Everyone will be wearing cloaks," Tram said, "So I don't see why they couldn't."

"What's the speech about?" Tal asked.

"He said he is going to address the problems in Akkron," Drew said, frowning. "All the fleet will be there."

"Can we go?" Wren asked her father. Drew looked at Brake and Brake sighed.

"How many people actually know we're the ones who opened the cave?" Graham asked. "I doubt anyone will go there looking for us."

"If everyone is going to be in cloaks, we'll blend in," Tal said, "And I want to know what my father is going to say."

"We're going," Ming Li decided. "We're part of the group and we will not stay here forever."

Zera's mouth turned down. "There is nothing to say you are safer here than anywhere else if The Dark Cloud has any way to track you. Still, I'm not sure it's safe to be in such a crowded place."

Wren shrugged. "Crowds are safer. Who's going to try anything in a crowd?"

"Let's vote," Tal said. "Who says we can go?"

Tal, Graham, Ming Li, and Wren's hands flew up immediately. Zera raised her brow and Tram, Brog, Karlof, and Brake shook their heads. Hamble and Drew raised their hands.

"Hamble, are you going to be so careless?" Austra huffed. "In a crowd that size, they can be snatched and no one will notice. Surely you won't place your daughter in danger, Drew."

"They shouldn't be in too much danger," Drew said. "But you are wrong about one thing, Graham. Everyone knows who you all are."

"How?"

"It came out immediately," Brog said. "The giants did not think as clearly as we should have and let your names be known."

"Oh," Graham said. That could make things difficult.

"I assume The Dark Cloud knows someone has you in hiding," Zera said. "They probably will not be expecting you there, but is it worth the risk?"

"I suppose I cannot go to help protect them?" Brog said.

"That wouldn't be a very good idea, my friend," Brake said. "You will draw attention we can't afford." Brog nodded.

"I don't think I can keep coming to these meetings for the time being," Drew said. "Governor Briggs is acting suspicious towards me. I'm pretty sure he's having me watched. I told him Wren hasn't been home since it happened, and I don't know why he doesn't believe that since he doesn't know where Tal is. Most of his suspicions about me have nothing to do with Wren, though. He probably knows I've been looking into him."

"He has been acting differently when you are around," Zera agreed. "It is for the best that you have less contact for a while."

"He keeps telling me to come a half an hour late to things," Drew sighed. "I think he wants to talk to the other fleet members before I get there."

"You probably shouldn't have come tonight if you are being watched," Austra sniffed. "You could put us all in danger."

"The governor doesn't know that we are using portals," Drew protested, "So even if he is having my house watched they won't know I left."

"He knows I can make portals though," Wren reminded them. "He saw me do it when Tal and I were getting away from him."

"I didn't think about that," Drew muttered.

"Okay, so we won't expect Drew for a while," Brake said. "Does anyone else have anything to add?" No one answered. "Alright, we're done for now."

"So, do we get to go tomorrow?" Graham asked.

"No," Brake said. "And the rest of us will go separately. It's best if nobody can link us. I want you all to stay here and stay out of trouble."

"Do you think you can do that?" Austra said, with narrowed eyes.

"No problem," Graham said. "No problem at all."

"I can't believe you lied to us," Ming Li said glaring at Jaaz. "I mean, I can believe it, but I can't believe I believed you."

"What are you talking about?" Jaaz asked, sitting cross-legged on his bed. Wren was going to let Ming Li deal with this one. Ming Li was mad and didn't want to go to the governor's speech until she confronted Jaaz. They decided they were going with or without permission.

She put her hands on her hips. "You do speak Flordillian, don't lie to me again."

"I told you. They taught me what to say."

"No, no. You were answering her questions which means you understood her. You don't even have an accent. A language isn't something you can learn that well and fast."

"I don't!" he protested.

"You're lying. Now we'll never trust you."

"Okay, okay, I speak Flordillian," Jaaz said, looking desperate. "I didn't think they would kill you though. I figured you were too valuable, although they did say they only needed one of you ..."

"We aren't even going to listen to anything you have to say again. I just wanted you to know."

"That's not fair! I can't stay here forever! It is so boring! Can't you let me go? I won't be on anyone's side. I'll go back to school and mind my business like I should have in the first place!"

"Not an option."

"Wren? You won't let them keep me here forever right?"

Wren sighed. She wished they'd never ended up with Jaaz. She knew they couldn't trust him, but she couldn't help feeling a little bad for him. He was like a little kid that wanted to fit in somewhere.

"What if I tell you something?" he said, hopefully.

"Like what?" Wren asked.

"I can't tell you unless you let me go."

"Not going to happen," Ming Li said, laughing angrily.

"But if you tell us, we might trust you more," Wren said.

"I'm not gonna tell unless I get something out of it." He sat on the bed with his arms folded. He looked like a pouting toddler. A massively tall toddler.

"How do we know that what you have to say is even worth anything?" Wren asked. "I thought you said you didn't know anything about The Dark Cloud."

"I don't. It's not about The Dark Cloud."

"You want us to let you go because of information that isn't even about The Dark Cloud? You are pretty pathetic," Ming Li said, shaking her head.

"I know who put the notes in your books."

Wren looked at Ming Li and raised an eyebrow.

"Ah, so you want to know," Jaaz said, smiling.

"Not enough to let you go," Wren said, crossing her arms.

"Not even close," Ming Li said, shaking her head. "That isn't actually information that changes anything."

Jaaz frowned. "Fine. I'll tell you who did it if you bring me a whole plate of Ming Li's mom's cookies."

"Fine," Ming Li said. "Who put the notes in our books?"

"You promise I'll get the cookies?"

"I promise," She said, rolling her eyes.

"It was me."

"What?" Wren and Ming Li exclaimed together.

"Yeah. I did it. I was too slow getting Tal's back to him. That's why I was at the window. I thought it was great luck at first, getting to become friends with you."

Ming Li ground her teeth. "We weren't friends."

"Well, I thought we would become friends. But that was the night my dad had me talk to The Dark Cloud."

"Wait ... You didn't talk to The Dark Cloud until that night?" Wren asked.

"Nope. I went home and told my dad everything that happened. He got really excited. He told two of The Dark Cloud members and had them come. They made a quick plan and told me how to help. They were excited that I could speak Flordillian because one of them could speak it."

"Hold on," Wren said, "If you hadn't talked to them before, why would you put the notes in our books? You had to know something about it."

"That wasn't The Dark Cloud, that was Coach Zalliah. She asked me to do it and not tell anyone."

"Why did she want us to go to Meegore?"

"I don't know. She gave me a hall pass to help her. That was enough for me. I hope you can see that you can trust me now that I've told you so much."

"Actually, I trust you less," Wren said.

"Seriously," Ming Li muttered, "You'll help anyone for a hall pass or a plate of cookies."

"Not the kind of friend we need," Wren agreed, shaking her head.

He frowned. "Does that mean I don't get any cookies?"

Ming Li rolled her eyes. "You'll get your cookies. We aren't liars."

"Do you think you could not tell the others all of this?"

"Why? So you can get something out of them?" Wren asked.

"It's not a bad idea."

"You should stop trying to have ideas," Ming Li said, "I don't think they agree with you."

"So it was Coach Zalliah," Tal said, pacing around the kitchen. "Not that it's surprising. We already thought it was."

"So did she see an aura around us and decided we weren't prepared enough to go to Meegore?" Graham wondered, drumming his fingers on the table. Brake sat next to him, deep in thought.

"Jaaz didn't know anything," Wren explained from the head of the table. "He was doing errands for Zalliah and she was rewarding him. He didn't care to find out why he was helping her."

"He's a little traitor," Ming Li muttered, sitting at the table across from Graham. "Well, a tall, skinny traitor. He's pretty much willing to do anything for a prize. We wouldn't do what he wanted, so he told us something for cookies. That's the type of person I'll never trust."

"Jaaz is a complicated situation," Brake said. "I don't know how we should deal with him. It seems like he is a greedy, misguided teenager. I don't think he's evil. Ming Li's right. We cannot trust him. He is bending in the wind towards anyone who will reward him. I wish we could let him go."

"Can't we?" Graham asked. He didn't think it was very useful holding someone who didn't know anything.

"No," Brake said, rubbing his chin. "He doesn't know where we are, but there's a chance he has overheard something he could tell The Dark Cloud."

"After they left him, I bet he isn't feeling very loyal to them," Graham said. "He might avoid them."

"I have no doubt he would tell them anything they wanted to know," Brake said. "All they would have to do is threaten him or bribe him and he would cooperate with them."

"That's true," Ming Li said. "That guy has no backbone."

"It might also be dangerous if we let him go. The Dark Cloud might not take his failure lightly. He might be a traitor, but I can't help but feel for him. He is still young and impressionable. I hope he can eventually see that his actions were not worth the consequences and he can make a better life. That also won't happen with his father. I'm hoping Brog will have a positive influence on him."

"So we still don't know what to do with him?" Tal asked, sitting.

"No," Brake said, shaking his head. "He also knows who some of our members are."

"Is anyone looking for him?"

"No. His parents are saying he's on a holiday. I assume it's because they don't want anyone to know he was helping The Dark Cloud. They probably know that they left him on the island and figure someone captured him."

"There's something I've been wondering about," Wren said to Brake. "How do you keep sending messages to everyone so fast?"

"Ah," Brake smiled, "I wondered if any of you would ever ask."

"So, are you going to tell us?" Graham asked.

"It's not a great secret. It's only kept from young people."

"How is that fair?" Ming Li asked, frowning.

"Do you realize what a mess it would be if teenagers and children could talk to their friends anytime they wanted, any hour of the day?"

"I could do that before I came here," Graham said. "It was called cell phones."

"Yes, cell phones." Brake shook his head. "I'm not ready to tell you all about my time on Earth, but I spent enough time there to know that cell phones were a tremendous waste of time for the young. Probably for more than just the young."

"What's a cell phone?" Tal asked.

Graham pulled his dead phone out of his pocket. He didn't know why he kept carrying it around. "This is a cell phone."

"What does it do?"

He handed him the phone, and Tal turned it around, examining it. "When it's powered, a screen comes up and you can type in a number and call someone. They use their phone, and you can talk to each other from almost anywhere on Earth. You can hear them like they are right next to you."

"Wow," Tal said, "That would be so convenient. I thought your world didn't have magic."

"It doesn't," Ming Li said. "It's technology, not magic."

"It sounds like magic to me," Tal said, and Wren nodded in agreement.

"That thing we drove in was like magic too," Wren said. "It was driving with no animals pulling it."

"We're getting off topic," Graham said, as Tal handed his phone back. "Are you going to tell us about the messages?"

"I suppose," Brake agreed. "It's something we rarely tell until after you become an adult. You have to promise not to teach it to your friends."

"Maybe you haven't noticed, but we are the only friends we've got right now," Ming Li said.

"I still want a promise."

"I promise," Graham said without hesitation. Ming Li was right. Who were they going to tell?

"Me too," Wren and Tal said.

"Ming Li?" Brake asked.

"Of course I promise."

"It's actually a very simple thing to do. All you do is cup your hands like this," he said, cupping his hands, "And you picture the person you want to send a message to and you whisper into your hands. The message goes right to them."

They all stared at him for a second.

"Seriously?" Ming Li asked. "That's it?"

"It would have been convenient to know this before," Tal muttered. "Kids should get to know this one. Parents are always wondering what their kids are doing. If they could do this, it would be so easy."

"It sounds super dorky though," Ming Li said. "I wish there were cell phones. At least it wouldn't look crazy."

"Younger children can't manage it. They don't have the concentration it takes to do it. It has been experimented with before."

"Let's try it," Graham suggested. "We can all go into different rooms. Can you talk to more than one person at a time?"

"You can, but most people don't because it's difficult to concentrate on multiple people. It can get garbled if you aren't concentrating properly."

"Can you talk to non-magic people?" Ming Li asked. Graham figured she was talking about her mom.

"Yes, but they can't answer back," Brake said. "That would take magic."

"I'm surprised my dad hasn't been yelling and threatening me to get home," Tal said.

"You can't do this with anyone."

"That would be too easy."

"You can only do it with people you have a connection with. A good connection. If you tried to talk to an enemy, it wouldn't work. If you try to talk to someone who wouldn't want to talk to you, it won't work. It won't work if it's someone you don't know well."

"So how do you get messages to those people?" Graham wondered.

"There are messengers in every city," Brake explained. "If you think you may need to send a message to someone in the city, you find a messenger you trust and develop a connection. We have a member in our group that lives in Akkron and is a messenger. He has proved very valuable.

You also need to know the general area the person you want to talk to is in."

"This is getting less and less cool," Ming Li said.

"It doesn't have to be a close area. It is enough to know the city they're in. If someone is lost, you can't call out to them and find them. You would have to search through every place they might be."

"That sounds exhausting," Tal said, "But still better than nothing."

"Let's try it," Wren said, standing up.

They all stood except Brake. "Make sure you whisper," he cautioned. "If you don't, it will sound like you are screaming right in someone's ear. When you whisper, it sounds like you're talking."

"I'll go to the first meeting room," Graham said, leaving the kitchen.

"I'll go in our room," Tal said, taking off down the hallway.

"You take our room," Wren told Ming Li.

Graham went into the meeting room and realized they hadn't decided who should talk to who. He sat on a blue chair and tried to decide what to do. Maybe he should wait and see if one of his friends would talk to him first. It might be depressing if nobody tried to talk to him, though. He would bet Ming Li and Wren would talk to each other.

"Can you hear me?" Tal's voice boomed into his head. He jumped. That was loud! It felt like Tal's voice was bouncing off his brain.

Graham cupped his hands and pictured Tal in his mind. *"You are supposed to whisper! I bet everyone in Akkron heard you!"*

"Right, sorry," Tal said a lot quieter, *"But we aren't in Akkron right now."*

"Exactly. I think you broke my brain."

"This is so awesome. Think of how helpful it will be. I can't believe the adults keep this stuff from us. It seems like it would have leaked out. I do feel a little peculiar talking into my hands like this."

"Maybe that's why you don't see people walking around talking into their hands. Nobody wants to look odd."

"Now that I think about it," Tal said, *"I can remember seeing a few people over the years doing it. I thought they were a little crazy."*

"I wonder if there's another way to do it. Once we aren't so busy, we should experiment."

"What if we whisper and don't do it into our hands?"

"I guess we could try," Graham whispered.

"I just did, and you heard me."

Graham dropped his hands and whispered into the air, *"All the adults know how to do this and none of them ever tried without cupping their hands?"*

"That is pretty sad. Everyone is too deep in tradition. No one likes change."

"I get that, but it seems a lot less dorky to do it without the hands. It still feels weird to be in a room all alone, whispering."

"I'm wondering if every crazy person I've ever seen talking to themselves was actually doing this."

"We should go tell the others. Maybe we'll surprise them all and they'll respect us a bit."

"Maybe," Tal laughed, a little too loud. *"I doubt Austra will ever respect us."*

Graham put a hand to his head. *"I'm getting a headache."*

"So am I, now that you mention it," Tal said.

Graham frowned. His head was pounding and his vision was blurring.

The door opened and Brake poked his head in. "I forgot to tell you. Only send brief messages. Don't have a conversation or anything. That will give you a colossal headache."

"Too late," Graham said, shading his aching eyes.

"Sorry. It's always best to be short and to the point. I better go tell the girls."

CHAPTER 17

I have an incredibly bad idea," Graham said the next morning over breakfast. He had spent part of the night tossing and turning with his horrible headache and part of it, thinking about The Dark Cloud.

Ming Li yawned. "If it's bad, do we have to hear it? My head didn't settle enough to sleep until the middle of the night."

"I'm always up for a poor plan," Tal said, tearing apart his toast and dunking it in milk. "I slept fine after I threw up. No more listening to Brake until he tells us all the small print."

"Is it about the speech tonight?" Wren asked, taking a small bite of eggs.

"No," Graham said. "We know that Professor Dovin is a member of The Dark Cloud. Why are we letting him run around free? He has to know who belongs to it and what they are doing. Shouldn't we be capturing him and bringing him here?"

"He would have to be a lot more useful than Jaaz," Tal agreed.

Wren's eyes widened. "You think we should go capture him?"

"I'm not positive," Graham said, running a hand through his hair. "We need to capture him soon, and we also need to talk to Coach Zalliah. She obviously knows something. I think they are the two people that could make a difference in what we should do next."

"So what's your idea?" Tal asked, picking pieces of toast out of his milk.

"That is so gross," Ming Li commented. Tal smiled and popped a piece into his mouth.

"Wren should go to the school and talk to Coach Zalliah." Wren dropped her fork. "Me?"

"Well, you are the only one who can open a portal. I thought a lot about it last night. You could let one of us through, but we wouldn't be able to get back. I also thought that you could take one of us with you … but she might talk to one of us better than with all of us. One on one is always better than talking to a crowd. It's also easier to sneak around alone."

"How would she keep from being seen?" Tal frowned. "If anyone sees her, it could be bad."

"Can you do that trick where you were invisible to Kaylee?"

"No," Wren said, tearing small pieces of her napkin and dropping them on the table. "That's an illusion, and it doesn't work on people from here."

"I should go with her," Ming Li said, narrowing her eyes.

"It would be better if I go alone," Wren sighed. "Graham's right. We need to talk to her. When should I do it?"

"Probably today," Graham said. "The more we know, the better."

"Ugh," Wren murmured, putting her hands over her face. She took a few breaths and looked up. "Coach Zalliah's prep period is in a couple of hours."

"You don't have to do it," Graham said. "We can come up with another way."

"No, I can do it. I'm just tired and I don't know what to say when I talk to her."

"Shouldn't we get permission from the rest of The Silver Eclipse?" Ming Li asked. "We promised them we wouldn't run off and do anything without asking them."

"They'll say no," Tal said. "They aren't into acting on anything."

"It's not like I'm going to try to capture Dovin or anything. I'm only going to talk to someone."

"Okay," Ming Li said, "But let it be known, I said we should ask the grown ups first."

Tal laughed. "Li is the one who wants to ask for permission?"

"Hey," Ming Li said, shrugging, "The more irresponsible you guys get, the more responsible I have to be."

Wren stepped out of a portal into the school gym. She hoped nobody had stayed after to talk to Coach Zalliah. No one was in the gym, but there were voices coming from the office. She took a deep breath and walked quietly over. The door was shut, but the voices were carrying outside. She pressed herself against the wall next to the door and listened. If she wasn't mistaken, Professor Dovin was in there.

"Don't come and talk to me during my prep," Coach Zalliah was saying. "I have things to do."

"I'm sure you think you do," he said bitterly. "My reason for being here is more important than anything you are working on."

Wren scrunched her nose. Definitely Professor Dovin.

"I've come to warn you," Dovin said. "We know what you are up to, and there are many people who don't like it."

"I don't know what you are talking about."

"You know exactly what I'm talking about," he huffed. "And I want you to go back to teaching and minding your own business."

"How dare you?" Zalliah spat, "Are you threatening me?"

"Of course not. A warning is not a threat."

"If you want to talk about someone who should go back to minding their own business, you should look in the mirror. You are getting caught up in things you are not admitting."

"I know you are trying to lead those kids. You sent them to Meegore."

"I don't know what you are talking about," she muttered. Wren could hear papers shuffling.

"Stay away from those kids! I don't need you meddling where you shouldn't."

"Why? Because it messes with your meddling?"

"Perhaps," he said. Wren could almost hear him smiling. "I'm watching you. I don't want you trying to contact them."

"All I did was give them a little help," Zalliah protested. "It would have been irresponsible to let them go to Meegore with no preparation. There is no way Wren would have made it through without the time I spent helping her prepare."

"Perhaps, but you were the one who gave them a time limit. It makes some of us wonder what your motives were. What did you want out of it?"

"I am their teacher!" Zalliah growled. "It is part of my responsibility to take care of my students. It's obvious you don't feel the same. I've seen no sign of you caring about anyone but you!"

"Keep away from them," Dovin said, swinging the door open. Wren covered her mouth with her hand and froze. Dovin slammed the door and stomped past her. She hoped he wouldn't turn around. Part way across the gym, he stopped and turned. He stared at her, but didn't look surprised. He walked back to where she stood.

Wren stared at him and dropped her hand. He looked at her with a small frown. She wasn't sure what to do. He was too close for her to open a portal. She could scream, but that might put her and Zalliah in danger. He reached for her arm and when he grabbed it, everything spun. When she opened her eyes, they were standing in a field of weeds and wildflowers.

"What happened?" Wren asked, shaking.

"It doesn't matter," Dovin said, looking at her with a scowl. "You sure have a bad habit of listening in on conversations you shouldn't."

"Or maybe you have a habit of having conversations you shouldn't be having," Wren said, standing taller, trying not to let him see her hands shaking.

He laughed. "That's true, but you still shouldn't eavesdrop. It can get you into trouble."

"I don't try to eavesdrop," Wren said, crossing her arms. "I can't help it if you are always talking about dangerous things."

"You are a hard one to figure out," Dovin said, walking slowly around her. She felt tense.

"Don't let me see you at the school again," he said. "And I don't want you to seek Zalliah."

"I don't actually care what you want," Wren said, hoping she sounded more brave than she felt.

"I'm going to let you go this time," he said, standing in front of her. "That makes two times I've let you go. Yes, I saw you in my office that day. I know you heard me talking to Melly. I could have done something about it, but I didn't. Next time, I won't let you go. I see the defiance in your eyes. You believe it's naïve of me to say I won't let you go? You think you can get away on your own. Let us be clear. You cannot get away from me if I decide you can't."

"You know I can cause trouble for you as well," Wren said, narrowing her eyes. "I know you are part of The Dark Cloud."

"Who is going to believe that?" he smiled. "I have an impeccable record. You have nothing except your word. The cave at Meegore opened and now you have a confidence you haven't earned."

Wren's mouth opened and closed. She glared at him then turned and ran. She placed her hands together to open a portal and pulled them apart. Nothing happened. Panic raced through her. She kept running.

"You see what I mean?" Dovin called. "If I want to stop you, I can."

"So he can block your power?" Graham asked, sitting on his bed. This was something he hadn't ever taken the time to worry about.

"He can block my portals at least." Wren said, sitting on the floor with her back against Tal's bed.

"And he just let you go?" Tal asked, leaning against the wall with his arms folded.

"Yes," Wren sighed, "I ran until I was sure he wasn't following me and then I could open the portal again."

"He must be super powerful," Ming Li shuddered, sitting next to Wren. "It's crazy that he can get around without opening a portal."

"It might have been a portal, but not the kind I make."

"I shouldn't have had you go," Graham said, looking at his hands. "It was too dangerous."

"Are we going to tell the adults?" Tal wondered. They all sat looking at each other.

Wren nodded. "We probably should. If The Dark Cloud can block some, or all of our magic, they need to know. It could put people in danger."

"I agree," Graham said, nodding. It would be irresponsible to not let them know. "We're going to get another lecture, though."

"I wonder where Zalliah fits into everything. She isn't part of The Silver Eclipse. Is she just a nice person trying to help us?"

"Who knows," Ming Li shrugged. "It makes sense that most people aren't part of any group. Maybe she saw an aura and knew how to help us."

"Why did she send us to Meegore, though? And only give us two days?"

"Does anyone feel like their life has gone from super boring to super crazy?" Tal asked. "I remember back in the good ol' days when all I had to worry about was avoiding my father and doing my homework."

"Come on Talon," Ming Li said, "You know you wouldn't go back. This is so much better than school."

"I actually like school, but I prefer hanging out with you guys to all those snobs I used to hang out with."

"You're the only snob we hang out with," Ming Li smiled, throwing his pillow at him.

He caught it and threw it back. "I'm glad you made an exception for me."

"One thing I have noticed is that we're either bored or way too crazy these days," Graham said. "I'm hoping the speech tonight is just boring."

"Oh, it will be boring," Tal assured him, "But that doesn't mean it won't be crazy."

Wren looked at her friends. They were a block away from the area Governor Briggs would make his speech. It was a bit of a walk since they didn't want anyone to see them come out of a portal. Graham, Ming Li, and Tal were wearing dark shirts and pants under their cloaks. Wren was the only one wearing a dress. She didn't have any black shirts. She pulled her red hair back into a careless ponytail and pulled her hood over it.

"Are we ready?" Wren asked.

Ming Li shrugged. "What is there to be ready for? All we do is go listen."

"And spread some rumors," Tal said, smiling.

Graham looked out of the side of his eyes at Tal. "What do you mean?"

"You heard the adults. There aren't many rumors about them," Tal explained. "Is that a good thing? People know The Dark Cloud is out there. They might try to ignore it, but they know. Don't you think they should know there are good guys out there, too?"

"So, what do you plan to do?"

"Send out a few whispers."

"I doubt the others would approve."

"Yeah, well, what are they actually doing? They've been working together forever and have they accomplished anything?"

"I'm sure they have," Wren said. "They haven't actually talked to us about the things they've done."

"Maybe that's because they haven't done anything."

"That's not true," Wren argued. "My mom died doing something for them."

"But what?"

"I don't know."

"If people don't know, what good does it do? People have to have hope. They can't have hope if they don't know anything."

"That's true," Graham said. "But let's not overdo it, okay?"

"No overdoing," Tal agreed. "It's amazing what a few whispers can do."

They turned the corner and walked to the Governor's Fleethouse. It was a large building that Wren thought was a castle when she was little. The large brass gate was open, and they packed people in the courtyard. The governor always gave speeches from a balcony in the front. Everyone was wearing a cloak. Most of them were colorful, because this was a public event. People liked to wear more color when there were a lot of people gathered together.

"We might look a little suspicious standing together," Graham whispered. "There aren't a lot of dark cloaks."

"That's what I was thinking," Tal said. "You and Li go stand over there and me and Wren will go to that side."

Graham and Ming Li walked in the direction Tal had pointed, and Wren followed Tal. They stopped in a spot that wasn't too crowded.

"They're more people than usual," Wren said, looking around.

"Yeah," Tal agreed. "People know something is happening and don't want to miss anything."

"I don't recognize anyone so far."

The woman next to them was gossiping loudly to her neighbor. "I can't believe what she was wearing!" The woman said, "Everyone knows you don't wear red with purple unless it's a special occasion. And she is in the fleet for goodness sakes! She should at least talk to her consultants before going into public."

"Too easy," Tal whispered to Wren. He positioned himself beside the woman and turned so she couldn't see his face, but she could still hear him. "Did you hear about The Silver Eclipse?" he said to Wren. He wasn't being loud, but the group near them could all hear if they were paying attention.

"The Silver Eclipse?" Wren asked, "Like the old magic?" She wasn't sure what Tal wanted her to say.

"The Silver Eclipse is the group that is fighting against The Dark Cloud."

"Did You hear that?" The gossiping woman said to her friend. Tal backed away into the crowd, and Wren followed. He grabbed her arm and led her far enough away they couldn't see the woman anymore.

"Are you going to do that a bunch of times?" Wren asked.

"Nah," Tal smiled at her. "I'm done."

"Seriously? That's all you wanted to do?"

"It's enough for now. That woman will get it around fast enough, plus there were at least four other people that probably heard."

"You didn't say much."

"I didn't need to. Trust me."

Someone bumped into Wren. "I always hate these things," she admitted. "They're so crowded."

"Not to mention boring. I haven't been allowed to miss a single one."

"Here they come," Wren said, pointing to the balcony.

The crowd fell silent. The seven fleet members filed out onto the balcony. They were all wearing blue tunics, dark pants and capes. The tunics had golden pins attached to them. They had a small picture of a golden ship. You couldn't see it from where they were, but Wren had seen it enough she had it memorized. They stood in a line. Petral, Drew, Anelle, Lyna, Zera, Mav, and Jayla. Everyone clapped.

"And here comes the King," Tal said.

The fleet members stepped back and moved to one side, leaving enough space for Governor Briggs to step through. He stepped to the center of the balcony with a big smile on his face. "Boo," Tal said, so low Wren wasn't sure he said it.

"Welcome!" Governor Briggs said, raising his arms in the air. The crowd clapped. "I know you are all here with questions. I will briefly explain what is going on in Akkron and then the press are welcome to come in and get a more detailed version."

"There are concerns regarding the Island of Meegore," he said. "The cave has been opened. As many of you know, my son was one of those who opened it. We have little information, as the four have all gone missing. We are doing all in our power to find them." The audience clapped again. Wren felt a knot in her stomach. What would happen if they were found? "If anyone knows of their whereabouts, I will reward them."

"Lovely," Tal whispered.

"There has also been some concern over a group called The Dark Cloud. We know you are all concerned. The Dark Cloud has been creating chaos all over the continent. The weather is out of control in many areas because of them. Akkron, thankfully, has not had to deal with those problems at this time.

"It pleases me to announce to you all that we have discovered one of their members," he smiled. The audience gasped and began whispering among themselves. The fleet members shared confused looks with each other.

"Why do I feel nervous?" Wren whispered.

"Because there's no way for this to be a good thing," Tal said, keeping his eyes on his father.

"Fleetman Drew, step forward," Governor Briggs said, still smiling. Wren gasped. Had her father turned someone in? Did he tell the governor about Jaaz? Her father stepped forward. He looked nervous. "Fleetman Drew, you have been accused of belonging to The Dark Cloud." A gasp followed by a hush fell over the audience.

"No," Wren whispered, grabbing Tal's arm for support. He frowned and put his arm around her shoulders. The other fleet members were not reacting, but a few looked like they were holding some emotion in.

"There has been evidence of Fleetman Drew sneaking around and meeting with people in secret. He will be tried and punished."

"Why is he still smiling?" Wren said through gritted teeth.

"Because he's evil." Two of the governor's guards came onto the balcony and took Drew by the arms and escorted him out.

"You are wrong!" Someone called from the audience, "If anyone is part of The Dark Cloud, it's the governor!"

"Yes!" Someone else shouted, "Down with Governor Briggs!"

"Fleetman Drew is being framed!" called another.

"He has deceived us all," said the governor. "I understand your anger. He seemed like a nice man, but it has all been a game to him and The Dark Cloud!"

"What about The Silver Eclipse?" someone called out.

"The what?" asked Governor Briggs.

"Does The Silver Eclipse think he's part of The Dark Cloud?" a woman called.

"I told you," Tal said, "It's already gotten through the crowd."

"I'm not sure what you are talking about," the governor said, a smile plastered on his face.

"I won't believe he is Dark Cloud unless The Silver Eclipse says so!" a man yelled.

"The press is welcome inside in five minutes," the governor said, waving and walking inside. All the fleet members followed. The crowd milled around, arguing with one another.

"We should leave," Graham said, coming to them with Ming Li at his side.

"We have to help my dad," Wren said as they pushed through the crowd. She felt like she might be sick.

"We can't do anything right now."

The crowd wasn't leaving, so it was hard to make their way to the gate.

"I feel like we should do something more." She couldn't imagine her father in prison. "What good are we doing if we hide?"

"So let's not hide," Ming Li said, grabbing Wren's arm and pulling them onto an enormous boulder to the side of the gate.

"My dad loves this stupid rock," Tal said, jumping up next to them. "He might put us in prison just for touching it."

Graham climbed up. They all turned to the disorganized crowd.

"Quiet!" Ming Li yelled, pushing down her hood. Her black hair blew in the breeze. The crowd all turned and looked at them. Wren pushed her hood off, and so did Tal and Graham.

"I actually have nothing to say," Ming Li whispered so only they could hear.

"Don't let the governor do this!" Wren called to them. "Don't let him wrongfully accuse people! Anyone could be next!"

"Uh-oh," Graham said, "I see some guards coming through the crowd."

"My father is corrupt!" Tal yelled, "Don't let him ruin Akkron!"

"It's the governor's son," someone nearby whispered. "Those must be the kids who opened the cave!"

"The Silver Eclipse is your best hope!" Tal yelled, then turned and said, "Let's get out of here." They leaped off the rock and ran out the gate. The governor's guards were right behind them. "A portal would be nice right about now," Tal said as they ran.

"They're too close," Wren said. "If I open one they could follow us through."

"I've got it," Ming Li said, turning and knocking them over with a gust of wind. Wren opened a portal, and they ran through.

CHAPTER 18

"We need to stop landing like this," Graham groaned, sitting in the dirt. "Tal landed on my head." he rubbed his head and stood up. Ming Li and Wren were already brushing the dirt off of their cloaks.

"It didn't feel that good on my backside either," Tal said, still sitting on the ground. "You've got a hard head."

"Haha," Graham said, looking towards a noise in the bushes.

"It's a rednax," Tal said, looking to where Graham was staring.

Graham stepped back. "How do you know that?" He'd never seen a rednax, but he had heard plenty.

"I just do." Tal stood and walked over to the bush. "Should I get him out so you can see him?"

"No!" Wren, Ming Li, and Graham all said together.

"We have enough to worry about without smelling like Rednax," Ming Li shuddered.

"We have to figure out how to help my dad," Wren said, kicking at the dirt.

"There's no way the fleet will convict him," Tal assured her. "My father might be corrupt, but the fleet members are decent for the most part."

"And Zera is there," Ming Li said, "She can convince them."

"She has to be careful though," Wren explained, "She doesn't want the same thing to happen to her. She's useless if she's captured."

"Let's go in before we run into the rednax," Graham said, climbing the tree. He wished animals didn't scare him so much. With any luck, his friends wouldn't find out about his fear of spiders ...

"I've noticed I don't feel drained after I open portals anymore," Wren said, climbing behind him. "It must be one benefit of Meegore. I still feel tired when I open them, but not the same at all. When I bring all The Silver Eclipse here, I feel pretty drained, but I can still do it."

"I don't feel drained when I use a little wind," Ming Li said, from behind her, "But when we were at the mall and I was holding down those two creeps, it felt hard. And tiring."

"I wish healing things didn't make me want to hurl," Graham said, as he fell into the hideout. He hurried off of the cushion before anyone else fell in. He entered the kitchen and grabbed a glass of water. What were they going to do? He didn't know enough about the government to know how they could help Drew. He was pretty sure Wren was holding back tears.

"At least the speech was short," Tal said, entering the kitchen. "He usually goes on forever. The poor press will get the long part I guess." He sat at the island and grabbed a banana and started peeling it. "He must have been going for shocking the crowd."

"Where are the girls?" Graham asked, sitting across from Tal.

"They went to their room," Tal said, biting the banana. "Wren was about to cry and didn't want me around."

Graham frowned. Now was probably not the time to tell Wren about Karlof. She had enough to deal with. "When we were out there, we saw Karlof."

"Oh, yeah?"

"Yeah. When the governor had Drew arrested, Karlof smiled."

"Are you sure?"

"Positive. Ming Li saw it too."

"So what does that mean?" Tal wondered, tossing his banana peel at the garbage.

"I can only think of two things. Either Karlof isn't actually on our side, or it's part of a plan the adults have and we aren't in on it."

"Which one would be better? I mean, if Karlof is a member of The Dark Cloud he knows too much. He knows where we are."

"Yes," Graham agreed, "But if the adults have a plan without us, that's bad too. They can't leave us out of something that big. Could Drew have gotten arrested on purpose?"

"It's possible, but what would be the benefit?"

"I don't know," Graham admitted. "Is Karlof Drew's brother?"

"If I remember right, he was Wren's mom's brother."

"Maybe he doesn't like Drew and was glad they'll lock him up?"

"I have no idea," Tal said. "So what do we do?"

"I don't know."

"Perhaps he smiled out of stress? Karlof looks like a bad guy. Just like my dad, so if he is bad, my theory is right. It's those evil eyebrows."

"They don't look alike at all."

"There are different ways to look bad," Tal said. "My dad has the 'handsome bad guy' look. Karlof has the 'I've been in lots of fights' bad guy look."

Graham breathed deep. None of this was getting them anywhere. "I guess we have to wait until someone gets back from the speech so we can ask them."

"Should we check on Wren?" Tal asked. "I'm not good at helping in these kinds of situations. It's so awkward."

"Me either," Graham admitted. "If she's crying, she probably doesn't want to see us right now."

"She's pretty tough. We should probably give her some time and then she'll be fine."

"Wren is tough?" Graham said, raising an eyebrow.

"More than people give her credit for," Tal said. "I've known her forever. Not well, because she never liked me. I've watched her over the years and she is always the first one to do what's right. She's brave too. I've seen her stand up to other kids that were bullying people."

"Is something going on with you two?" Graham asked.

"What do you mean?" he asked, chuckling.

"I mean you two keep ending up together whenever we split up."

"That's mostly coincidence," Tal argued. "At Meegore we didn't realize we would end up separated from you after the slides, and she had to go with me to see my dad because she's the only one who can open a portal."

"Yeah, but today you chose her to go with you." It didn't matter, but he was curious.

"That was only because she was standing closer to me and Li was standing by you."

"You said it's 'mostly' a coincidence."

"So? What are you saying? You think I've secretly had a crush on Wren for years and now that she's finally talking to me I'm trying to seize the opportunity?"

"I was just wondering."

"Why are you asking? Are you interested in Wren?"

"No!" Graham answered a little too fast. He wasn't, was he? He liked her of course. But he liked all of them. She did have excessively pretty hair and stunning green eyes. He also liked the way she wanted to do the right thing. She was willing to leave her comfortable life to change the world.

"That was a very defensive no," Tal said, smiling.

"It wasn't."

"It seems like a strange time to bring this up."

"I was just curious," Graham said, wishing he hadn't said anything. "I thought you liked Ming Li at first. You tease her a lot."

"She's always been fun to tease. I used to tease her before we were friends, I always wanted friends like Wren and Li.

Since everyone thought I was stuck up, I only got to be friends with stuck up kids. It's so annoying to be around that all the time."

"People *thought* you were stuck up?" Graham smiled, raising an eyebrow.

"I'm not stuck up, I'm confident."

"You are totally stuck up," Ming Li said entering the kitchen. Graham's face felt hot. He wondered how long she had been there. She sat next to him on a stool. "If you're hot, and you know you're hot, and you act like you're hot, you're stuck up."

"Not stuck up," Tal smiled, "Able to accept the truth."

"Graham is as hot as you are and you don't hear him saying it," Ming Li said, putting her elbows on the island and resting her face on her hands. Graham groaned but smiled. He sipped his water. "And me and Wren are both pretty, but we don't go bragging about it."

Graham snorted, and water came out his nose. He hoped Tal didn't notice through his own laughter.

Ming Li looked at them both and shook her head. "You really shouldn't be laughing. Wren is in our room with puffy eyes trying to pull herself together."

Graham and Tal stopped laughing. "Is she going to be okay?" Graham asked.

"Yeah, she cried for five minutes and now she's mad. I'm not even sure who she's mad at. She's pacing around the room muttering about Briggs, Brake, Drew, pretty much everyone. I think she wanted to be alone, because she told me to come check on you guys."

"Did you tell her about Karlof?" Graham asked.

"You mean about his creepy smile? No. I didn't think she needed anything else to worry about."

"Do you think Karlof is with The Dark Cloud?"

"No. I think he just doesn't like Drew."

"Why?"

"Karlof blames Drew for getting Wren's mother killed," she explained. "He said he was over it, but I assume he wasn't. He's probably happy he's getting punished for something."

"That's a better option," Tal said. "If he is part of The Dark Cloud, our meeting house would be compromised. Plus, he knows who all the adults are. He could make it terrible for them."

Wren came into the kitchen. Her eyes were red, and a little swollen. "I heard someone come in. Was it Brake?"

"Yes," Brake said, entering the kitchen behind her. He eyed all of them with the look they all hated. The one that felt like he was gazing into your soul and judging you. "Are you alright?" he asked Wren. She nodded. "What do you all think you were doing?" His voice was controlled, but sounded angry.

"When?" Tal asked.

"Oh, I don't know ... When you went to the speech when you were told not to. When you announced The Silver Eclipse to the world. When you revealed yourselves. When you blew over the governor's guards and jumped through a portal in front of everyone. You choose."

"The world needs hope," Graham said. "Now they know that someone is fighting on the right side."

"Now instead of people wondering what you are all doing, they know," Brake said, frowning.

"Good," Tal said. "I want people to know that I'm working on a good cause. I don't want to be linked to my father."

"But now they know we don't have any element of surprise," Brake said. He sat at the table and looked tired. "Now The Dark Cloud will be more careful."

"The Dark Cloud already knew," Ming Li said. "We just let the rest of the world know. Now they can choose sides."

"We don't want people choosing sides. We wanted to deal with The Dark Cloud without involving the world."

"You can't solve an entire world's problems without involving people," Graham said. "How long have you been trying to capture The Dark Cloud? What have you all risked? Has there been any progress?"

Brake sighed and rubbed his eyes. "We have all been trying. You don't understand. You don't know what some of us have lost. We have made progress, and we have stopped certain people. Whether they were Dark Cloud or not is irrelevant. We don't advertise it because we are being careful. It won't do any good if they all go into hiding."

"You guys can be careful," Wren said, "And we're going to do something."

"I don't want you to act hastily, Wren," he said. "Acting when angry is never a good idea."

"I'm not talking about doing something crazy," she said, crossing her arms and glaring. "I know we can't break my dad out. He's bragged to me about how well the governor's prison was built. I tried to whisper a message to my dad, but it didn't work."

"No, they would have precautions to stop that. So, what do you think should be done?"

"You can all keep hiding," she said. "You all have your places in Akkron. We don't. Everyone knows who we are and what we're doing. The four of us should fight this a little more forcefully."

"I agree," Graham said.

"Me too," Tal added.

"If we aren't trying to blend in, I'm wearing my new jeans." Ming Li said.

"You don't want to stand out too much," Brake said.

"What should we do?" Graham wondered.

"We should go to Meegore again," Wren said. "We need more magic. Afterwards, I think we need to go to Boztoll. We can try to help them get rid of the clouds."

"None of this will help your dad," Graham said. He thought she would want to do that as soon as she could.

"I know, but we might have to leave that for the rest of The Silver Eclipse. Hopefully, the fleet will vote to free him. If the majority vote, they can overpower the governor's vote. I'm hopeful the people will help as well. My dad is popular in the polls."

"What if we help the people in Boztoll and take them in small groups to Meegore?" Graham suggested.

"That way, they could all get magic and they wouldn't be loyal to my father," Tal said.

"I'm not sure that's a good idea," Brake said, "And not safe."

"We wouldn't advertise. We could do it slowly. Wren could take people by portal and only take one or two people at a time."

"It would take a while," Wren said. "But if everyone at Boztoll could have magic, they wouldn't have to be scared anymore."

"It sounds good to say out loud," Brake said, "But if you think it through, it isn't as cut and dry as you think. If everyone who isn't magic gets magic, you have a bunch of people who have never been taught magic running around untrained. That could cause a hundred problems of its own. There are also quite a few of them that might hold grudges."

"Okay, I get that," Wren said. "We'll have to figure out a way to do it safely. I'm not giving up on it."

"First, let's concentrate on figuring out how to get rid of the clouds," Tal said.

"It's pretty obvious what we have to do," Graham said.

"And that would be what?" Ming Li asked.

"We have to leave," Brake said with wide eyes.

"How would that help?" Ming Li asked.

"Zera sent me a message. She said we need to get out of here immediately."

"Where's Walter?" Graham asked.

"He's always with Brog," Tal said. "I'll go tell him we need to leave."

"I'm here," Brog said, walking in. He had Jaaz slumped over one shoulder, and Walter was bouncing around beside him. "I have superb hearing," he said, bowing his head and giving Graham a look he didn't understand.

Brake pulled a map out of his pocket and showed it to Wren. "Can you take us here?"

"Yes," she said, taking a deep breath. She opened a portal. "Careful how you step. It looks like it's raining."

Graham sighed as they all stepped through. He had been hoping for a good night's sleep before a long day of planning. It didn't look like that was going to happen. He stepped through the shimmery portal and came out on his feet. That was the first thing that had gone right today.

Wren looked around the old cabin. It was almost the opposite of the meeting house. It was made of logs and only had minimal furniture. The rain was pounding on the roof and they were all dripping on the floor. Everyone was folding their arms and shivering. The only one who seemed to be happy was Walter.

"It's not as bad as it looks," Brake said, lighting a fire in the fireplace.

"It looks like it's probably full of spiders," Graham said, shivering.

The cabin was only one room, and it had a staircase going down. "The basement should be full of supplies."

"I will go look," Brog said, putting Jaaz on the floor. He was snoring quietly. Brog must have given him some ailam powder.

Wren was so tired. She felt like she could sleep for two days at least. Her friends probably felt the same. They all looked tired, and no one was talking. They all stood there, shivering. Brog came back up the stairs with an armful of blankets and clothes and handed them around.

"We'll go change downstairs," Ming Li said, grabbing Wren's arm and dragging her down with her. Once they got downstairs, Wren felt a small surge of relief. The downstairs looked a lot better than the upstairs. It looked more like the last place. It was painted white and had shelves full of supplies.

Wren yawned as she looked at the clothes Brog handed her. "This is the ugliest color of green I've ever seen," she said as she pulled it over her head.

"It looks like there's a lot of stuff on the shelves," Ming Li said, pulling on a dry pair of pants. "You could find something else."

"I'm too tired," Wren admitted, wrapping the blanket around herself. It felt wonderful.

"Do you think the boys are done?"

"I don't know," Wren said, sinking to the floor. She was glad it had carpet. "They can come find us when they're done." Ming Li followed her example, wrapping herself in her blanket.

"I guess we should have worn our cloaks when we left," Ming Li yawned.

The next thing Wren knew, she was being shaken out of sleep. "What is it?" she mumbled.

"Zera is here," Graham said, leaning over her.

Wren sighed and stood up. Ming Li was already standing. They walked up the stairs. "How long was I asleep?" she asked.

"About four hours," Graham told her. "We were all asleep when she came in."

Zera stood in the cabin, looking like a drenched cat. Wren's eyes widened. She had never seen Zera like this. She was wet and shivering, and her hair was a mess. Mud covered her boots and the hem of her dress. Brake was wrapping a blanket around her, and Brog handed her something hot to drink. A large crate stood beside her.

"How did you get here?" Ming Li asked. "You look terrible."

"Yes, thank you, Ming Li," Zera said, taking a sip from her mug. "I came by unicorn. I didn't have time to find anything more suitable."

"Is that my mom's hot chocolate? Why didn't we get any?" Ming Li asked, glaring at Brog.

"You were all asleep when I finished it," Brog replied. "I assumed you needed to sleep more."

He went back to an old stove and ladled more hot chocolate into mugs. Everyone watched him. Wren didn't know why she felt so numb. Even her brain felt numb. She wondered if the others felt the same. They needed to sleep better. Brog handed everyone a mug, and they all stood slowly sipping.

"Are you going to tell us why we're here?" Ming Li asked. She seemed to be the only one who wanted to talk.

"We should sit," Zera said, looking at the three old chairs in the room. They looked like they were full of splinters. She sat on the floor and the rest of them followed. Wren thought of how funny they must look sitting on the dusty floor, wrapped in blankets, drinking hot chocolate.

319

"Do you think the fleet will let my father go?" Wren asked.

"I am not sure," Zera said, looking into her hot chocolate. "I hope they will, but I cannot be certain. All of us were surprised. The fleet does not want to make any decisions while they are still in shock."

"And we are here because?" Tal asked.

Zera sighed, "Karlof has agreed to testify against Drew."

"What?" Wren exclaimed, trying not to burst into tears. She was too tired to cry.

"I am not sure about all the details. I only know that he sent word to the governor. They also granted him temporary custody of Wren."

"That doesn't make sense," Wren muttered. "He knows I'm not going to be home."

"I knew his smile meant something," Graham said, yawning.

"I had you all come here because we can't trust Karlof now. He knows where the meeting place is."

"He doesn't know where this one is?" Tal asked.

"Karlof wasn't an official part of our group," Brake said, "He only came to meetings occasionally. That was the only one of our places he has ever been to."

"I am not saying he is with The Dark Cloud," Zera said. "I believe this is more of a personal matter between brother-in-laws. We can't be sure though, so we need to cut ties with him. If he was Dark Cloud, he could have betrayed us many times. He knows a lot of our plans."

"Could he have been the one that told The Dark Cloud when we were on Earth?" Graham wondered. "He could have overheard when we were talking to Drew."

Zera set her mug on the floor. "It's possible, but it is also possible it was someone else. I am not ready to blame him for that yet."

Wren wanted to cover her ears. Karlof looked scary if you didn't know him, but he had been like a second father to her. A strict, grumpy second father, but still. They all sat in silence, listening to the rain hit the roof.

"What's in the crate?" Wren asked.

"Oh, that is Ben," Zera said. "I didn't want to leave him with Karlof, so I stopped by and grabbed him."

Wren untangled herself from her blanket and got to her feet. She wasn't as stable as she would like to be. She walked over and opened the crate. Ben was sound asleep.

"It wasn't easy carrying that here on a unicorn," Zera admitted. "He didn't seem to mind though."

"Thanks for bringing him," Wren said, rubbing his back. It sounded like he was purring.

"Do you all need to go into hiding now?" Graham asked. "Karlof knows who you all are."

Brake and Zera looked at each other.

"I do not believe Karlof is part of The Dark Cloud," Zera said. "I am not willing to give up my place on the fleet. I will risk it and trust Karlof will not turn us in."

"We can let all the others choose for themselves." Brake added.

"We should capture Karlof and we won't have to worry," Tal said, frowning. "It's the most logical option. We need to act more. We were all talking about it this morning. If we capture the people we know are bad, we can question them, lock them up, and stop worrying about them."

Brake shook his head. "Not that simple."

"It actually is," Ming Li said. "You all overthink things."

"And you underthink them," Brog said. They all turned to look at the giant. He had been standing silently by the stove. "What do you suppose would happen if members of The Dark Cloud disappear? You will have more people out looking for you."

"Brog is right," Brake said, rubbing his chin.

"And remember what happened this morning," Brog said, tilting his head and looking at Wren.

"What happened this morning?" Brake sighed.

Brog shrugged. "I told you, my hearing is superior."

"I went to talk to Zalliah," Wren admitted.

"That was careless," Brake said. "What did you talk about?"

"Nothing," Wren said, looking at the floor. She explained what had happened with Dovin. Brake paced and Zera sat frowning.

"So he can block your magic and he can transport," Brake said, still pacing, but now he was rubbing his head. "Were you going to tell us all of this if Brog hadn't ratted you out?"

"Things have been happening too fast," Wren said, throwing her hands up defensively. "By the time we process one thing, something else happens."

"They have also talked of capturing Dovin," Brog nodded.

"I can't believe you're squealing on us, Brog," Ming Li frowned. "We trust you."

"It is only what they need to know," he said.

"We should send Jaaz home before he wakes up," Brake said, looking over to where Jaaz slept. "It would be best for him to not even know we left the last place."

"Is that a good idea?" Zera frowned.

"I don't know," Brake admitted, "But we can't keep him here. We don't have the same setup to keep him. Wren, can you open a portal?"

"I can try," she sighed. "I feel so drained." Brake told her where to open a portal and she did the best she could. It could have been bigger. Brog picked Jaaz up and stepped through with Brake close behind. They were only gone a minute, but the portal felt like it was tearing at Wren's brain. When he came back through, she released the portal and everything started spinning, and went dark.

CHAPTER 19

The next morning, Graham and Tal sat on the dock, by a lake, near the cabin. It was still damp and cold outside, but the rain had stopped. It was freezing, but better outside than inside. The cabin wasn't very big, and there were way too many people pacing around inside.

Throughout the night, members of The Silver Eclipse had been trickling in. Every time a new person came, someone had to fill them in on what was going on. Wren was still out, but Zera assured them she was just overly tired. Ming Li was staying close to her friend, but Graham and Tal were feeling claustrophobic.

Graham pulled his cloak tighter. Tal was picking up rocks and tossing them into the icy water. They couldn't stay out much longer. It was way too cold.

"It shouldn't be this cold," Tal said, breaking the silence. "We're still months away from winter."

"But we don't even know where we are," Graham said. "It could be winter here."

"How could it be winter here and not in Akkron?"

"Maybe we're on the other side of the world or something."

"That wouldn't change the season," Tal said skeptically, raising an eyebrow. "Besides, the only thing on the other side of the world is the ocean."

"I guess I still haven't learned much about your world," Graham admitted.

"The weather is abnormal all over these days," said a voice behind them. They both popped up and turned to see Brog. "If you pay attention to other cities besides Akkron, you would notice they are all experiencing problems with ice storms and snow."

"Everywhere but Akkron?" Tal asked, frowning. "I wonder why."

Brog looked out at the small lake. "I would assume it is because the people responsible for the bad weather live in Akkron."

"Is it possible for a few people to control so much of the weather?" Graham wondered.

"The Dark Cloud are not just a few people," Brog said. "I believe most of them are in Akkron, but they are in all lands."

"We flew over a lot of land on the way to Meegore and it didn't seem cold," Graham said.

"Yes, but there are few people between Akkron and Meegore. There wouldn't be much of a reason to bother the weather there."

"How long has it been going on?" Tal asked. "I haven't heard anything about it."

"Only a few weeks," Brog said, "At least the snow and ice."

"I hope Wren wakes up soon," Graham muttered. "Then we can make a plan."

"Wren is awake. That is why I came out here."

Tal shivered. "Oh good. My backside is about to freeze off."

They walked down a dirt path to the cabin. Graham's head hurt. They desperately needed to get more sleep. It was no wonder no one had come up with a good plan. Everyone was too exhausted.

"I hope we aren't going to be staying here long," Tal said as they opened the door. "The last place was much better."

"It was better," Brake agreed, as they entered. "This place is only temporary. We have better places, but this one is the safest, because we never use it."

Graham looked past all the people and found Wren sitting on a chair next to Ming Li, drinking out of a mug. "You should have slept longer," he said, walking over to her.

"Probably." She yawned. "But you all should have slept more, too."

"It's hard to sleep when your friend passes out," Tal said, joining them.

"I call a rest day," Ming Li yawned. "No getting into trouble or going anywhere."

"I can handle that," Tal said, sitting on the floor. "How are you feeling?"

"Abandoned," Ming Li said, glaring at him. "You all act so concerned about Wren and you leave me in here to watch her all by myself. Yes, I know you were talking to Wren. She's fine, but tired."

"You could have come with us," Tal said.

"Then I would have been part of the abandonment."

"It feels weird to know I was passed out while all these people were here," Wren admitted, looking to where Austra and Tram were arguing in the corner.

"Don't worry," Ming Li said. "You didn't drool or anything."

Graham smiled and shook his head. "Did we miss anything?" he asked Ming Li.

"Not really. Everyone was arguing about what to do with Karlof and The Dark Cloud and wondering if we should have let Jaaz go."

"I've been thinking about that," Graham said, feeling a little worried. "Jaaz knows who some members of The Silver Eclipse are. That might put Brake and the others in more danger."

"We aren't as big of novices as you believe," Hamble said, walking up beside them. "You don't have to worry about Jaaz. Brake erased his memory."

"You can erase memories?" Graham exclaimed. All the talking and arguing stopped as everyone looked at him. "Why didn't you tell us you could do that? How much did you erase?"

Brake sighed and walked over to them. That seemed to be the sign for everyone else to gather around. "Erasing memories is a tricky thing. I can either erase it completely or erase some of it. I can't control how much. It usually erases about two weeks to a month."

"Usually?" Tal exclaimed. "How many times have you done it?"

"I told you, we have been working against The Dark Cloud for years. We have done more than you all seem to think. I could get better at erasing certain parts of memories, but that's not a skill most people want to volunteer to be tested with."

"So, Jaaz won't even remember talking to The Dark Cloud or betraying us or anything?" Ming Li asked.

"And The Dark Cloud might talk to him again and he might try to betray us again," said Wren. "Especially since his dad was the one who had him talk to them in the first place."

"But now he wouldn't be as useful because we already know," Tal told her. "We have the advantage when it comes to Jaaz."

"I still think we need to capture all the people we already know are bad," Ming Li said. "I know you all believe it's a terrible idea, but it's better than letting them go free."

Graham agreed with Ming Li, but it sounded like The Dark Cloud had a lot more members than The Silver Eclipse.

"The more I think about this, the more pathetic it sounds," Wren said. "Okay, so we can't go capture Dovin, Melly, or Jaaz's dad."

Austra's head snapped up and her eyes were wide.

"I get that he'll be missed, but what is our real problem here, right now? It's Karlof. He's the only one who can rat everyone out, and he is the only reason we can't be at the meeting place."

"That's right," Graham said. Wren had a point. "If Karlof disappeared, it might not be as obvious. He seems to do his own thing, so people might not care. If he's only sent a message to the governor, there's time to grab him now before he can tell anyone anything."

"We can't lock him up just because he *might* do something," Brake said, shaking his head.

"If we do things like that, we are not much better than those we oppose." Zera agreed.

"He can't be completely innocent," Wren said, wiping a tear from her eye. "If he was, he wouldn't want to testify against my dad. He knows my dad isn't in The Dark Cloud. If he's going to say he is, then he isn't good."

"That's true," Brake said, rubbing his chin. "We will have to think about this some more."

"We don't have time to think," Graham said. "If we wait, it might be too late."

"What did you say about Melly?" Austra asked, clenching her teeth.

"I was just saying we can't capture the people in The Dark Cloud," Graham said.

"When has Melly come up?"

"She was the person Professor Dovin was talking to about The Dark Cloud," Wren said. "Nobody seems to know who she is."

"I don't believe you ever asked about her," Austra said, narrowing her eyes. "You only said a woman."

"Do you know her?" Zera asked.

"Of course I do," she said, frowning. "She's my sister."

Everyone looked around at each other with wide eyes.

"I don't think so," Ming Li said. "She didn't look a thing like you."

"She is my half sister. No need to look so concerned. We were never close. I'm not even shocked. Melly was always a follower. I always knew that could cause her problems."

"She might not be in too deep," Graham said. "From what Wren said, it sounded like the only Dark Cloud member she knew was Dovin."

"You don't have to make me feel better," Austra said, "Like I said, I'm not shocked. It surprised me for a moment. It changes nothing."

"At least we know who she is now," Brake said. "So, what's our first move?"

"The first thing we need to do is get control over the weather." Professor Hedder said. "It has gotten out of control. The entire world is going to suffer if we can't get the crops in."

"That is true," Austra said nodding, "If we can fix the weather, there's still time to replant before the real winter happens."

"But if we fix it, can't they mess it up again?" Graham asked.

"Some of us believe that The Dark Cloud lost control of the weather. They messed it up so much that we think it has gotten worse than they intended," Brake said, rubbing his temples.

"I don't see how we might fix it," Austra frowned. "What can we do?"

A pounding on the door made everyone jump. Brake stood as the door opened and a filthy Drew walked in.

"Dad!" Wren said, jumping up and running to him. He swung her around in a big hug. Everyone swarmed around him and talked at once.

"Quiet!" Brake yelled. "Let the man breathe."

Everyone stepped back. Drew laughed and kept his arm around Wren. "It's good to see you all missed me. It's been a whole day. You're not the easiest people to find."

"Isn't that the point?" Brake asked, smiling at his friend.

"The governor didn't let you go, did he?" Zera asked. "We haven't even had an official meeting about you yet."

"No, he didn't," Drew said, frowning.

Wren fanned her hand in front of her face. "You smell awful."

He chuckled. "I'm sure I do."

"There's no way you escaped that prison by yourself," Tal said. "My father is always bragging about how much stronger it is than before he was in office. Nobody should be able to escape."

"That's what you said too," Wren said, looking at him. She scrunched her nose and took a step away from the smell.

"Ah, yes," Drew said, smiling again, "But who was put in charge of making sure the prison was secure?"

"You were," Zera said, shaking her head.

"I was."

"So you knew how to escape?" Tal asked. "How did you do it?"

"When I helped design the prison, I was already suspicious of the governor. I knew things could easily go badly for me. I made a way to escape any of the cells in case it ever came to that."

"Good thing you did," Wren said.

"Yes. Well, the way to open it is easy. I figured it was best to get out as fast as possible. If they were expecting anyone to break me out, they would expect it would take them time to come up with a plan."

"So how do you open it?" Tal asked, leaning forward.

"What wrong Talon?" Ming Li joked, "Afraid you're going to end up there?"

"I'd say it's about a fifty-fifty chance," he said, winking.

"You have to lick the bars."

"Really?" Austra said, rolling her eyes. "That is disgusting and not very secure."

"You have to lick them to the tune of *The Old Troll in the Hills*. Each bar is like a piano note. It doesn't make a sound, of course. That made it a little difficult. I also felt incredibly silly."

"I would imagine," Austra said, shaking her head.

"It took me four tries. I'm not sure my tongue will ever be the same again."

Graham wanted to laugh at the look on everyone's faces. They went from mild disgust to close to gagging. Tal was grinning.

"So you licked the bars, and they popped open?" Austra asked, crossing her arms. "And you just walked out of there?"

"Nothing is that easy. When you get the bars right, the floor opens in the corner and you can go into the pipes."

"Oh gross," Wren said. "They weren't sewer pipes were they? You smell terrible, and you touched me." Everyone took another step back.

Graham wished he had a camera. Austra looked like she was ready to heave.

"I'll be downstairs changing," Wren said, speed walking to the stairs.

"Well, freedom doesn't come without sacrifice," Drew said. "I went straight to the meeting place, but nobody was there. The governor made me drink something that blocked my magic. I couldn't send a message. It's wearing off, though. Why are you here?"

"Karlof agreed to testify against you," Zera said. "I thought it would be best to come to a place he did not know."

Drew frowned. "I guess I shouldn't be surprised. Shouldn't we capture him? We can't risk him telling them anything."

"Exactly what we've been saying," Graham said.

"Let's bring him to the meeting place and at least question him," Tal suggested. "If it doesn't go well, we can either capture him or come back here."

Graham raised his hand. "I agree."

"So I guess we aren't getting that day of rest," Ming Li said, sighing.

"I suppose we could try talking to him," Brake said, looking unsure.

"Wren, are you strong enough to open a portal?" Drew asked as Wren came up the stairs.

"I can try."

"Why don't we have the kids go to the meeting place," Zera said. "Brake, Austra, and I can go to Drew's house and talk to Karlof. If he won't cooperate, we'll take him. Everyone else can go home for now. Drew should stay here."

"I should go instead of Austra," Drew said.

"Really?" Austra said, raising her eyebrow. "You can't even use your magic right now, and you look like you were spit out of a dumpster. If Karlof doesn't know you have escaped, it won't be good for him to see you."

"Sorry Drew," Zera said, "You need to sit this one out. If this turns into a fight, we will need Austra."

"You think she can fight better than I can?"

"I have seen her take down two goblins without breaking a sweat," Zera said. "Without using magic."

That impressed Graham. Goblins were supposed to be strong and tricky. Austra didn't look like the type. She seemed more like the one who would be scared to mess up her fingernails.

"I will stay here with Drew," Brog said, "And I will take care of Walter and Ben."

"Wren doesn't look in any condition to be making lots of portals," Professor Hedder said. "I'll stay here until she can send me back."

Ming Li nodded. "So Thor and Loki will take care of Drew. Let's go."

"I'll stay as well," Hamble said. "I'll at least wait until the ground dries."

"So, I'll send you three to our house and the four of us to the meeting place?"

"Yes," Brake said, putting a hand on Ming Li's shoulder. "If we don't come to the meeting place within the hour, I want the four of you to come back here. Under no condition are you to come looking for us. Do you hear me?"

"Of course we hear you, Uncle Brake," Ming Li said, smiling, "But since when has that ever made a difference?" Brake shook his head.

"Capturing Karlof shouldn't be too hard," Drew said, looking at the ground. "I promised I wouldn't tell, but he has violated any trust between us."

"Karlof is huge!" Tal said. "I don't think it would be easy to make him do anything."

"He can't do magic."

Wren narrowed her eyes and looked at Drew. "But I've seen him."

"That was a long time ago," Drew said. "I bet you can't remember anything recently."

"No, I guess not."

"But how is that possible?" Graham asked. He thought once you had magic, you always had it.

"We don't know what happened," Drew said. "When he escaped from the trolls, it took him a while to recover. He could never do magic again. We paid a lot of healers to help him, but none of them could make a difference."

"I've heard similar stories before," Brake said, "But I wasn't sure if they were true. It was always after a traumatic event."

"Well, if he doesn't cooperate we should be able to take him with no trouble," Austra said. "Let's stop waiting around and go finish this."

Wren landed in the meeting house and stood by her friends. They were all staring at the corner. She looked over and saw Karlof lounging in a chair. Her mouth popped open, but she didn't know what to say. Karlof slowly got to his feet and opened his arms.

"Wren," he said, "I've been looking all over for you."

"Don't overreact," Graham whispered.

Wren walked over and hugged her uncle. She wasn't sure how to interpret all the emotions going through her. Anger seemed to be the strongest. She couldn't believe he would betray her dad like this.

"I've been worried," he said, looking down at her. "I'm going to take care of you until this mess with Drew is dealt with."

"I don't need to be taken care of," Wren said. "I'm fine staying here."

"The governor has appointed me your temporary guardian, and I don't think this is the best place for you. I'll take you somewhere safe."

"I would rather stay," Wren said, taking a step back. "We have things to do."

"Yes, I know," Karlof said snorting. "Saving the world. You think four kids can do that?"

"We have help," Ming Li said. Tal whispered something to her that Wren couldn't hear.

"And where is that help?" he asked. Wren took another step back, and he grabbed her arm.

"What are you doing?" she asked, "Let go."

"I need to take care of you Wren. I'm not letting you stay here with these people."

She tried to pull away, but he was strong. "What do you mean by these people?"

"This entire group is a joke. It's time we left them."

"You're hurting my arm," she said.

"I wouldn't be if you weren't pulling."

"Let her go," Graham warned.

"You three all look like you are about to pass out or throw up," Karlof laughed. "What kind of magic are you trying to use on me? You might as well stop because I have coated this place with rednax venom. If you want to fight me, you're going to have to use your fists, and I don't think you're gonna win." He flexed his free arm and laughed again.

"Why are you doing this?" she asked. Graham stepped beside her. Wren hoped he wouldn't do anything crazy.

"I told you, I'm taking you somewhere safe. Of course we'll make a quick stop at Meegore on our way."

"Meegore?" It was making sense. If Karlof lost his magic, of course he would want to go to Meegore to get it back. "So you want to use me?"

337

"Wren," he said, looking at the ceiling and shaking his head, "You are all I have left of my sister. I care about you, but I need you to take me to Meegore. My principal goal is to keep you safe though."

"I'm not going with you. I know you're planning on testifying against my dad."

Karlof growled. "You put too much faith in that man. All of my problems in life are caused by him."

"How so?"

"If it wasn't for him, Magnalee would still be here. She only joined his pathetic group of vigilantes because of him. Now you're following in his footsteps. Hasn't it ever occurred to the four of you that you are underqualified for this fight? What have you learned about The Dark Cloud? Nothing worth your effort, that's what."

"We've learned things," Wren protested.

"Yeah? What are they doing? Why are they sending people to Boztoll and then harassing them there? Who are they? If they're so bad why does everyone survive the 'accidents' they cause? They have to have a goal. What is it? You're out of your league. I've let you waste enough time. I'm only looking out for your welfare."

"Why did you use the rednax venom if you're so innocent?" Tal asked.

"I know you all. You won't let Wren go without a fight."

"You know that's right," Ming Li said, running forward and smashing a lamp into Karlof's arm. He yelled out and let go of Wren's arm and Graham immediately punched him in the face. Tal was only a second behind kicking him in the knee. Ming Li jumped on his back and pulled his hair. He grabbed her and swung her off his back and threw her at Graham and Tal. The three of them all landed in a heap on the floor.

"You are all going to pay for that!" Karlof growled, right before Wren hit him in the head with the lamp. He fell to the ground and didn't move.

"Did I kill him?" Wren squealed, throwing the lamp to the floor. "I wasn't trying to kill him!"

"He's breathing," Graham said, "But that's a lot of blood." Wren looked at her uncle and felt sick. He had a big gash on his head and it was bleeding a lot.

"What do we do?" Wren asked. It was hard to breathe. This had all gone so wrong.

"The adults will come when they can't find Karlof," Ming Li said, holding her side.

Graham kneeled by Karlof. "We need to stop the bleeding."

"So we help the enemy?" Tal said, taking off his cape and handing it to Graham. Graham rolled it up and pressed it to Karlof's head. Tal already had a black eye, probably from being smacked by Ming Li's head.

"I'll go outside," Wren offered, wanting to get away from all the blood. She felt like she might be sick. "I'll send a message to Brake."

"Take someone with you," Graham said, still pressing on Karlof's head. "I need one of you to help me though."

"I'll stay with you," Ming Li said, kneeling by him. "Tal looks like he could use some air." Tal nodded and followed Wren. They hurried to the exit and opened the door.

A blast of cool air made her stomach feel better. They stepped out into the jungle.

She pictured Brake and whispered, *"Karlof is at the meeting place."* Before she could open a portal someone grabbed her from behind. She screamed and threw her head backwards, hitting them in the face. They yelled and let go. She ran a few feet and turned around. A thin man in a brown, worn tunic was coming at her grimacing. His nose was bleeding, but he didn't seem to care.

"Get away Wren!" Tal yelled. She looked over and saw him lying on the ground. It looked like his arms were stuck to his sides. A thin woman with greasy, blond hair was standing above him smiling.

"Where's Karlof?" the man asked as she walked backwards. She could open a portal, but she couldn't leave Tal.

"We captured him, now leave her alone!" Tal commanded.

"You captured him?" The man asked, still walking towards Wren. He wiped his bloody nose on his sleeve. "We went through a lot of trouble for him, and we ain't leavin' without gettin' what he owes us."

"That's for sure," the woman said, kicking Tal in the ribs. He grunted.

"And what is that?" Wren asked.

"A trip to Meegore to get Frenk here some magic," the woman said. "And your three friends for The Dark Cloud."

"Quiet!" Frenk said, yelling at the woman.

The warning was too late. Wren smiled. He didn't have magic. Frenk must have read Wren's mind because he rushed her. She levitated rocks as fast as she could and flung them at him. They weren't very big, but he stopped to cover his face.

"You stop that!" the woman yelled. Wren kept the rocks coming. The woman's magic must not be strong enough to do anything besides hold Tal down. Frenk backed away.

"Do something Melly!" he called. He had small bloody spots on his face and arms.

"I can't or this one will get away!"

Wren was getting tired, but she kept the rocks going. Frenk finally turned and ran into the trees.

"Frenk, get back here!" Melly yelled.

"I'm still here!" he called. "This is all your darn fault Melly! You best fix this!"

Wren looked around for a bigger rock. She saw one and lifted it off the ground. Before she could throw it at Melly, Tal turned and knocked her over with his legs. She fell over as Tal leaped up.

Melly scrambled to her feet, "Listen you rotten kids," she snarled, raising her arm. "We did not come this far for nothing." Something was crackling in her hand. It almost looked like lightning. "Don't move or you are dead."

Wren wasn't sure what to do. She didn't know what kind of magic Melly was holding. Frenk came back out of the woods holding a big rock. He was smiling.

"If you cooperate, you don't have to get hurt," Melly said. "You take us to the Island of Meegore and we turn your boyfriend here into The Dark Cloud, and everyone's happy."

"You have a funny definition of everyone," Tal said. He looked calm, except his fingers were twitching.

"Believe me, this is for the best of everyone," Melly laughed. "Frenk will finally have magic and The Dark Cloud will finally take me seriously. It's better for you two as well. Now you don't have to keep hiding. The Dark Cloud will help you a lot more than anyone else could."

"Just because Karlof joined The Dark Cloud, doesn't mean we will," Wren said, not daring to move.

"Karlof? In The Dark Cloud?" Melly laughed, "They do have standards, you know. He isn't in The Dark Cloud any more than Frenk. That doesn't mean that he wasn't willing to bargain to get our help."

"I'll be in The Dark Cloud as soon as we go to Meegore," Frenk said.

"Yes, and we are wasting time."

"There's a big ol' tree growin' behind you," Frenk said, pointing behind Melly. He was right. Well, it wasn't an enormous tree, but a tree was growing and was now taller than Melly.

Melly turned around and Tal fisted his hand. The tree bent over and wrapped around her. She screamed and something shot out of her hand and hit the ground, leaving a scorch mark. Tal was twisting his hands around each other and the tree branches kept growing and twisting around Melly. Her screams pierced Wren's ears. Frenk stood there with his mouth hanging open.

Wren wished she had magic that made fighting easier. She took advantage of Frenk's distraction and ran at him. Her shoulder made contact with his stomach as she plowed into him and they both fell over. He grabbed her and tried to throw her off him, but she wouldn't let go of his shirt. Frenk wasn't very big, but he was still stronger than she was. He rolled her onto the ground and sat on her stomach, holding her wrists above her head.

He laughed in her face as she struggled and she almost gagged. His breath was horrible, and the blood smeared across his cheek seemed way too close to her for comfort. Without warning, he screamed and let go of her wrists. He waved his arms above himself as two red and blue birds pecked at his head. Wren grabbed his shirt and pulled as hard as she could, knocking him over. The birds kept pecking at him as he tried to roll away.

Wren leaped up and looked at Melly. All she could see was her face. Tal stopped moving his hands and ran over to Wren.

"Are you okay?" he asked. She nodded as she watched Frenk fight with the birds. "Sorry I couldn't help sooner," he said, waving his hand in the air and causing vines to wrap around Frenk. "It took me longer than I want to admit to realize I could call on the birds."

"It's fine," Wren said. "And thanks." The two birds stopped attacking Frenk and landed on Tal's shoulder. Now besides the black eye, his head was bleeding, and he was holding his stomach.

Graham and Ming Li seemed to step out of nowhere. Ming Li was holding an ice pack on her cheek and Graham's lip was swollen.

"Were you guys ever going to come back?" Ming Li asked, with a hand on her hip. "We could have used your help in there." She looked from Tal to Wren and then at Frenk. "Oh ... what happened out here?"

"Karlof had friends," Wren told them. "It sounds like Karlof was going to make me take that one to Meegore," she said, pointing at Frenk. "And she was going to take the rest of you to The Dark Cloud."

"There's a person in there?" Ming Li asked, walking over to the tree. Melly glared at her. "That's a pretty cool power, Talon."

"Sometimes I think you say my name just so you can call me Talon," Tal said, with a half smile.

"I'm not denying it."

"You two look worse than when we left you," Wren said, pointing at Graham's lip.

"Yeah, Karlof wasn't as knocked out as we thought," Graham said with a wince.

"But he is now," Ming Li added. "We tied him up this time before we bandaged his head."

"Karlof is strong," Graham said, rubbing his jaw, "But, he's slow. That's the only reason we won.

"I'm going to open a portal to my house and see if Brake, Zera, and Austra are still there," Wren said. "If Brake answered me, I didn't hear him. I don't know if he got my message."

She opened a portal outside her house and saw the three of them standing by the door. They looked towards it and moved cautiously forward. Wren hopped out and motioned them forward. They came faster and entered the portal.

"We were worried when you did not answer," Zera said, looking at each of them.

"You'll all be sorry if you don't let us go." Frenk said, struggling with the vines.

"Frenk?" Austra said, squatting beside the man. "What are you doing here?"

"Wouldn't you like to know?" he said through gritted teeth.

"Karlof was going to give Graham, Tal, and Ming Li to The Dark Cloud and make me take him and Frenk to Meegore."

"The last thing the world needs is Frenk with magic. He causes enough trouble without it." Austra said, standing. "Where's Melly? I'm sure she's around here somewhere."

"There," Tal pointed.

"That's impressive," Brake said, walking around the tree.

"Where is Karlof?" Zera asked.

"In the meeting place," Graham said. "He's unconscious and tied up. He needs a healer."

"The four of you captured all three of them by yourselves?" Austra asked, raising her eyebrows.

Ming Li nodded. "Yeah, so now maybe you'll take us seriously."

"Well, from the looks of you, you almost lost."

Wren felt it. They could have lost easily. They were exhausted before they came here. Now she was pretty sure they needed a week at least to recover.

"I hope you aren't going to tell us we have to turn them loose," Tal said, tilting his head.

"No," Brake said. "The three of them are going straight to our prison."

"The real prison, or the 'nice cozy room full of books' prison?"

"The real one."

"I might be able to make a portal," Wren said, "But it's going to be hard. If we get them all together and do it fast, that would be best."

"I could try to heal you first," Graham offered.

Wren looked at her friend and shook her head. "No." He looked as beat up as she felt. "If you heal us, you can't heal yourself, and it will take even more out of you. I can heal most of my problems with sleep."

"Let's take these two in and try opening the portal from inside," Brake said. "They'll be easier to move than Karlof."

"They put rednax venom all over inside so we couldn't do magic." Ming Li said.

"That will take too long to clean," Zera said. "We will have to bring Karlof out."

"You ain't really gonna let them lock us up, Austra?" Frenk asked, frowning. "That's a mean thing to do to family."

"Is he your brother?" Brake asked.

"Cousin," Austra said, "And yes Frenk. You need to be locked up."

"Ya always thought you are so much better than the rest of us," Frenk said. "Always acting like the queen and treating us like scum."

"I'm not having this conversation with you," Austra said, rolling her eyes. "You have no one to blame but yourself." She turned to Zera. "I didn't even know Frenk existed until a few years ago. He's been trying to get me to do things for him or give him money ever since we met."

"I know you got money, and yer perty stingy to yer family. You shouldn't blame me anyhow. Melly was the one with the idea," he said. "I shoulda known it wouldn't work. If she hadn't a gone tellin' them I didn't have no magic, it woulda worked."

"Don't blame me!" Melly screeched from inside the tree. "If you had hit them with the rock, we wouldn't be in this situation."

"Raise your hand if you think it's time for some ailam powder," Tal said. "Looks like it's unanimous."

"You should all be in bed," Brake said, shaking his head. "And why are you all lying on the hard floor?"

Graham, Wren, Tal, and Ming Li were all lying on the floor, looking at the ceiling. While Austra, Brake and Zera took Karlof, Frenk, and Melly to the prison, they'd tried to scrub away all the rednax venom, but it was a slow process. It was like cleaning oil with water. It smeared around, and it didn't help that they were all beat and sore.

"We finished cleaning and decided this was as good a place as any to die," Ming Li said with a weak smile.

"We're only resting before we go to bed," Graham said.

"Resting in bed would be a better option," Brake said, sighing. "I'm going back to the cabin to tell everyone what happened. I don't want Wren to make a portal, so it's going to take a while. We locked the entrance, so nobody can get in until we get back. When I return, you better all be rested and on the way to recovery, alright?"

"Alright," Tal said, "But does that have to involve getting off the floor?"

Brake shook his head. "I'll be back as soon as I can. Don't go anywhere. Except to bed." He turned and walked out the door.

"Remember how we thought we were tired yesterday?" Graham said.

"I wish I was as tired as I was yesterday," Ming Li said. Wren nodded in agreement.

Tal rubbed his side. "I think I have that witch's shoe print on my ribs."

"I could heal you guys," Graham said. "It would be better if only one of us was miserable."

"Nah," Tal said, yawning, "We can heal the same way as you."

"I'm feeling better than I did yesterday in some ways," Wren said. "At least I know my dad's safe and Karlof can't do anything."

"That's true," Ming Li said. "We put three people behind bars. That's progress."

"Yeah, it makes me feel like we aren't doing this for nothing," Tal said. "I mean, a lot of today was luck, but we did it. It makes me feel more motivated to move forward."

"Yeah, I feel like we can actually do this," Ming Li said.

"So, what's our next move?" Wren asked.

"I've been thinking about that a lot," Graham said. "In my opinion the most important thing we can do is figure out a way to summon the silver eclipse."

"But it's only been done three times," Wren said.

"Yeah, but we are the ones who have to make it right. We are the ones who were chosen. I think we'll figure it out." Graham didn't know how they would do it or when, but something was telling him it had to be them.

ACKNOWLEDGMENTS

Thank you for reading my book! I hope you enjoyed it. If you did please go and give it a review on Amazon. Reviews make books more visible.

A special thanks to my husband Tom and all of my kids for making this possible. Without them I never would have made it. Their ideas and technical help were invaluable. Thanks to Xander for the website.

Thanks to Michelle Clark for all of her help and patience. Without her I would have a mess.

Thanks go out to Mary Thompson, Rylee Penrod and Becca Wolford.

About Author

Kristy Dixon graduated with a degree in English from the University of Utah. She started writing stories when she was seven and has been writing ever since. In the beginning she tried writing historical fiction, but soon found that to be boring. She started writing The Silver Eclipse at the urging of her children and found fantasy writing to be more fun. If she isn't writing or playing board games with her kids, she is probably eating cookies or wishing that she were eating cookies.

ALSO BY KRISTY DIXON

Boztoll (The Silver Eclipse – Book 2)

Coming Soon

The Other Continent (The Silver Eclipse – Book 3)

Made in the USA
Monee, IL
13 December 2023

49050011R00208